Joe Parzych is the sort of writer whose story you can't lay down, and when you have finished reading it, you can never forget it. He will not let us completely lose the world of American immigrant families when a mother washed clothes for thirteen children without a washing machine and a father "wearily trudged into the house after work, the caustic smell of paper mill chemicals clinging to his dingy work clothes." This book is rich with a gentle humor that comes from surviving the confusion of growing up.

--Pat Schneider, author of nine books, including *Writing Alone & With Others,* Oxford University Press.

Here is a memoir told with honest precision and abundant insight, a coming of age story of a boy of Polish descent growing up on a farm in the 30's in western Massachusetts. Parzych was one of thirteen children and his voice rings with individuality. I laughed out loud many times reading it. "Our farm," Parzych writes, "was a 'Noah's Ark' type of operation with a little bit of almost everything--" And this is what we get with this work; and we are the wiser for it.

--Genie Zeiger, author of *How I Find Her: A Mother's Dying and a Daughter's Life,* and *Atta Girl!*

Growing up in a little house with two rooms upstairs and two rooms downstairs, Joseph Parzych of Gill has poignantly brought back New England farm life in the early part of the 20th century. Writing about his early days in Gill, MA, the reader can easily picture young Joe trying to snuggle down under his feather quilt in a room, frigid enough to see his own breath on a cold winter morning. There's no electricity, no running water, the girls slept in one room, the boys in the other. Attending his first Mass is a big adventure that Parzych writes colorfully from a young boy's view. Anyone wanting to enjoy reading about life on a farm in the 1920's and 1930's will find Jep's Place a real pleasure. Parzych has remembered the day-to-day incidents that become a charming, and often humorous memoir.

--Irmarie Jones, columnist for *The Recorder,* and contributor to *Yankee* magazine.

"In his memoir <u>Jep's Place,</u> Joe Parzych of Gill, a first generation American, writes of helping his mother make feather quilts, "It gave me a good feeling to hear my mother tell stories as we all sat around the kitchen table. A cheerful circle of light fell around us, cast by a kerosene lamp hanging from the ceiling. 'Tell us about the old days Ma' we'd say' and she'd begin."

  --Anna Viadero, editor of The Good Life, and Local Color.

Joe writes of the struggles of his Polish family to establish their home in Gill .The memoir is a treasure of early twentieth century rural life. The harsh or tender moments and laughter are images woven together with insight and compassion by the voice of a true story teller. I was quickly in empathy with the boy and the gentle spirit that came of hard times.

  --Joan Coughlin, teacher and painter.

Not since Titus Moody has a New England original emerged from this flinty soil to crack wise and wax profound on the verities of work, family, and community. How much more insightful are Joe Parzych's perceptions of small town New England, as he views Massachusetts life with the precocious eye of a hardscrabble first generation Polish immigrant. Written with humor wrung from experience on a sharecropper farm, the rag room of a Depression-era paper mill, and a backwoods still in Prohibition ....

  --David Detmold, editor of Montague Reporter

Jep's Place:

Hope, Faith and Other Disasters

Joseph A Parzych

10-Digit ISBN 1-59113-937-6
13-Digit ISBN 978-1-59113-937-9

Printed in the United States of America.

Booklocker.com, Inc.
2006

Jep's Place:

Hope, Faith and Other Disasters

by

Joseph A. Parzych

In memory of my daughter,

Deborah Parzych Lambert

Contents

Introduction

I was born in the town of Gill, Massachusetts, in a small farmhouse at the end of a dirt road far from electricity or telephone. Grass grew between the wheel tracks with wild roses along the sides. The white, clapboarded house had two rooms up and two rooms down.

The farm was in a basin with hills all around. A trout stream curving through the low-lying pasture borders the property. In spring, peepers in the marshes signaled the awakening of life. Not long after the peepers fell silent, barn swallows returned to nest. We fished and swam in the brook in summer and coasted on the hills in winter. I loved the place.

Chapter 1: Mystery Trip

There were 13 kids in our combined family—15, counting two of my father's sons by his first wife. They died in infancy. Not even my mother knew about those two.

Ma and Pa each brought three kids to the new family. They had seven more children, two years apart. Emaline was the first, then Gladys, Irene, me, Lora, Louis, and Julia. In the two upstairs bedrooms, girls slept in one room, boys in the other. It was kids, wall to wall.

The entire 13 kids did not live at the farm at the same time. There was always someone coming or going, running off or being run off, so it was hard to get an accurate headcount. I can only say it looked like a load of pumpkins when we all piled into our Essex sedan for a ride into town.

The last five kids were born at the farm in Gill. The mid-wife who delivered them had once worked for a doctor and she assured us that she knew all about delivering babies. Years later, she told us how she had learned midwifery by listening in on the doctor's dinner conversations while working in the kitchen as cook's helper.

She was a bit addled, but the price was right. She did not charge for her midwife services. That might have been because we were her only customer. But, her heart was in the right place and she certainly was a comfort to my mother who otherwise would have given birth unattended.

Our farm was a "Noah's Ark" type of operation with a little bit of almost everything—cows, pigs, chickens, ducks, geese, goats, pigeons, rabbits, bees, and a horse. The author M.G. Kains wrote Five Acres and Independence. If my father had written such a book, it would have been titled Seven Acres and Poverty.

When I was about four years old, my father converted the back shed to a kitchen. I clearly remember a family friend standing waist deep in the middle of the floor nailing boards onto supports. The floor slanted, so they slanted the ceiling to match. It made the kitchen appear to list like the Titanic. Water periodically coursing through the cellar completed the illusion. When it rained, the roof leaked like it had been shot full of holes. In springtime when the drain became sluggish, jars and bottles floated in the cellar in water a foot deep.

The well was a different story; that went dry before the ink dried on the deed. My older brothers helped my father dig a new well, but it was often on the verge of running dry by the end of summer. For some reason, my father seldom drank water, perhaps in the spirit of conservation.

With so many kids, it was easy to get lost in the shuffle, so it was a pleasant surprise, one frosty winter morning, when my father singled me out to go with him. Snow creaked under our feet as we walked out to the garage to my father's pride and joy; his beautiful tan Essex.

The tarpaper sided garage my father had built was a long rectangular box that fit our square-backed car well. The older boys said it was the crate that the Essex came in. I was never sure whether they were kidding or not. When Pa opened the garage doors, the faint smell of tires, gasoline and exhaust conjured up thoughts of adventure. As the only one going, I got to sit in the prized front passenger seat. Pa turned the car ignition key on, set the choke, throttle and spark, got out and inserted the crank in a hole under the radiator. He put his foot on the crank. With one quick thrust of his foot, the car engine responded with a throaty strumming. He backed the car out and closed the doors. We were off, with me sitting next to Pa, ecstatic to have him all to myself, gloating that my brother Louis was too young to go along and had to stay home with the girls.

It had all started that cold winter morning. From my bed, I could hear murmuring in the kitchen, downstairs. Usually, I liked to get up early, but the bed, piled high with quilts, was warm and cozy. The room was frigid enough so that I could see my breath in the air. Icy frost covered the boards of the slanted ceiling. Drafty cold air seeped in between the wooden laths on the walls where horsehair plaster had fallen away, and it had taken most of the night to get the bed warm enough to fall asleep. I snuggled down under the feather quilt next to my brother Louis to snooze a while longer.

I once asked Ma why we could not have heat upstairs. "Be thankful you have a roof over your head and food on the table," she said. "Think of the starving kids in Africa and China." When saying my nightly prayers, I gave thanks for the roof over my head despite its being leaky. I thought about the kids in Africa and China pictured in the pamphlets that missionaries sent Ma, soliciting funds. There was usually some pitiful little kid holding an empty bowl, standing in front of a hut made out of mud and sticks. Those pictures made me glad we were not poor.

My sister Emaline had burst into the bedroom.

"Joey, wake up, wake up," she cried.

I burrowed deeper under the covers. Emmy laughed.

"Do you want to go with Pa?"

There was no need to ask twice. I jumped out of bed, and ran downstairs in my long underwear. The floors were so cold it hurt my feet. I stood close to the wood stove in the kitchen, grateful for its comforting warmth. Frost ferns had completely covered the windows with their breath-taking beauty. Emmy took the tea kettle from the stove.

"Never mind staring at the windows, you've got to get washed and dressed."

I followed her into the pantry where the pump stood, with the handle raised, next to the black iron sink. She poured hot water into the pump and worked the handle up and down. Soon water poured out of the pump's mouth. She filled the wash basin and tempered the cold well water with hot water from the kettle. I shivered as I washed up, but soon I was back by the warm stove. My other sisters joined Emmy, helping her to get me bundled up. I couldn't stand still for the excitement, wolfing toast, washed down with coffee while standing by the stove as they dressed me.

"Hold still, Joey," Emmy said.

Getting to go with Pa in his pride and joy—his tan Essex –was all I could think about. I headed for the door.

"Hang on," Emmy," said. "Your hat looks grungy."

She whipped off my hat, clapped a brown beret on my head and wrapped a scarf around my neck. I looked like a French explorer setting out for the North Pole.

Pa sported a new haircut with the smell of barbershop hair tonic still lingering. He looked especially handsome in his polished black high top shoes, blue serge suit, white shirt and tie. When he put on his navy blue overcoat, it gave him the look of royalty. I felt a surge of pride in having him for a father. Sunday clothes transformed Pa. He stood straighter and taller, with an air of confidence, unlike the slump-shouldered man who wearily trudged into the house after work, the caustic smell of paper mill chemicals clinging to his dingy work clothes. Dressed in his Sunday best, he had the confident look of a man of means.

Sometimes, after conserving water, he liked to tell us how he had left home at 13 or 14. His father had sent him out to make his way to America with little more than the clothes on his back, a new pair of shoes and 50 cents. As a boy Pa could neither read nor write, and the 50 cents was soon gone. He told how he had found food and a place to sleep at the end of each day. Somehow he made his way on foot across Poland to Germany.

He worked for about a year to earn his ship's passage. He told of coming to the New World as a "greenord" and working his way up to become a prosperous businessman. Seeing him dressed, as grandly as Prince Albert pictured on his tobacco can, left little doubt in my mind that Pa would soon be rich, again.

He put his English driving cap on at an angle; I adjusted my beret to match.

"Such a pair," Ma said in Polish, as we went out the door. My chest seemed to expand to be so grandly dressed, going where, I knew not, but glad just to be going out into the world beyond our isolated farm. My sisters had returned to cooing and fussing over our new baby Julia. A blast of cold air swept into the kitchen from the open door.

"Hurry up and close the door before the baby catches a death'a cold," they called out in a chorus.

Joy and self-importance swelled my head as we drove off in a swirl of steam from the exhaust of the fancy Essex, sporting real crank-up windows and bud vases on the door posts. We went down the dirt road, bordered by high snow banks, barely wide enough for one car. The stately Essex rumbled over the planks bridging the brook that bordered our farm. Pa continued out onto the graveled main road. Here, the snow-packed road was wide enough for cars to pass. Pa gloried in the Essex's powerful "super-six" engine with aluminum pistons and adjustable louvers on the radiator. It even had an automatic oiling system to lubricate the chassis. Pa pressed on the gas pedal to get a running start as we came to a hill. The car surged up the slope with a powerful roar.

The carburetor had a heater. Unfortunately the passengers had none. Our breath came out in little clouds. Pa took off his cap, from time to time, to wipe the frost forming on the windshield. He lit up a Lucky Strike by igniting a wooden match with his thumbnail. The smell of sulfur and tobacco smoke drifted in the frigid air. I blew out puffs of breath, pretending to be smoking, just like Pa. The love I felt for him seemed to rise from my heart toward him, but he was busy navigating his powerful car and hardly noticed me. The car seemed to get colder as we drove through the frigid air. I began to shiver, and was glad my sisters had bundled me up in long underwear, a heavy woolen coat, mittens and beret. I only hoped no one would notice that it was a girl's beret when we got to wherever we were going.

I began fantasizing. The cone-shaped nickel-plated headlight reflected the side of the road. I watched images of proud trees and poles topple and get dragged down into the back of the headlight, swiftly humbling them. I imagined that we were riding in a powerful ruthless machine, unmercifully mowing down everything we encountered on the way to our mysterious destination.

Pa was usually not one to talk much to children. But it was enough for me just to sit beside him, just the two of us, together, though I yearned to hear him say he loved me, just once. Pa sat up straight as he drove, looking very masculine with the Lucky Strike clamped in his lips. I gazed up at Pa in adoration. He could have posed for a cigarette advertisement. His eyes were intent on the road as he fiddled with the choke, the knobs for the radiator louvers and the carburetor heat control. He handled the big wooden steering wheel as though he were piloting a river boat. When he parked the Essex in Turners Falls, the car doors closed with a solid "thunk".

"Not tin, like a Model T Ford," Pa said with a smug smile.

We walked to an enormous brick building with a wide flight of steep stairs going up and up. I hung onto Pa's hand, struggling to keep up. At the top landing, a tall oaken door opened onto a hushed interior with ceilings that seemed to go as high as the sky. I grew fearful. Sunlight streamed through stained glass windows, casting spectacular red and yellow and blue patterns where it fell. The heady smell of incense, statues, ornate altar and paintings of angels on the ceiling made me wonder if the stairs had somehow led us to heaven, or at least partway there. The scene looked every bit like the holy picture in our dining room where light beams drew good people up into the air while others suffered in a fire pit, begging for mercy with outstretched arms. My fears built as we walked down the aisle past statues of people with bloody wounds adorning the walls. This was one scary place. I could not see to the front where I feared the fire pit most certainly was located.

Suddenly, the beret vanished from my head; and my preoccupation with bloody bodies vanished. I looked around to see who'd taken it. No one was there. I looked up at Pa. He solemnly continued walking, looking straight ahead with his head high. He was bareheaded, hat in hand, with no sign of the beret. Apparently, he hadn't noticed that anything had suddenly vanished. I followed him to long rows of wooden seats; worried, not knowing what to do. Pa ushered me to the right side where men sat. Women sat on the far left, while families sat together in the middle rows. To be the only boy sitting with the men made me feel grown up.

Once seated, Pa pushed a brass button on the back of the seat in front of us. A little hanger sprang open and he hung up his hat. I had hoped that my beret was hidden inside his hat, and he would hang that up, too. But, no such luck. I stared at the little button and empty hook in front of me. I tried to puzzle out the vanishing beret. I prayed for a miracle. Ma was always praying for something, but it never seemed to pan out. The beret didn't reappear. My luck with prayer wasn't any better than Ma's.

Everyone sat in silence, neither speaking nor looking at each other. Socializing, apparently, was against the rules. I dared not ask my father about

5

the beret for fear of getting cuffed for breaking the silence. I pondered what to do.

My thoughts about the dilemma soon faded as a person entered from a side doorway at the front of the room. The person wore a long black dress with a fancy white lace over-blouse, and a little beanie. I couldn't decide if the person was a man in a dress, or one homely woman. A deep voice, sounding stern and masterful, left little doubt that the person was a man. He began rattling off what sounded like Polish, but he talked so fast, I couldn't make out a thing.

Two boys in red dresses with white over-blouses followed him around, fetching things for him. I caught a few words of prayer in Polish. "Mi Oicha ee sina ee duha--Our Father and Son and Holy Ghost."

His rapid fire talk sounded like a cross between an auctioneer and a machine gun. Once he got into the swing of things, his voice rose and fell, and then rose higher yet, until his fierce hollering scared me. His scowling gaze roamed about the room, then seemed to zero in on our direction. His face grew redder as he got wound up. I wondered if he was hollering at me for walking in without taking off my beret. At this point I gave up trying to understand what he was railing on about. The distance from him to me was comforting. I figured I could probably outrun him to the door if he started after me.

As he ranted on, I resumed dwelling on the mystery of the vanishing beret. I knew I was going to get a good licking for losing it. A vision of that nice beret appeared in my mind's eye--- brown felt, with a little curved tail sticking up at the top. Losing it wasn't even my fault. Well, maybe a little bit. I shouldn't have been so proud of myself being all dressed up and gloating about being the only one to go with Pa. I'd been warned about being proud.

Despair swept over me. I began to hope. Maybe Pa would not notice the beret gone, and when I got home, I could throw myself upon the mercy of my sisters. They might holler, but at least they wouldn't spank me. Despair won out. Pa was sure to notice when we went outside and I just knew I would get a licking. I just hoped that it would not be in front of everyone.

I tried to see if there really was a fire pit at the front of the church, hoping the fierce sounding man in the dress would not throw me into it for the double sin of being so proud and for losing the beret, or even for not removing it, like all the other men did. I reasoned that I could claim that it was a girl's beret, and since all the women in church wore hats, a girl's beret would be permissible to keep on. The more I thought about it, the more I wondered if being thrown into the fire pit wouldn't be better than facing Pa or the guy in the dress hollering his head off.

6

What would I tell my sisters when they asked what happened to their beret; when I had no idea what had happened, and Pa hadn't seen anything, either? Perhaps God had snatched it from my head. Maybe he gave it to some woman who'd forgotten to wear a hat. The whole thing was baffling. Both my head and stomach began to hurt.

Organ music burst forth, startling me back to reality. People began singing. At first I liked the music and singing, but when the music stopped, my thoughts drifted back to the missing beret. The outing with Pa wasn't fun anymore. Here, I'd felt so fortunate getting to be the only one to go with Pa, and now I was in a jam, again. Why hadn't he left me home and taken one of my sisters or my brother Louis? Then I wouldn't be in all this trouble.

My knees hurt from kneeling on the hard little wooden benches down by the floor. I couldn't see what was going on, nor understand the priest's Polish half the time, droning words like "dominius pobiscum". The boring rigmarole seemed to drag on forever. The only thing to break the deadly monotony was a fierce cracking and banging of steam pipes that started up. As the place got warmer, my heavy coat made me hot and sweaty. My long woolen underwear began to itch, and I dared not scratch for fear of getting cuffed. I wondered, in the depths of my despair, if this ritual would ever end. There seemed to be no limit to sitting, standing, kneeling, sitting, and back to standing in this strange silent game of Simon-says which I mostly guessed wrong.

We got a little break when two men came around with baskets on the end of a long pole. Pa and the other people put in money. It apparently was for refreshments, because people got up and went to the front to line up at a railing. They knelt there waiting for the man in the dress. Folks opened their mouths like baby robins and he would feed them a little morsel like a mother bird to shut them up. It didn't seem like all that commotion was worthwhile for what little they got and I figured that was why Pa didn't bother with it.

Just when I felt like we were going to spend the rest of our lives jumping up and down, folks began acting more lively. Women began picking up their pocket books, straightening their hats and pulling on their gloves. Men began unsnapping their hats and flipping the hard little kneeling benches up. People stood looking relieved and happy to be finished with the ordeal of it all. The bloody statues, partially hidden by the restless crowd, were not as disturbing, and the atmosphere took on a festive air. People who had completely ignored each other nodded and smiled as though their sight had been miraculously restored by the torment they had endured.

Pa got his hat off of the little hanger, briskly stepped out into the aisle and stood in the line headed for the door. He still hadn't noticed that I wasn't carrying the beret. I tagged along, keeping my eyes peeled for the damned thing. My hope lay in someone finding it and putting it where I could see it. Maybe God would take pity on me and would put it back on my head just as quickly as he'd snatched it off. No such luck. I began trying to think of an excuse. Nothing came to me.

Outside, the long set of stone stairs looked frightfully steep. I hesitated. Pa reached into his pocket, slipped out the beret and put it on my head, all in one motion, like a magician pulling a coin out of the air. I looked up at him and smiled. His eyes twinkled as he took my hand. The lump in the pit of my stomach eased; the world became bright and cheerful, and I was able to breathe normally. My small hand in Pa's big calloused grasp made me feel safe as we walked back to the car.

On the way home, the Essex seemed to run better. It climbed hills with little effort and cruised along the flats at a swift pace. Trees and telephone poles were felled and swept away into the shiny headlights in a twinkling as the car sailed along. It reminded me of workhorses who wearily plodded in the fields, but then, after a hard day at work, would break into a trot with renewed vigor, once they knew they were heading home.

When we entered the kitchen, the wood stove radiated warmth to the four corners of the room. The ferns Jack Frost had left on the windows were gone. The aroma of chicken soup filled the air. Lemon pie, baking, added to the delicious smells. The room seemed filled with peace and harmony. I took off the beret and handed it to my sister Emmy. I hung my head, waiting for Pa to tell everyone what a fool I'd made of myself. Depression began to come over me. It seemed that I could not go one day without doing something wrong, and getting scolded, spanked or called a bad boy or mischief-maker. I headed for my refuge, the big wood box built-into the wall by the stove.

"How did everything go?" Ma asked, half listening, as she cuddled Julia and murmured, "jes ciekocham"—I love you"—the very words I longed to hear. Pa shrugged, "Church is church. What can happen in church?"

My despair evaporated and a warm glow returned to the kitchen. I watched Ma and my sisters coaxing the baby to smile. Julia kicked her feet in delight with each happy grin. No one dreamed that something terrible would soon happen to Julia.

Chapter 2: Snow Plows

One of my earliest recollections is toddling out to watch my brothers, Stanley and Walter, repairing a bicycle. They had the rear wheel off.

"Get that kid out of here so he don't scatter the parts and lose them," Stanley said

Walter picked me up and moved me out of the way. That did not endear them to me. Later, when the new Sears & Roebuck catalog came, Johnny spotted a snow plow attachment mounted on the front of a car.

"Do you think the Old Man's Essex could push that plow?" Johnny asked. "It'd be nice to be able to plow out to the main road."

"It's got power enough," Stanley said, "but the ass-ache's got a cork clutch and it'd burn right out."

The reason they showed so much interest was that the town only had one hired truck to plow out the entire town. The truck driver didn't start plowing until it stopped snowing, and then he only plowed once. Days or even weeks went by before the driver cleared the road to our house. If snow drifted into the road, we could only hope for a minor miracle. Like everyone else, Pa had tire chains to get through the snow. But when the snow was deep, or the road drifted several feet deep, chains were insufficient. If there was a big storm while Pa was at work, he stayed with friends in Turners Falls until the road was cleared. If he got caught at home, he would walk to the main highway and someone would usually give him a ride to work. Because we had no telephone, Pa would walk home to see if our road had been cleared, a few days after a storm.

When snow drifted deep, the town used an Oliver Cletrac crawler tractor with a V plow to break through the drifts. The sight of the Cletrac tractor created a vivid sight. It often showed up at night with bright lights blazing, high up on a big wooden cab, shining both front and rear. The stubby tractor enclosed in the V plow with wing plows extended looked like a huge mechanical June bug, buzzing fiercely. With no muffler the tractor engine roared, the tracks clattered and the ground shook. The house reverberated as the alien looking bug-like monster advanced down our road, to our utter delight.

One night, we kids ran out to follow behind the tractor as it rattled and clanked along, lights ablaze, exhaust roaring. The crawler traveled just a little way beyond our house where the traveled way ended. It suddenly spun around, and came straight at us. We didn't know whether the operator could see us or not. We shrieked, and high-tailed it back to the house. Snow made life difficult for older people, but the first snow was always an exciting time for me. I once ran outside barefoot and never felt the cold. Emmy chased me back inside telling me I would die of pneumonia. Ma just shook her head.

Chapter 3: Sliding

We loved sliding on the snow-covered hills. All the other kids in the surrounding neighborhoods had sleds. The only sled we had was one that had once been the steering section of a traverse, or "rip". It was a clumsy thing made of heavy wood with a strip of steel for runners. The clumsy thing could not be steered, and we felt inferior for not having a sled like the Flexible Flyers that most kids had. Though Pa never bought us birthday or Christmas gifts, he occasionally bought us things at the Salvation Army Store. When Pa came home with a re-varnished Flexible Flyer, we were thrilled. If it had been gilded with gold we could not have been happier.

On cold, crisp winter evenings, we gathered in impromptu sliding parties with other kids from far and wide. We took turns using the new sled and the old traverse front sled. Cold never seemed to bother us. We stayed out until Ma called out "Yoo-hoo" from the porch. Sound traveled far in the crisp air. And the sound of her summoning us was comforting, making me feel good that Ma was concerned enough to call us home.

The only time the heavy wooden sled became really useful was when we used it on a traverse, or "rip", essentially a long plank with a rigid wooden sled, front and rear. The front sled pivoted to steer. The rear sled did not. A dozen kids, or more, could pile aboard. The combined weight would cause the rip to go charging down hill at a ferocious speed. The neighbor family had a steep hill going down from their barn. The hill was sparsely sanded, if at all. Only older kids rode the rip down the treacherous hill.

After an ice storm, the hill iced over beautifully. Sliding was nearly suicidal. The narrow road had the tops of bare boulders sticking up in places. I begged my sister Emmy to let me ride on the rip. "It's too dangerous," she said. "You are not old enough to ride."

The rip lived up to its name, ripping down the treacherous hill like a luge, bouncing off boulders, and throwing showers of sparks in the dark of night as it scraped over stones in its downhill plunge toward a narrow bridge at the foot of the slope. The bridge was edged with more boulders. The helmsman could not control the careening rip full of screaming kids on the run-away rip. Emmy put out her foot to try to slow it down, but it hurtled on in run-away fashion, smashing into the bridge abutment boulders, spilling everyone off, and wrecking the front sled. Emmy wrenched her leg, but other than that, no one was seriously hurt. With the front sled smashed, the rip was out of commission. The kids put it back into the barn.

A couple of years later, when I felt old enough to ride, I approached the neighbor kids about loaning our front sled to replace the smashed one so that we could rip down the hill. Attaining the age of rip riding was a rite of passage, and I felt compelled to take a ride on that rip, just to experience the thrill of it. Danger only made the ride all the more alluring. We replaced the smashed front sled with our sled and brought the rip to the brink of the icy hill. Down we hurtled. One wild ride bouncing off boulders was sufficient. They put the rip back into the barn, saying we would try it later. But later never came and the neighbor kids refused to return our sled. Eventually, I summoned up enough courage to confront their father, who grudgingly returned our sled. I suspect he felt that, since Emmy was aboard the rip when it smashed into the boulders, the temporary replacement sled should have become permanent. The father's extreme irritation at having to give up the sled made me feel like a bad boy all over again.

Chapter 4: Bad boy

Early on, I learned that I was a bad boy and, despite all that my parents did to change me, I still got into trouble. My mother often spanked me and asked in despair, "Oh, why, why can't you be good like Johnny?" He was her son from her first marriage.

My father thrashed me with a heavy strap until he complained of getting arm weary, but I still got into mischief. Pa fancied himself a Sherlock Holmes in detecting guilt. Often, to avoid getting hit, my sisters would say, "Joe did it." That was sufficient evidence. Trouble dogged me at every turn. I loved my parents and yearned to be praised, but discouragement weighed me down. Because the spankings did not keep me out of trouble, I reasoned that it was my nature to be naughty.

One day when Ma was making donuts, she made the mistake of letting me help carry donuts from table to stove. She grew impatient at my slow pace and began hurrying past me with them. "I wanna' be a baker man," I wailed. "I don't have time to have you help," Mama said, handing me a ball of string. "Go play."

Her voice told me she meant it. I went to the pantry. From there I began stringing a telegraph line, tying the end of the string to the cover of her prized green butter dish to anchor it. I looped the string around everything I came to. The string crossed the kitchen, looped around door knobs, the Latouraine coffee can filled with silverware sitting like a centerpiece on the kitchen table, around food tins planted with flowers on the window sill, and anything that I came to. The telegraph line ended at the handle of the corn broom standing in the corner. Busy with the donuts, Ma took little notice that I had strung the line.

As she hurried from the table to the stove, the string blocked her way. She put down one handful of donuts and with a sigh of annoyance, yanked the string to snap it. Half of the kitchen and virtually all the contents of the pantry came crashing to the floor, including her favorite green butter dish. I headed for her bedroom and dove under the bed.

"You naughty, naughty boy! Now look what you've done; you broke my green butter dish. Can't I have a single thing in this house without you breaking it? You're going to get it, but good. Now, come out of there, right now!" She picked the corn broom out of the carnage and stormed into the bedroom. She poked me with the bristles.

"You come out of there, this minute—you're going to get it good. My beautiful green butter dish, "she lamented. "How could you?"

13

I knew I'd eventually get spanked, but figured she'd go a little easier on me if I could put it off until she cooled down. I waited a long time that day, knowing how much she prized that butter dish. Later, when I came out from under the bed to take my spanking, Mama said, "Why can't you be good like Johnny?"

I would have rather had a spanking. I thought long and hard about my not being "good like Johnny." Maybe it was because Johnny was older, or had taken after his father, because Johnny really was good. I'd never seen him get scolded or hit even once. He was good to me and once took me to a bakery and bought me a jelly doughnut. When Pa bought me a tricycle at the Salvation Army store, Johnny ran alongside me, laughing, as he kept me from tipping over as I furiously pedaled down the sidewalk.

"Will I ever be good like Johnny? I once asked. But Ma did not answer.

Chapter 5: Washday

As I grew older, washday held out a chance for me to redeem myself. I helped Ma lug water from the outside rain barrel, pail by pail, to fill a big copper boiler sitting on the glowing kitchen wood stove. The kitchen soon became an inferno.

I lugged more rain water to fill the rinse tub while Ma filled the wash tub with hot water from the boiler. She refilled the boiler from the rain barrel, added a couple of bars of brown P&G lye soap, and put Pa's work clothes in to loosen the ground-in grease and grime. Without stopping to rest, Ma grabbed a piece of clothing from the wash water and began scrubbing on the metal washboard. After scrubbing a section, she looked to see if it was clean, then, turned the clothing to scrub another place. Soon, steam from the top of the boiler came rolling across the low ceiling. The stench of lye filled the air. Wash water soaked the front of Ma's apron. Sweat showed in dark circles under her arms. Ma stopped, from time to time, to rest her head on her forearm. She went back to scrubbing, hurrying, always hurrying, with quick steps, snatching at laundry. The worst of it was; she never quite got her washing caught up.

When Ma got a piece of clothing scrubbed, I cranked it through the wringer into the rinse water and, later, back to wring it dry. As I cranked, my imagination took hold. I became Cranker Man—who could overcome the toughest piece of wet laundry that dared defy him. It was a time when I knew I was being good. I went to take a break out on the porch, away from the heat and steam and stink of lye, when I spotted a pickup truck racing down the road to our farm, trailing a rooster tail of dust. It pulled into our driveway. A sign on the side of the pickup read SEARS & ROEBUCK CO. A washing machine sat on back. I figured the driver was lost and wondered whatever possessed him to turn down our road. A neatly dressed man, wearing a tie, got out.

"Why don't you show me where your mom's at, Sonny?"

Water stood in puddles on the kitchen floor, the boiler billowed steam, and Ma stood hunched over the tub, scrubbing. A huge mound of laundry sat on the floor. Her hair was coming undone, and her face showed weariness and despair.

"Lady, have I got the machine for you," the man said.

"We got no 'electric," Ma said, with a sigh.

"I know that, ma'am. But this machine doesn't need it. A gasoline engine makes it go. And I'm here to give you a free demonstration."

I figured the Sears man couldn't have known Ma would be doing the washing that very day. It was a sure sign that somehow she would have that washer. The salesman seemed to glow as he talked about the end of her drudgery with this miracle of modern science. Ma cut him off. "You jus' wasting your time, mister; my husband will never buy it."

"When he sees how easy it makes life for you, he'll buy it. I know he will. Won't hardly cost more than a pack of cigarettes a day."

Ma's eyes brightened as he told her about the Sears & Roebuck easy payment plan. He unloaded the washer onto the back steps' landing, pulled out the choke knob, stepped on the kick-start pedal and had it puttering merrily in no time.

"I'm gonna' leave the washer here for you to use all day—free," the Sears man said. With that, he hopped into the truck, gave a cheery wave and took off in a swirl of dust. It all happened so fast Ma could only stand there with a big grin on her face. Her eyes were fixed on the purring machine. She hadn't smiled that much since before Julia died. And it made me feel good to see her so happy. Then, with a start, she swung into action to take advantage of this temporary respite presented by God, Sears Roebuck, or maybe St. Jude, patron saint of the hopeless.

She loaded the washer and pulled back on the gear shift lever sticking out on the side. The agitator went into motion swishing the clothes back and forth in the sudsy water. As soon as one batch of washing was done, she'd start another, pausing only long enough to change the water when it got too murky. Soon the clotheslines were full, and we began hanging clothes on barbed wire fences. Then the machine died. Ma clapped her hands to her head. "Yesus Maria, we've worked the poor thing to death."

"No, Ma, maybe not," I said, checking the empty gas tank. I siphoned gas from the saw rig we cut firewood on, and soon had the machine running, again. We took down curtains and stripped the beds. "Take off your clothes," Ma said, and she washed those also. When the fences by the house were full, we spread laundry on bushes and the lawn to dry. Soon, clothes reached out into the hayfield. When we finished spreading the last of the laundry, the farm looked like a clothing factory had exploded. But every last piece of dirty clothing in the house was clean. Ma was caught up at long last. When Pa got home from work, Ma was ecstatic. Her words came out in a jumble as she told Pa about this wonderful washer that only used a little gasoline and could be bought for a pack of cigarettes a day. But Pa just shook his head.

The next day, Ma watched, shoulders slumped, tears brimming, as the Sears & Roebuck man drove off down the road with that wonderful washer.

"Don't worry, Ma," Emmy said, putting an arm around her, "Someday I'll get a job and I'll buy you that washing machine."

Chapter 6: Julia

After Pa refused to buy the washing machine, Ma's eyes sunk into her head. She sighed mournfully, and walked around like a zombie, as she had when Julia died. A strange sound had awakened me on that terrible morning. At first, I thought my mother was singing. My parents and the older kids went to church before Julia was born, and sometimes, while getting dressed for church. Ma sang songs she learned when growing up in Poland. But this didn't sound right. I ran downstairs, half asleep, to see what it was. On the way down, I realized it wasn't Sunday and it wasn't singing. It was wailing—scary wailing. I found Mama in the bedroom, crying in a sing-song voice, over and over, "My baby, my baby, my sweet dear baby," as she washed blood from Julia's mouth. Ma's eyes were red, filled with tears, and there was a terribly sad look on her face.

"What's the matter with Julia, Mama?" I asked. But she didn't seem to hear or even see me. Pa paced back and forth, gesturing with his hands, palm up, looking at the ceiling, saying, "Why? Why?"

When he turned, I saw a big blood stain on his white shirt.

"What's wrong with Julia, Pa?" I asked. But he didn't hear or see me, either. I felt as if it were all a bad dream, with me just looking on, not able to do anything about it. Julia lay on the bed as though she were sleeping. Mama would stop dressing her every little while and pick her up to cradle her and sit on edge of the bed, rocking and crooning the way she did when she put Julia to sleep. From time to time Mama would close her eyes and turn her head back and forth as if she were saying "No, No, No." Tears came, and a terrible moaning sound came from somewhere deep inside her.

As she put a white christening dress on over Julia's head, she had trouble getting her arms into the sleeves. Julia was limp all over. Mama kept brushing away tears as she struggled to dress her. Emmy led me into the kitchen.

"Julia's dead, Joey," Emmy said, putting her arm around me. I remembered how happy Ma and Pa had been when Julia was born. When her labor pains began Ma lay on her bed calling for Emmy.

"Quick, go get the baby lady. Tell her it's time."

Because the mid-wife had once worked for a doctor, Ma had great faith in her. She lived more than a half mile away. Emmy and Irene ran all the way.

The midwife had waddled down the dirt road to our farm, taking her sweet time, her cane in one hand and a mysterious black bag in the other, calm as could be. At the farm, she went into the bedroom to see Ma. When she came out, she took off her shoes and put on worn-out bed slippers. "You boys get behind the stove and stay there," she said. "I got work to do."

The cook stove sat a couple of feet out from the wall. My younger brother, Louis, and I got behind the stove and slid under it on our bellies. The midwife stood by the stove, heating water. Her toes stuck out of holes in her slippers, tempting us. We pinched them, but she just laughed, taking all the fun out of it. From time to time, she went into the bedroom to check on Ma.

When Pa came home from work, she sent him into the bedroom. On one trip, she stayed in the bedroom with Pa for a long time. We all waited in the kitchen, watching the bedroom door. We heard Mama cry out, occasionally, and the midwife murmur. The only sound in the kitchen was the tea kettle singing on the stove. After a while, we heard a baby cry. Pa came out, his shirt sleeves rolled up, carrying a baby wrapped in a towel. The baby lady followed. She had a wash basin of warm water ready on the table. Pa smiled as he put the baby in the water. It was a cute little thing. Pa washed it carefully, as though it would break. We all watched. No one spoke. I kept wondering where that baby came from. It seemed like the magic trick Johnny did, pushing a penny into his arm and getting it out of his ear. I wanted to ask Pa where the baby came from, but I knew we had to keep as silent as wallpaper. We watched in surprise. We weren't used to seeing him taking care of kids, especially a baby, but he seemed happy with the little thing and I wondered if he was going to keep it, seeing as he always said there were too many kids. I asked my sisters, in a whisper, where the baby came from, but they just got embarrassed, grinned and whispered, "God sent her."

The baby had seemed as pink as the baby mice my older brothers used to find in nests in the corn crib. They gave me the babies to keep as pets. And I'd keep those little pink mice in a wooden Kraft cheese box, but they always died and turned grey. I wondered if this baby would be as hard to keep alive as the baby mice.

The midwife came for a few more days to help take care of Ma, the baby, the house and the farm animals who had to be fed and watered. She wanted to help out a few days longer because Ma was still moving pretty slow, but Ma wouldn't have it. Later, she explained. "The baby lady doesn't charge, and it's not nice to ask people to work without paying them. We'll just have to get along as best we can." Mama thanked her and gave her a hug.

At Julia's christening, friends and relatives came to celebrate. They each laid a dollar bill on Julia in her crib to make a blanket of money. People talked and laughed and joked. Someone said, "Being the 13th must be lucky, seeing how healthy she is."

Pa acted a little funny and stopped smiling when they said that. We didn't know he had a secret. Ma and Pa seemed happier than they'd been in a long time. Ma smiled wide when people exclaimed, "Oh, what a healthy baby—so fat and so happy."

One morning, Julia woke up sick. Her face turned white and her body went limp between spasms. She wouldn't eat and grew worse and worse. Ma and Pa were scared. Julia had never been sick before. They tried all kinds of home remedies because Pa didn't have much faith in doctors. "What's a doctor going to do?" he said. "They just take your money."

Julia cried more and more. She began doubling up and kicking her feet. Her stomach swelled and she cried ever harder. Late in the day, Mama wrapped Julia in a blanket, and she and Pa went off to find a doctor. When they got back, Ma was biting her lip. Julia wasn't crying or fussing, anymore. She just went, "Uh, uh," panting in little breaths, as though it hurt her to breathe.

Pa was scowling. "See? What did I tell you? That miserable doctor wouldn't even look at her. He was more worried about his dog catching cold from running in the wet grass."

"Well, doctors don't like to be bothered at home," Ma said in a low voice. "And we've never been to him before. We'll just have to try to get her to take some of the medicine the druggist gave us, and wait until tomorrow when the doctor will see her at nine o'clock."

Ma's lips began to move in prayer as she laid Julia back in her crib. But, at about 6 o'clock next morning, Julia vomited blood and died.

With Ma and Pa both in shock, Emmy took charge.

"Gladys, take the kids and go pick some flowers; I'll keep Louis home."

Before long, we each had a big bunch of flowers, but Gladys kept saying, "Oh, look, there's some blue flags over there," or "Oh, look! Let's go a little farther and get some Purple Gentians."

Gladys, read a lot and knew the names of all the flowers, or pretended to. "Gladys," Irene said, "I know what you're up to. You're dragging us all over creation to keep us away from the house. Well, I'm soaking wet, I'm cold, and I'm going home."

"O.K., O.K. But first, we have to stop and tell the Studers about Julia."

Mr. Studer answered the door. When we told him about Julia, he just stood there in the doorway with his mouth open, like he wanted to say something. But no words came out. Then, Mrs. Studer came to the door, put her arms around us and herded us in for hot chocolate. When we left, Mr. Studer gave Gladys $5, but it was the hot chocolate and the softness of Mrs. Studer's hands I liked best.

When we got back with the flowers, Ma and Pa were gone. Emmy said they'd gone to see the priest and to find an undertaker. We tiptoed into the bedroom to look at Julia. She lay in her crib in her christening dress and bonnet with a blanket tucked up under her chin. She looked the way she always did when she slept--- except that her cheeks weren't pink anymore. She was turning a yellowish gray.

"She doesn't look dead," Emmy whispered.

Emmy was right. She didn't look dead. She looked like she was sleeping. But I knew what dead mice looked like and she was beginning to look like them.

"What's going to happen to her?" I asked.

Emmy put her arm around me. "Julia's going to heaven."

The only thing I knew about heaven was from the big holy picture hanging on the dining room wall. In the picture, a priest was giving communion to a family who all looked right up at God without a one of them hanging their head or anything, like they'd never done one single thing wrong in their whole life. It was a kind of open-roofed church with God floating up above with his arms stretched out. Angels were flying around him. A bright sort of spot-light beam shone down out of God's right palm to the good people who were receiving communion. The light was drawing them up so that their feet were off the floor. God's left palm gave off a darker beam shining down on this sorry-looking bunch, kneeling in a fire pit, at the other side of the altar. They were hanging their heads and had their hands together as if they were begging to be raised up out of the fire. I did not want Julia in the fire pit.

Ma and Pa came home and took Julia away. They returned without her, and didn't say anything. They just sat on the bed together, next to the empty crib, with their shoulders slumped. Pa looked at me and said, "There's our mischief maker," and mussed my hair and smiled a little. I wished I wasn't such a mischief maker and that they would love me. I wanted to be good like Ma's son, Johnny, and I wondered if they would be sad if I died.

Along toward evening, the undertaker came to the farm. He brought two sawhorses into the dining room and draped them with a white cloth to make a stand. He carried in a small white coffin and set it on the stand, then stood two tall candles on the floor on either side, lit them, and opened the coffin. He did not speak except to say "Goodbye" as he was leaving.

Julia wasn't yellow or gray, anymore. She looked like a doll, all powdered and rouged with pink lips and cheeks, nestled in a box with white satin around her. After the family knelt to pray for Julia, we went to bed, leaving the candles burning. I couldn't sleep, thinking about Julia. Late that night, I crept downstairs. Julia looked lonely in her little coffin. It seemed all very mysterious to see her lying there so peaceful, and I wondered why she had to die. The candles flickered and scary shadows leaped on the wall. I worried that the candles would fall against the curtains and set the house on fire. I went back to bed, wondering what was going to happen next.

In the morning, a lot of people came to the farm, including my sister Helen and her husband, Ludovico Magrini. They lived in another state. His right arm was blown off when he was a boy. His wooden right arm just hung there, covered by his white shirt sleeve buttoned at the wrist. The hand had a glove covering it. People tried not to stare, but it never bothered him. I looked up to Magrini because he could do anything he wanted with his good left arm.

The undertaker set up Julia's coffin out on the lawn. Everyone passed by to have a last look at her, and say goodbye. Ma started crying like her heart would break. She kissed Julia, over and over, sobbing, and wailing, not letting the undertaker close the cover until someone took her away. Cars lined up behind the hearse for the ride to the cemetery. At the cemetery gate, the caretaker held up his hand like a cop. The undertaker talked to him for a while, then, walked back to our car.

"The priest isn't here. He wants five dollars before he comes to say the prayer," the undertaker said, "and we can't bury the baby until he gets $16 for the burial plot."

The muscles in Pa's jaw bulged and jumped. He swore, calling the priest a bad name.

"You stay here. I'll take the Missus to the church to see the priest."

Everyone sat waiting in the cars. No one in our car talked. We just waited and waited. The sun beat down; it got hotter and hotter. The only sound was that of the caretaker's push mower as he trimmed the grass. My sisters fanned their faces with their hankies. My shirt was sticking to my back. Just when I thought the undertaker was never coming back and we'd all die of the heat, he drove up and said something to the caretaker, who was still acting very important. The undertaker showed him a paper. Their voices got loud. The undertaker pointed at the sky and said. "We don't need the priest to come to say a prayer. I'll say a prayer that God will hear just as well as the priest's five dollar prayer."

The cars moved along past neatly mowed grass. When Pa saw the hearse going through the brush way out to the back of the cemetery, he looked like he was going to say a bad word, again. I really didn't know what that meant, but it didn't sound good, the way Pa said it.

Someone had dug a hole in the brush. A big pile of dirt stood next to it. The undertaker said a prayer about Julia going to heaven. Everything got real quiet. Women began sniffling and wiping their eyes. When the men lowered the coffin down into the hole, tears ran down Mama's face. She threw a handful of dirt down on Julia's coffin. My sisters and Pa cried. A lump stuck in my throat. I couldn't cry and my stomach hurt. The men took off their jackets and bent to shovel dirt down over the coffin until the hole was full. They mounded up the left-over dirt on the grave and patted it smooth. It didn't look at all like the holy picture. I began to worry. How was Julia ever going to get out of that hole and go up to heaven with all that dirt heaped on top of her?

The undertaker poked two holes in the mound to hold the flowers people brought. He took the wild flowers from Irene and scattered them over the dirt. Everyone stood around for a little while before driving off. I wanted to go to sleep and wake up to see Julia smiling and kicking her feet. I wanted everything to be the same again. But it never was.

Chapter 7: The Old Green Car

After Julia died, Ma sent us out to play in the old green car, more and more. We spent hours and hours pretending we were royalty going for a ride. The car really wasn't old. In fact it still looked practically brand new. Pa had parked it out behind the barn when the engine bearings burned out. He went back to the Essex agency to buy another Essex—a tan one.

"For $50, I buy a better Essex than the first one that cost $1000," he said. "The Depression is a bad time. But if you got money, it's good. Everything is cheap."

I loved that old green car and made up my mind that someday I'd get a good motor somewhere, maybe in a junkyard, and I'd drive that car all over the country just like the trips we imagined. There was something magical about being inside the car. We were transported to another land away from the outside world. We became royalty, rich beyond belief, going on fabulous journeys to far off lands, attending Cinderella balls, royal weddings and tours to exotic places. As driver, I was a skillful chauffeur and not a bad boy. I couldn't wait until I was old enough to fix up our friend, the old green car, and drive endlessly on real adventures. Parking that car out behind the barn was the best thing Pa had ever done for us kids. We never ceased to wonder at Mama's quick consent whenever we asked permission to play in it.

"Go, go. Play as long as you want. I fix you lunch."

The girls dressed up in the fancy cast-off clothes that people were forever giving Mama, nowhere near her size, and usually some strange style. I don't know if they expected her to wear those gowns when slopping the hogs, but they were perfect dress-up clothes for our fantasy trips. After my sisters got their finery on, I'd unsnap the top of my cap and play the part of chauffeur. I'd hold the door open for them as they climbed into the car in their grand attire. "To the opera, James," they'd say in a snooty voice, and we'd take off on our fantasy trip with appropriate engine noises provided by the chauffeur. We stuffed the emerald chariot's cut glass bud vases on the door posts with daises or Indian paint brushes. I never dreamed that our beloved old green car would ever be gone. It had been a part of our lives as long as I could remember and I always thought it'd be there until the day I died.

Chapter 8: Potato Pancakes

Late one evening we were eating potato pancakes, our absolute favorite. Ma didn't like to make them because it took too long to peel and grate the potatoes and to fry them in lard. She only made them when we were low on food and there wasn't much else to eat. Cooking them smoked up the kitchen, so she kept the kitchen door open even in cold weather. We loved it because we didn't have to sit crowded on the long benches at the kitchen table, and could go out on the porch to eat the pancakes. For us it was a party. We could talk and laugh, and we didn't need to keep quiet as we did when Pa was home. We just loved everything about it.

One evening, Pa was at work on the night shift, and we were polishing off pancakes faster than Ma could fry them. As soon as they were done, she scooped them out of the frying pan and flipped them right into our hands, still piping hot. We'd juggle our pancakes, and go outside on the porch to cool them enough to eat.

I was standing on the porch next to my older sister Irene when someone appeared out of the darkness. It was a little scary. The shadowy figure stood on the ground, below the porch, in the shadows.

"Hey, kid, gimme me one of them pancakes. I'm hungry."

I didn't know what to make of it. I was too scared to hand him my pancake, but Irene gave him hers. As he came closer to reach for the pancake, I could see he was just a boy. As soon as Irene came back with another pancake, he asked for it, again. She kept making repeated trips and he kept wolfing them down. It didn't seem to bother him that they were hot. He asked me for mine, again.

"Who are you, anyway," I asked, trying to get a good look at him in the darkness.

"Stanley," he said, "your half brother."

I vaguely remembered Stanley talking to Johnny about the snow plow, but the concept of a half brother still confused me. The shadowy figure looked a little thin, but otherwise seemed whole enough to me. When Irene came back, he asked her for yet another pancake. Irene balked.

"Go in, and get your own; I haven't had one to eat, yet, myself."

"Don't tell your Ma I'm out here, just give me another pancake."

Someone gave him one. The way he'd bolted those hot pancakes, he seemed terribly hungry.

"Do they ever talk about me?" he asked between bites. "Do they ever wish I'd come home?"

No one answered, and he slipped away into the night as silently as he'd come.

Chapter 9: Sweet Potatoes

One day when Pa was at work, Ma bustled about in the kitchen with a happy look on her face. I saw something that looked like cooked squash sitting in a bowl.

"What's that?" I asked.

"Get away from there, that's sweet potato for Johnny."

I'd never tasted sweet potato. We never grew anything but white potatoes. Ma must have sneaked the sweet potatoes by Pa when she went into the store to buy groceries at the First National. He usually sat waiting in the car while she shopped. He kept control of the money, even when only Ma was working. He might have been especially overbearing that day. Ma went in the front door of the First National. I followed. She zipped out the rear door of the store, slipped in the back door of the adjoining tavern, slapped money on the bar, the bartender quickly poured her a shot of liquor, she tossed it down and hurried back into the store to finish shopping. She dutifully deposited the change into Pa's outstretched hand. She seemed calmer and at peace, with a bit of a smug smile on her face with the sweet potatoes that she had tucked away in the grocery bag and her quick trip to the tavern.

I pestered for a taste until she gave me a spoonful, to get rid of me.

"Yuk." I said. "That tastes like someone dumped sugar into mashed potatoes."

"Good! Because there's only enough for Johnny."

Ma continued bustling around the kitchen, eyes shining bright and a contented smile on her face.

"Johnny is coming home from the CCC," she said, as though she could hardly believe it. Just talking about Johnny coming home made Ma happy. He was good to me and came to my defense one day, when the girls teased me when I had an accident on the way to the outhouse. I was sad when he left home.

Even after Johnny froze his ears walking the six miles from school, Pa still did not transport the kids, though he was paid a stipend to do so. All three of them were Ma's kids from her first marriage. Pa worked the swing shift, the time didn't come right for him to transport them, he was sleeping, or gas cost money. He reasoned that if he could walk across Poland to come to America, they could walk to high school. Pa had already taken his daughter Helen out of school to work in the onion fields, and later got her a housekeeping job. Walter and Stanley, Pa's boys by his first wife, had already quit school at about age 13, so they were spared the walk. By the time Mary, John, and Elisabeth trudged the six miles through snow-clogged roads to get to school, they often shivered so much the teachers would let them stand by a radiator to thaw out until their hands stopped shaking.

Mary didn't have any overshoes. She wore a pair of men's rubber barn boots. When she got in sight of school, she put on her shoes and hid the boots in a snow bank, ashamed to be seen wearing them. After school let out, she'd hang back until the other school kids had gone along, so they wouldn't see her uncover the boots to put them on for the long walk, home.

When Mary quit, Pa got her a job taking care of a grocer's kids and doing the housework in their apartment over the store and working part-time in the store. Johnny quit next, and without him to walk with her, Bessie quit, too. Pa got her a job as housekeeper and nanny for three dollars a week. Pa came around on pay day to collect her wages. However, it wasn't unusual, back then, for working children to give part of their pay to their parents. Here they gave it all.

Chapter 10: Johnny and the CCC

Johnny couldn't find work after quitting high school. There wasn't a job to be had, anywhere. On October 12, 1934, Johnny joined the Civilian Conservation Corps. The enlistment age was 18. He was only 17, but they enrolled him anyway. The CCC furnished room and board, a uniform, related clothing and $5 a month. In addition, the government sent a $25 monthly allotment check to each family. It was tough going during those lean years and the CCC check helped us get by.

The CCC was a make-work project to keep young men occupied, where they learned useful occupations, to give them hope and to keep them out of trouble. The CCC was one of the first of Franklin Delano Roosevelt's many projects to get the economy going during the Great Depression. They wore WWI Army uniforms and got off to a quick start using Army officers to organize the project. It was a huge success. The enlistees built camp housing and furniture, cut hiking trails, built dams and small bridges, cleaned forests of underbrush, helped fight fires, cleaned farmers' barns and dug water holes for fire protection. The CCC sent these young men, who had seldom traveled outside of their community, to other parts of the country. It gave them a better self-image and broadened their horizons.

The CCC certainly changed Johnny. He had never traveled far from home. Going to Camp Lewiston in Maine with the CCC was a turning point in his life. He saw some of the country, received some education, gained self confidence, and it got him away from the stress of living with his stepfather—Pa.

John hitchhiked home with gifts he'd made in the camp craft shop. He arrived in Greenfield at his sister Mary's house in the dead of night. The neighbor's dog raised such a ruckus it woke up the neighborhood. Lights went on in other houses. The man who lived in the downstairs apartment yelled at Johnny, "Get the Hell out of here before I call the cops." Mary explained that Johnny was her brother and got the man calmed down.

The next day, Johnny came to the farm and gave me a coin bank made from a section of popular tree with an Indian figurehead burned into the side. We saw a lot more of Johnny than we did of Stanley and Walter after they ran away from home.

Stanley and Walter were Pa's kids, and were close. Stanley had been the first to run away, in the dead of winter at about age14. He knew he was in trouble because he went to work for a neighbor to help saw wood, instead of giving me a bath in the washtub.

"It snowed a foot of snow during the night," Stanley later said. "The Old Man didn't come home because the road wasn't plowed out. Your mother said I was going to get a good licking when Pa got home, so I threw a few things in a burlap bag and headed out in that foot of snow. I didn't know where I was going, or what I was going to do, or where I was going to stay. I just didn't want to stick around for another whipping."

Walter waited to leave until spring, when the snow was gone. As he was going out the door, Ma warned him not to try sleeping in the barn, telling him Pa would jab a pitch fork into the hay to find him when he got home from work. Walter went to stay in the empty tobacco barn across the field from our house. He waited there, hoping someone would come to ask him to return home. But they never did.

"It was cold and damp on the dirt floor, and I was hungry," Walter later said, shaking his head. "Johnny knew I was there. He could have brought me something to eat. Bugs crawling over my face kept me awake at night. It was awful. After a few days, I went looking for Stanley."

I was often reminded of Johnny, Stanley and Walter when I used the outhouse and looked through the Sears Roebuck catalogues that the boys loved to study.

Chapter 11: Outhouse

I first saw real toilet paper when we went to visit some city folks in Holyoke, MA. We used scraps of newspaper, or the Sears & Roebuck catalog, which made was a lot more interesting than looking at a roll of toilet paper. Buying toilet paper seemed foolishly extravagant, as well as boring. The catalogue sent me into a dream state. The visions of paradise that Sears & Roebuck held out to us were far more attractive than the ones the priest droned on about on Sunday. We couldn't wait to read the new catalog when it came in the mail. When a new one arrived, the next stop for the old catalog was the outhouse, where it furnished reading material as well as toilet paper.

The outhouse was at the end of a long woodshed attached to the house. The woodshed was nothing fancy; just a big sloping box built with log rafters and rough lumber that weathered silver gray on the outside. A door, at the far end, opened onto a room the size of a closet with just enough space for a "two-holer".

The "two-holer" seat, nailed onto a raised platform the size of a blanket chest, had a small hole for children and a big hole for adults. The hole edges were "smooth and rounded for utmost comfort in colonial maple or walnut finish" as described in the Sears Roebuck catalogue. We were careful to first tear out pages of the catalog that were of least interest. Pages showing jewelry and watches, Winchester rifles, Daisy BB guns, fishing and trapping equipment, Coleman kerosene lamps and lanterns, stew pots, spiders, and ladies undergarments were saved as long as possible. Horse harnesses, wiffle trees, sulky plows, snaths, and pre-cut houses complete with front porches were of interest but not essential. Anything to do with electricity or plumbing was fair game—since we had neither on our farm. I sometimes read them as a kind of fantasy or science fiction, wondering what life would be like with indoor plumbing, electric lights and a radio. It was something to dream about, but totally out of the reach in our present state of finances. But, I was content to look and dream. Selecting a suitable page grew increasingly troublesome as the catalogue grew thinner. Not only would the person have to make a tough choice, but they had to consider the wrath of someone who wanted to save a particular page of interest. I sometimes flipped to the corset pages to guiltily invade the privacy of the demure models who modestly cast their gaze downward or to the side.

The outhouse seemed like a world of its own. The enchanting daydreams brought on by the catalog were accompanied by flies buzzing in the soft light, gliding in circles perilously close to webs cast by spiders lying in wait. A shovel stuck in a pail of wood ashes stood ready to scatter a covering after each toilet use. Motes drifted in a shaft of light angled down from a small open triangle where the top of the privy door sagged away from the door frame. The atmosphere created a fantasy world that made hope real and the owning of treasures, displayed in the "wish book," possible.

After dark, it was another story. Even after I'd started grammar school, and slept outdoors when visitors were given in our beds, I'd sometimes ask Ma to go out to the outhouse with me at night. I think it was from my earlier experience of falling through the hole. Or it could have been just to get her undivided attention. It never failed to amaze me that Ma would take time from her bustling about, light the lantern, and go out to sit with me to wait patiently. There wasn't much conversation, but I felt close to her and cherished our time together. To have her to myself even for those few minutes presented me with the illusion that she loved me despite my flaws. It never dawned on me that she might have regarded this time as a respite from her unending chores, rather than the mildly annoying sacrifice and the act of love that I imagined. But the time together, sharing the comforting glow of the lantern seemed to signify that she did love me, after all; though she never seemed to be able to ever bring herself to tell me that, even once in her lifetime.

The disaster of falling through the hole began one Sunday afternoon when I'd begged my older sisters to read me the comics. They didn't want to be bothered. But Helen, arriving home for a visit, took pity on me. She sat next to me on the running board of the Essex, reading me the funnies. It was Pa's first Essex that we sat on, the emerald beauty that we later played in as the "old green car", out behind the barn.

Helen showered me with affection, kissing and hugging me when she arrived. I think it was because Pa had given Helen the honor of naming me. She chose to name me after Pa, the most important person in her life, not knowing Pa had once had another son named "Joseph" who no one in the family knew about. In a way, it was just as well I didn't know. The sheer number of kids in the family was already confusing enough. Someone had once tried explaining the relationships in our combined family, with brothers and sisters, half brothers and half sisters, and stepbrothers and stepsisters, but it only confused me more. Years later, when I discovered the other Joseph, I wondered if Pa was especially hard on me because I reminded him of his first-born who had died in infancy.

Helen and the older kids flitting in and out of our lives seemed quite natural. It didn't seem at all strange that Helen should suddenly appear one day to read me the funnies. She read the balloons over each character's head, patiently explaining what was taking place as she read. When she'd finished narrating the funnies on that memorable day, I went to the outhouse by myself to show her how grown-up I was. Curiosity got the best of me, and since I was grown up enough to go to the outhouse alone, I decided to try out the big adult hole. Down I went, like Alice in Wonderland. It wasn't very far to fall—three or four feet, at most—but it seemed a lot more. The landing was soft and dark. But it stunk, and the outside world was now high above me like two holes in the night sky. Panic gripped me. Some unnamed horror was sure to get me in that foul smelling pit. I sensed something stirring. There was no telling what lurked in the dark. Bugs and rats, maybe, or even snakes posed to strike. I cried out for help, and then cried some more when no help came. At last, Helen, hearing my cries, called to my sisters.

"Joey's fallen through the hole. Come and get him out. I'm all dressed up."

"Well, we're dressed up, too," was the answer.

Helen went to the back of the outhouse, opened the clean-out door, and pulled me out. The outside world, that had seemed such an impossible distance away, suddenly looked safe in the bright sunshine. I was grateful for Helen's rescue, holding her in high regard from that day forward, even though she'd held me out as far away from herself as she could. Fortunately, I was considered too young to go to church and Ma later told me that I was not wearing Sunday best clothes. Ma later explained that usually only the kids able to dress themselves went to church on Sunday, and that she had enough to do without that. Helen washed me up in the brook and dressed me in clean clothes.

Chapter 12: Church Collection

One Sunday, after I was considered old enough to go to church, the usher sat us way up in the front of the church. During collection, he waved the collection basket close to Pa's nose when he didn't drop in any money. Pa quickly ducked his head back to keep from getting hit. The priest glared at Pa from the pulpit, "Some people don't have money to give to God but have money to spend on drink."

The muscles in Pa's jaw started working. I felt ashamed, and wished Pa had more money. I began wondering why God would need money since He could do anything He wanted to do.

Soon after that, Pa went to see the priest to make arrangements for our first communion. There were five of us who had yet to do so. When Pa came home his eyes were wild looking.

"The priest said it would cost $10 for each kid. I told him that would be more than I made in a month if I was working steady. But he wouldn't budge. I told him that he should be hung from a lamp post."

Ma tried to calm him down, but Pa hit the table with his fist. I hid in the built in wood box. We didn't go to church for a long time after that. Time went on. And when it didn't look like we would get a new priest any time, soon, Ma went to St Mary's, the Irish church, to see if we could go to church there. The priest was very nice about it, and Ma enrolled us in Sunday school. When it came time to make our first communion, Pa told us to ask the nuns how much it would cost. The nuns said an offering of 50 cents would do—if we had it. By now, Gladys who was four years older than me was already in high school and didn't want to parade in the public procession with all the little kids. I wasn't all that crazy about it either. I felt embarrassed, towering over the other little kids going to the altar to receive first communion from a visiting bishop.

Soon, so many parishioners of Our Lady of Czestochowa switched to St. Mary's that the diocese began sending a Polish-speaking priest to St. Mary's to hear confessions during Lent. Pa never got over the shabby treatment by the Polish priest during Julia's burial and vowed to have Julia transferred to the St. Mary's cemetery. But when we heard some of the parishioners saying, "Why don't they stick with their own kind and go to their own church," Pa gave up. He stopped talking about having Julia's body moved, and quit going to church altogether. Years later, after the Polish church lost a large majority of parishioners, a fine priest took over. Membership surged back strong, but Pa was disgusted with the whole thing and said he would deal direct.

Sometimes on Sunday afternoons we'd drive up to the cemetery to see Julia's grave. There wasn't any marker—just a little mound of dirt out in the bushes. Ma would kneel to pray, and her eyes would fill up as she tugged at the sprigs of brush that crowded in on the grave.

Mama always worried that the brush would take over and no one would know where Julia was buried. But there was no money for a gravestone. She began getting so worked up when we visited the grave that Pa would put it off as long as he could. But that just made it worse the next time when she saw more brush had crowded in.

One day, when we went to the cemetery, we saw the grave had settled. Ma began to cry. I wanted to tell her it was O.K. because that meant Julia had somehow gotten out of there and had gone up to heaven to be with the angels. But, Ma never seemed to smile anymore. I hoped Pa would get more steady work so we could buy a stone, but the mill laid workers off more often. Pa began spending more time at the Polish club. His heart trouble and ulcers got worse. While money was scarce, we usually had enough to eat because we raised a lot of our own food. But the coal bin had long since been empty, and the wood fire in the kitchen stove did not last the night. If a water glass anywhere in the house were left out, the water froze and the glass broke The door to the upstairs bedrooms, where we kids slept, was kept closed. On windy nights, curtains moved by gusts that found their way around the loose-fitting windows.

The wind howled and the windows rattled all one wintry night. In the morning, Emmy found a little pile of snow next to her bed. "Time to put on more quilts," She laughed. "I thought I'd freeze to death last night."

Emmy hunted for more quilts and, when she found none, she piled old coats on us. In the end she took Johnny's army overcoat from the CCC and laid that on, too. But by the time she piled on enough quilts and coats to keep us warm, we could scarcely breathe from the sheer weight. The sheets were ice-cold when we first went to bed and seemed to take forever to warm up.

Sometimes, we heated flat irons on the kitchen stove to take to bed to warm our feet. The irons held heat for quite a while. But one night Louis and I tried something different. We filled two quart whiskey bottles with hot water to take to bed. During the night, the bottles banged together, or maybe the bottles got too far down to the foot of the bed, froze, and broke. Next morning, icicles hung from the foot of the bed. Ma began crying when she came up to wake us for school. Soon after that, she announced we were going to make down quilts.

Chapter 13: Story Telling

Feather quilts are warm and light. Goose down is best, but our geese had long since been served up on the table. Arnold Studer let us have all the turkey feathers we wanted. But we had to strip them.

We'd start with a huge mound of turkey feathers in the center of the kitchen table, and strip the vanes from either side of the quill. That was to keep quills from stabbing through the covering, and to make a softer quilt. We piled the curled vanes on the table in front of us, and put the stripped quill in a cloth on our lap. Stripping was tedious. As the evening wore on, the mound of turkey feathers in the center of our table grew smaller and the down in front of us grew larger. If anyone sneezed or laughed, stripped feathers flew everywhere. Saying anything funny was strictly forbidden. Unfortunately, there was a tendency to get silly as the evening progressed. Though we were forbidden to say anything funny, I never could resist saying something to make everyone explode in laughter. The feathers would fly, and Ma wouldn't be able to keep from laughing. But it didn't keep her from cuffing me.

A safer pastime was story telling. Though Ma never told funny stories as we stripped feathers, we looked forward to her stories of days gone by. Her story-telling gave me a good feeling. It was comforting to hear her talk of earlier times, as we all sat around the kitchen table with the hanging kerosene lamp casting a cheerful glow over the gathered family.

"Tell us about the old days, Ma," we'd say, and she'd begin.

The stories of her childhood in Poland reminded me of the book Heidi. I could imagine Ma's log home in the mountains, never dreaming that one day I would visit that very same house, still there, in the Tatra Mountains looking very much like Heidi's grandfather's still vivid in my memory.

One evening while we were stripping feathers, Ma told us of neighbors coming to her family's home to strip goose feathers on long winter nights. They'd always have food and sometimes a drink before they began working. Those were happy times. Neighbors talked and joked as they worked. When one family finished stripping their supply of feathers, the group would move on to another house. The work bee also served as a social gathering to ease the long dreary months of cold and isolation.

Ma told us about a wolf that howled one evening as a group of women began leaving Ma's home. The women beat a hasty retreat to the house.

"Tata went outside," Ma said. "The wolf howled, again. Then, we hear other wolves, 'AWOO, AWOOO.' None of the women wanted to go home."

Grandfather poured kerosene on a homemade broom, made of brush bound to a stick. He set it on fire. Raising the torch overhead, he led the frightened women home. "I always feel safe around Tata—he so brave," Ma said.

Sometimes she told about the good times in America—living in Chicago, meeting her boyhood sweetheart in Housatonic, and sharecropping at Cold Brook Farm in Montague. Sometimes the stories were sad. Leaving Cold Brook Farm had been hard for Ma, especially since my half sister, Mary, had stayed on to work taking care of the new sharecroppers' baby. Mary was Ma's first-born by her husband, Franz—or "Frank", as he was later known in America. Ma's other two children, Bessie and Johnny, came later. Franz was Ma's childhood sweetheart and her whole life. That former life was but a lingering memory—a memory that got better each passing year, as she reminisced about those bygone days on evenings that Pa worked the night shift.

"If not for Mary, Johnny, and Bessie, I think I dream it," she said, her eyes looking far beyond the pile of feathers. "This life, not like the other life. Pa is not like my first husband. I am glad Pa took me and my children, but sometimes," she said, "too many children—his, mine, and more together—too many." She shook her head.

I knew what was coming next. Ma would sigh and wonder out loud if there would be no end to childbearing and taking care of youngsters, working in the fields, keeping house, cooking, cleaning, and scrubbing endless mounds of dirty laundry only to have the clothes grow dingier with each washing. Then there was a barn full of animals to feed, and water to carry. The orchard and garden meant fruit and vegetables, but with them came weeding and hoeing, picking and canning. "Too many children," she'd say. "And too much work."

Hearing her despair weighed me down with guilt for being one of the "too many children." Sometimes it made me feel resentful and frustrated, and I'd try to divert her attention by changing the subject.

"Tell us about coming though the war."

Her eyes would brighten and she'd begin, "Mary was just a baby, then. I live in Housatonic with my first husband." A trace of smile would appear and the lines in her face would soften.

"I'm not twenty years old, yet, and I miss my Mama and Tata. I not see them for two years—maybe more. After I have Mary, I get such an ache in my heart for my family in Poland. I just want to see them again and our home in the mountains, made from big logs, smoke coming from the chimney. That's all I can think."

Ma's eyes sparkled as she backtracked to how she and her first husband met, "Franz and me, we grow up next door to each other. When he was a little boy, he says he is going to marry me some day. But life is very hard in Poland and everyone talks of going to Ameryka. One day, his family goes away with him. Where, I don't know. I only know they go to Ameryka. Later my Tata goes to Ameryka alone. We have only enough money for one ticket."

Arriving in America in 1910, Grandpa didn't find his skills as a tailor of sheepskin coats much in demand. He got work in the Chicago stockyards, saved money and sent for his wife Aniela and three of their children—Ma, eleven, her brother Frank, nine, and Jan, four. Baby Aniela stayed behind with relatives in Poland. Three years later, they sent for Aniela. For her trip to America, relatives in Poland entrusted little Aniela in the care of a man from their village who was also bound for Chicago. They pinned the name and Chicago address of Aniela's family to his coat lapel so he wouldn't lose it. When Aniela and her protector got to Ellis Island, he got drunk celebrating his arrival, and lost the address card. Because he could not read, the man had no idea what was written on the card. With no address they'd be sent back to Poland, immigration authorities said. But Aniela said she could remember what the numbers and letters looked like. The officials gave her pencil and paper. From memory, she wrote out the address—Blazef Gawel, 8870 Houston Ave. Chicago, Ill. Immigration authorities took her word that the address was correct. Aniela and her "caretaker" left detention on Ellis Island and continued on to Chicago.

"When my Matka got here," Ma said, "She and my father opened a boarding house. When fellows hear about a boarding house serving Polish food and where people speak Polish, they come from all over. Sometimes three men, who work on different shifts, sleep in the same bed at different times. Someone was always sleeping in the bed. It was hard to change sheets."

For five years, Ma's parents prospered. Then, life took a dark turn.

"Fella' comes in with a side of beef, slams it on the table and says, 'Give me money'. Charges more than it worth, and it stolen for sure. My Mama gets scared and says to Tata, 'Better we go back to Poland. We already saved enough money. We can live good in the old country and not be scared of gangsters bringing stolen meat.'

"My Mama goes back to Poland. But she leaves me and Tata to sell the furniture and the house. One day, I'm poking the coal fire to start cooking for boarders. I'm about fifteen then. A man comes in the kitchen—Tata is away. He grabs me and kisses me. I say, 'Let go,' but he just laughs. He says, 'What you going to do? No one here but you and me.' He won't let go. I get scared and take the hot poker out of the fire and hit his face. It gives him a scar. After that, nobody grabs me. But my Tata says I have to go to live with relatives in Housatonic in Massachusetts if I want to stay in Ameryka."

Ma left Chicago for the little town of Housatonic in Massachusetts.

Chapter 14: Re-united

One Sunday, as Ma was leaving church, Franz, her childhood sweetheart, appeared.

"Maria!" Franz said. "I thought I would never lay eyes on you again on this earth. Come and visit my family. They will be so happy fate has brought us together again."

Love between the young couple rekindled and they soon married. She was 16; he was a year or two older. "I am so happy, I did not think anything bad would happen," Ma said, pausing for a moment.

"A year goes by and Mary was born two weeks before Christmas, December 11, 1912. All I can think is to go back to Poland to see my family, to show them my baby." A smile came across her face and Ma's eyes lit up, as if seeing something only she could see. I felt lost amidst the family gathered around the table mounded with feathers, envious of Mary for being so wanted and so treasured.

"My husband has a good job working for a school. He helps teachers when boys play baseball and football; nights, he works for a plumber. He was a volunteer fireman, too."

Her fingers flew stripping feathers; the pile of down grew.

"One time I come home with a new dress. He says, 'Take those rags back to the store and buy a good dress. No—buy two.'"

More and more homesick for her family, Ma set out for Poland with baby Mary in the spring of 1913. Mary was about six months old. Ma had no idea what an ordeal they would endure. As she got ready to leave, her husband said, "You must take plenty of money with you. No one knows what can happen."

So she made a little sack for the extra money, pinned it to her corset, and took a train with baby Mary to New York where they boarded a ship for Poland. The journey took two weeks crossing the Atlantic, a long train trip across Europe, and then a horse and wagon ride to her village. My mother and Mary arrived at her ancestral home in the village of Bialka, in the province of Nowy Targ, close by the Czech border. It was cause for celebration.

"It is the first time I see my two baby sisters, born after my Mama and Tata go back to Poland. The whole village came to see us. At the end, they play the Polish National Anthem—'Poland will never vanish as long as we live.'"

Tears wet her cheeks. Her eyes had that far-away look, once again.

"Someday, if I ever have the money, I want to go back to Poland, again." She wiped her eyes with her apron and began putting stripped feathers into a pillowcase. She looked at the clock. "Time to put away the feathers and go to bed."

Chapter 15: Ma Goes Through the War

The next evening Ma began to tell us about getting caught in Poland by WWI. "We have such a happy time. But war breaks out. Now, I was afraid the fighting comes to us. I tell my Mama, I want to go back to Ameryka before winter storms make the ocean rough. But she says stay, stay. Winter is far away. It is just a border fight; it will soon be over—you'll see.' I stay another year. But the war gets worse and worse."

Back in the U.S., her husband, now called "Frank", had all but given up hope of seeing Ma and Mary ever again, since she had no way of contacting him to inform him that they were alive and well. Ma said she made up her mind. It had been over two years since she'd seen Frank, and she decided she was going to Holland to get on a ship to America, war or no war. Her parents were aghast.

"How will you get to Holland to board the ship? The Army has taken over the railroads. You can't take a two year old baby, and travel on army trains filled with soldiers. It's crazy. You are just a girl. You'll never get through the fighting alive."

But, Ma was not to be deterred. She gathered what possessions and food she could carry, pinned her remaining money to her corset and got ready to leave.

"Leaving my village was very hard to do," Ma said. "Everybody is crying."

She knew there was a good chance her family would be killed in the war. And there was a greater chance she and Mary would be killed going through the fighting. But even if they all survived the war, both Ma and her parents knew in their hearts that they'd never see each other again. Her father could not bring himself to come out of the house to give his blessing or even to bid farewell.

At the depot, there were no civilian trains running. Rail car after rail car stood filled with Polish troops. Ma came to a rail car where a soldier stood on the platform between cars. She asked if she could come aboard. He reached down to help them up.

"Where are you going?"

"To Holland. And, then, to Ameryka."

"To Ameryka? Are you crazy? There's a war on." He shook his head. "You would have to go through the battle lines—through the fighting—to get to Holland. Go back to your village, foolish woman."

But they were already aboard with their bundles.

"The train whistle makes a toot," Ma said. "And the train starts. I feel scared. Nothing but soldiers on the train. I think about what Tata says about soldiers going crazy."

The soldier found them seats. He asked Mary's age, and then showed them photos of his wife and children. Other soldiers crowed around, showing photos of their families, and wanting to hold Mary. They shared food and blankets. After many starts and stops, and long waits, the steam train arrived at a town near the front. Artillery fire rumbled in the distance. An Army officer spotted Ma and Mary. "You—get off the train."

Ma found a man who agreed to guide her though the fighting.

"Big guns make noise; boom, boom, like thunder," Ma said. "A Polish soldier lets us go through. Soldiers in ditches have eyes sunk in their heads, dirty and not shaved, living in worse place than for animals."

They crossed over from the Polish Army side into no man's land, toward the German lines. The guide turned to my mother, "We wait until dark. We have yet to go through the woods and hope someone doesn't shoot us."

At dusk, they began the trek through the woods. Shell fire pinned them down.

"We wait, and I wonder why I do not listen to Tata. Why I am so foolish to try to cross the fighting? We will be dead and my family will never know what happened to us."

At last, their guide called a halt in the tattered woods. "We wait for daybreak."

When the sun finally began to show light on the horizon, the man said, "Wait here. If there's shooting, go back the way we came. Don't wait for me. Just go. Go back and don't try to cross, again."

The guide came back to show Ma which way to go and how to walk towards the trenches she had to cross to get to the town in the background. "Don't stoop or run," he said, "Stand up straight and don't run or walk too fast. And pray they don't shoot."

She walked, standing as tall as her slight figure would allow under the burden of her bundles. Two-year-old Mary held tight to her skirt.

"I scared someone shoots us, but I just kept walking."

I looked at my mother, now work-worn and middle aged, her brown hair pulled back into a pug and flecked with gray. I imagined her as a young woman walking through the fighting like Joan of Arc.

When she got to the trenches, German soldiers just stared.

"No one said anything, no one stopped us. They just watch us."

Once past the trenches, a column of German troops appeared. Seeing them, marching in formation, was frightening. Ma quickly took Mary to hide in the cellar of an abandoned house. Footsteps approached. She was sure the soldiers had spotted them. They cowered, hearts pounding, listening to the drumbeat of feet as the soldiers marched by.

They continued walking, afraid of the future. Winter was setting in. Buildings were in ruins, bombed or burned out. There were few civilians. She began to see more German soldiers wandering about as she got to a town. When they ignored her, she began to get over her stark fear of them. A train filled with soldiers stood at the depot. She hesitated before asking to be taken aboard. But, fearing the train would soon leave, she got up courage to ask, using gestures. A soldier helped them aboard. The train was carrying troops away from the front.

One of the German soldiers heard her say "Ameryka" as she tried to tell them her destination. He began speaking in broken English.

"Wife, children, New York City," he said. "I come home to Germany to visit, war comes. I no want to fight."

The soldier spoke of only wanting to go back to New York, to his wife and children. He took out pictures of his family.

"Other German soldiers take out pictures of their families, too, just like the Polish soldiers did." Ma said. "They gave us food, too. I couldn't believe it." Later, the English speaking soldier helped them find a train leaving towards Rotterdam, Holland, where she'd planned to board the Lusitania.

Ma's train chuffed away from the station toward Holland, while the German's train went in another direction, she knew not where. She had not thought to get his New York address so she could get word to his wife and family that he was alive.

Once in Rotterdam, Ma learned the Lusitania rested at the bottom of the sea, sunk on the way to Liverpool. There were no civilian passenger ships traveling on the high seas because of the danger of U-boats. Her spirits fell. She was marooned in Rotterdam and her money was running low. That evening, Ma wandered down to the waterfront with Mary. A Dutch freighter, the Nieuw Amsterdam, sat tied up at the dock. A sailor came down the gang plank. With gestures and broken English Ma was able to ask him about the ship's destination. When he said, "New York," she pointed to herself and Mary, and offered him money. He took them aboard the freighter, down into the hold.

After the ship got underway, officials discovered them and listed them on the ship's manifest as steerage passengers. The ship's master took eight dollars of Ma's, writing in the ship's manifest that she had twelve dollars remaining. In steerage, they had no privacy; sailors walked through the open hold, and brackish bilge water sloshed back and forth under the duck boards.

The North Atlantic seas became rough and soon everyone was seasick. Ma was so weak she couldn't get up to take Mary to the toilet. When she asked a sailor to take Mary, he cheerfully scooped Mary up and sat her on his shoulders. But frightened, she wet all over him. The sailor cursed and quickly put her down, never to offer again. Until she was well, Ma told Mary to pee into the bilge water sloshing beneath the duck boards. The ship seemed to wallow through the sea forever. After thirteen miserable days, the ship docked in New York.

"What will we do, now?" Ma asked the sailor who'd brought them aboard. "We have no proper papers."

"Not to worry," the sailor said. "We wait here for customs to inspect part of the ship, then we take you there, while they inspect here. Then, you hide there until night comes. Not to worry."

After nightfall, as they descended the gangplank lugging their bundles, a newspaperman spotted them. When he started asking questions, Ma told him the truth about arriving on the ship. "Wait right here. I'm going to get a camera man—this is a great story," he said, running off.

"As soon as he went around the corner, I quickly go to the train station, as fast as Mary can walk," she said. "After I buy train tickets for Housatonic, I have just one dollar left."

When they got to Housatonic, their apartment was dark. The thought that Franz might have moved away alarmed her. She knocked on the landlady's door. "Ghost, ghost," the landlady screamed, slamming the door. After reassurances that they were alive and not ghosts, the landlady opened the door.

"I am so sure you were both killed in the war; I thought you'd come to haunt me," she said. "Frank is down at the tavern. I send somebody to get him."

When the messenger said, "Hey, Frank, your wife's home," Franz took him to task for trying to play such a cruel prank, and he stayed on at the bar. At closing time, Frank came home. It was a joyous reunion. But Mary, who hadn't seen her father since infancy, was not at all sure she wanted to be around this stranger who was hugging her mother. She was afraid and wouldn't go to him.

"I was so happy to be home again," Ma said. "Life was good. Two years later I have Johnny and then I get pregnant, again, with Bessie. In 1918, comes influenza. People get sick and die in just days. Doctors and nurses can't take care of everyone. Many of them die, too. So the firemen go from house to house helping sick people. Frank goes to help, and he gets sick and dies in a few days. I had a good life with Frank. Now I am left with two small children, I'm pregnant, I'm alone, I have no money, and I don't know what to do. In this life, happiness is like a soap bubble. Poof—and it's gone." She began gathering up feathers.

"Tell us what happened, next, Ma."

"No more stories; time for bed."

****

The next time we stripped feathers, we asked Ma to tell us what happened after her husband died and how she met Pa.

"After my husband died, I ask myself, what I'm going to do?--no social security, no welfare, no family here to help. Money goes fast. I know I have to do something, so I get a job in Monument Mills sewing bedspreads. Neighbors are very good to me; they take care of my children when I at work. But one man likes little girls. Mary is afraid of him. I am afraid, too. Worry, worry, all the time—makes my hands shake. And I'm getting bigger with baby. I can't keep up at my job. Other ladies walk slowly by my machine and, quick; shove finished bedspreads in my basket so I do not get fired."

As Ma got closer to her due date, some friends helped with a plan. She quit her job, and went to Hartford, Connecticut to stay with friends to have the baby. Other friends in Housatonic took care of Mary and John.

"After Bessie is born, I come back to Hart Street in Housatonic, where the neighbor is a bad man."

Ma showed Mary, six, how to tie a bit of bread and some sugar in a piece of cloth and dip it in milk to give to baby Bessie as a pacifier. Mary would prepare the pacifier for Bessie to suck on while she rocked the cradle until the baby stopped crying and went to sleep.

A coal stove heated the apartment. The fire died down, one day, and the apartment got cold, so Mary poured kerosene on the hot coals. The stove exploded. Stove lids flew everywhere, flames shot up to the ceiling and singed Mary's eyebrows and hair. After that, Ma still worried, even more, if that was possible. And the man in the downstairs apartment was still after Mary. It was a desperate situation.

"Just before Christmas, I heard about a job at a hotel—the Manaco Inn. The McDonald family owned the hotel, and they were looking for a cook. I ask them for the job and tell them, true, that I have three small children. They hire

46

me and give me a room on the third floor. I sell my furniture to pay the bills, and I move in the hotel."

Mary took care of Johnny—not yet two—and baby Bessie, in the hotel room, heating the bottle on an electric hot plate.

"I bring food from the kitchen, and run upstairs every chance I get, to make sure everything is O.K. The McDonald family is good to me; they don't complain."

The inn was a gathering place, located at a cross roads of sorts, and not far from the train station. Travelers as well as local people frequented the inn. The son of the hotel owner got married, but his wife soon ran away with another man. The heartbroken husband told Ma that the small hotel room was too small for a family. "Take my furniture and get yourself an apartment."

"He gave me a thick rug, green like grass, and mahogany furniture, a beautiful lamp with a colored glass shade, and lace curtains, too. He is such a good man. I get an upstairs apartment next to hotel. It is not far from Monument Mills, so I go back to work there, again. The pay is better and I need more money to pay rent. At noon, I quick go home to feed Mary, Johnny, and Bessie. But, still, I worry. The landlady says she will watch the children, but I find out later that she drinks."

A week or two later, the landlady let some kids give Bessie a ride in the baby carriage. They left the carriage to play, it trundled down the slope toward the river, tipped over, and Bessie fell out, rolling to the brink of the river bank.

"I'm getting more and more nervous. My hands shake so I can barely work. I think to myself—danger is everywhere. The road and then the railroad tracks are on one side of house, and the river is on the other. I wonder what's going to happen next.

"I find out. I'm working sewing a bedspread. Something tells me something terrible thing is going to happen at home. I don't ask boss, can I leave? I just jump up from my sewing machine, and I run home—fast as I can. When I get close to home, I see Johnnie is sitting on the railroad track playing with stones between the railroad ties. I hear train whistle--Too-o—to-o-ot! The train is coming. I run, but my knees go weak. Almost there, I fall down. The train is coming fast—whistle blowing, and blowing. I crawl as quick as I can and pull Johnny away, just in time. Train goes by—Whoosh! The ground shakes and I am shaking, too. I lay on the ground holding him.

A few days later, I come home and Mary has a rag around her hand—blood all over her. Her finger is gone and the stump is bleeding. The landlady, who takes care of my children, is drinking, again. Mary says the landlady's son told her to hold a stick of wood. He's going to split it. He misses, and chops off her finger. His mother throws Mary's finger in the river and ties a rag around the stump to try to stop the blood. She tells Mary, that maybe I not notice the finger is gone. I take Mary to the doctor. He sews up the stump.

I am scared. Right after that, I meet your father. He had relatives who knew both him and me. They say to me, 'Man with three children—his wife die, he needs a wife; you have three children and need a husband. We have him come here to meet you.'" Pa proposed marriage on the first date. Ma accepted before he finished asking.

She turned to look at the clock, and jumped up. "No more stories. Put away the feathers. To bed; time to go to sleep."

Before going to bed, Ma lit the lantern and went with each of us to wait patiently as we took turns going to the outhouse on the end of the long dark woodshed. Like most rural homes, in our area, we did not have a flush toilet or running water. We felt fortunate to have water in the well.

Chapter 16: Water Problems

Water always seemed to be a problem on the farm—either too little or too much. I sometimes wondered why Pa settled in Gill. Perhaps it was because Pa could assume the mortgage and take possession without a down payment. Unfortunately, when the family moved to Gill they didn't have any more luck at with the farm than the previous owner, Jepherd Carey. I never found out what happened to Carey. All I know of him is that old timers in town called our farm "Jep's Place."

First Jep's house burned down, according to local legend. Then, after rebuilding it, he couldn't scratch out enough money to pay the mortgage. He hadn't done much in the way of maintenance or finish building the house. We never knew what became of him or whether he was even dead or alive. We often heard strange sounds in the night. Even during the day, the back shed was dark with empty barrels standing in the shadows. My older sisters speculated that it might be Jep coming back at night to retrieve something hidden in the barrels, or his ghost coming to haunt us. I don't know what was more scary—the thought of Jep, or his ghost.

Though someone had dug a shallow well in the front yard, it wasn't very productive. That isn't to say there wasn't any water on the farm. At times in the spring, water flooded the cellar a foot or more deep. And during rainstorms the roof leaked like it'd been riddled with bird shot. We'd awaken in the dead of night to hear the dreaded sound of rain on the roof and jump out of bed to light the kerosene lamps. While some kids ran to get pots and pails to catch the water, others moved beds away from leaks. After positioning receptacles to catch the water, we'd climb back into bed under damp covers for an uneasy sleep, listening to the "plinking and plunking" into assorted containers, knowing the leaks would migrate as the roof got saturated and we'd soon be up moving things around, again.

The one place on the farm that didn't seem to accumulate water was the well. That went dry before the ink dried on the deed. When the family first moved in, Ma and the kids lugged water from the brook and collected rain water off the roof until Pa and the older boys dug a new well. When Pa wasn't around, Ma often wondered aloud, "Why'd he buy such a place?"

Pa put Walter, Stanley, and Johnny to work digging a new well, and left for work. The boys were in their early teens. They dug down as far as they could but struck no water. That night it rained. The clay at the bottom of the well became saturated with rain water and turned to muck.

49

The next day, Pa borrowed a mud pump from the Montague Highway Department. On his way home, he stopped at Starbuck Plumbing to ask the owner, Mr. Starbuck, to sell him well tiles on credit. "I suppose you want them delivered, too," Starbuck said. Pa got riled up by the retort. Polish families buying up farms in the Connecticut River valley irked the earlier settlers, as immigrant families displaced old time Yankees. Resentment often surfaced in dealing with the immigrants, as it did that day in the plumbing shop.

"Well, I can't carry them on my back," Pa snapped back, and paid him off as soon as possible, never to buy anything at the plumbing shop, ever again.

On the following day, the rain-soaked clay made slow digging. The well didn't get much deeper before Pa had to leave for work. The hole wasn't shored up. Afraid they'd be buried alive, the boys spent most of their time keeping a wary eye on the dirt walls, getting their feet free from the sticky clay, and looking to head up the ladder.

The next morning, Pa helped them dig deeper. The clay became wetter and harder to toss up out of the hole. Pa set up a tri-pod and pulley. He tied a rope to a pail and they began hauling clay out, pail by pail. Soon, water began seeping in at the bottom. Small chunks of clay began ominously dropping from the sides. More clay fell. Pa decided it was time to set the tiles before the whole thing collapsed on the boys.

After the tiles were in place and backfilled, Pa covered the top with thick planks. He nailed a sheet of galvanized metal over them to shed rain. The sheet metal acted as a hinge when he lifted a plank to check the water level.

The new well didn't produce much water. Recovery was slow and the water was often cloudy, especially during dry times as the level got lower. Clothes became dingier and dingier with each washing. Ma began lugging water from the rain barrel to scrub clothes.

One day, Pa went behind the house to check the water level in the well. I tagged along. He tipped the plank back to peer into that deep dark place. "Want to take a look?" he asked.

I moved forward to take a place beside him. He got a firm grip on the straps of my overalls. I leaned forward to look. The well seemed to go down, down, to the center of the earth. The still water far down at the bottom looked like a round looking glass. Cool air rose from the well. Goose pimples popped up on my arms as I gazed down into the void. The well seemed to be drawing me in. The world turned sideways, making me feel I was losing my balance. Pa's firm grip on my back felt reassuring. While still keeping a secure hold of me, he counted the tiles--"Jeden, dwa, trzy"...his voice trailing off to a whisper. A frown came over his face. The well was very low.

He pulled me away from the brink and lowered the plank cover, warning me never to open it. Though my father, my mother, and my sisters all warned me, repeatedly—to never to open the cover, I couldn't help but be drawn to that well. The hinged plank cover, shaded by fragrant lilacs, held a fascination—beckoning me—to lift the plank and view the forbidden depths. The warnings made it all the more irresistible. The well seemed to draw me like a magnet.

One day when Pa was away, I looked to see if anyone was watching, then slipped into the cool shade of the lilacs. I knelt and lifted the plank—heart racing—hands shaking—to gaze down into the cool depths. This time the well seemed to go even further into the earth, with that odd feeling that an increase in the force of gravity drew me toward the void. I felt enlivened by the fear that I'd lean too far and the depths would pull me down, to tumble, head first, down, down, into the water far below. The fear of getting caught only made the experience more daring, more thrilling, and more satisfying. The cool air rising from the well filled my lungs. I felt a heady feeling of not being quite in control. When I felt the pull of the well drawing me and I felt that I was losing my balance, I quickly closed the cover and went away with my secret safe, my heart pounding, and my hands shaking.

Chapter 17: Potatoes and Strawberries

The clay soil that slowed the passage of water to the well made the heavy farmland very productive when conditions were right. But in spring, the fields were usually wet during planting, often delaying it. The farm was mostly lowland with clumps of cat tails in the pasture, and cranberries growing wild in the swamp across the brook. If we'd wanted to grow rice, the farm might have been perfect. Problem was, seeds often rotted in the ground in a wet year. Then, when the surviving seeds spouted, the sun sometimes baked the fields as the weather turned hot and dry. But other years, under ideal conditions, the heavy soil produced a bumper crop, keeping my father's dreams of prosperity alive. We raised a variety of vegetables, but after hoeing and weeding all summer, whatever we chose to raise always seemed to be selling for about three cents a peck.

Pa liked Khatadyn potatoes. We cut the seed potatoes so that there were at least two eyes on each piece. As we set the seed potatoes along the furrow, invariably someone would say, "It must be Joe's birthday—we're planting potatoes." Every one would laugh and we'd go back to planting. After a few years, it dawned on me that Pa was probably planting potatoes by the phases of the moon. Or maybe it was just coincidence. Still, it was nice to be remembered. But I longed for a birthday party.

Pa didn't believe in celebrating birthdays or in giving gifts, even at Christmas. But I liked to think that he was honoring me by planting potatoes on my birthday. He may have, but I never knew, for sure. Perhaps I did not ask so as to keep the illusion alive.

We grew strawberries as a cash crop, first on a sandy hill at the far end of a meadow, and later on a lower meadow. We sold boxes of berries door-to-door. But strawberries don't bear a crop until the second year. With the endless battle against witch grass, weeds, bugs, fungus, mold and disease it was hardly worthwhile and Pa eventually gave it up. We continued to raise berries for our own use, preserving them for winter. None of the kids were at all sad to see the end of our having to go door-to-door peddling.

Most of the housewives were kindly. But some shrews would dump the berries into a bowl before buying them to see if the big ones on top were hiding small ones underneath. Pa told us to always put a big strawberry in the bottom of the basket, so the housewife would exclaim at the pleasant surprise. She would then tell her neighbors about it and we'd sell an extra basket, or two, the next time.

Often customers would ask if the berries were "native." I never knew what to say. I dodged the question by saying we raised them on our farm. Irene said she answered "yes." But my older sister Gladys always said, "Oh, no, these are imported berries," so the housewives would think they were expensive foreign commodities. Unfortunately, Gladys's ploy did not increase her sales.

When strawberry season was over, we picked wild low bush blueberries to sell to stores. It took five or six of us picking, to earn what Ma earned working in the Keith Paper Mill. With merchants offering us so little, we often preserved those berries, too. Ma made jam in a long process of boiling the fruit down to thicken it. Keeping the stove going on hot summer days made the kitchen unbearably stifling.

A neighbor told Ma about a new product called Certo. Ma bought some of the jelling agent, probably from the Raleigh man, who came around each month peddling household products out of the covered pickup bed of his little truck. Certo cut the hours of preserving to a matter of minutes, plus the fruit went farther. Ma regarded the product as a godsend, and was grateful for the blessings that came her way. She would have nominated the inventor for sainthood, along with the Raleigh man. In addition to preserves, Ma liked to make cheese.

Chapter 18: Cows, Milk, Cream and Cheese

We kept milk cows. Since we didn't have electricity for refrigeration, or an ice house for ice to cool milk until the milk truck picked it up, what we didn't drink we processed into cheese and butter, feeding the rest to the pigs. I don't know why my father didn't have an ice house. We had a pond on our farm that froze solid. It would have only meant storing blocks of ice in a building with a layer of sawdust, or hay, insulating the ice. But without ice, we couldn't sell milk.

Ma made "farmer's cheese" by pouring soured milk into a cheese-cloth bag and hanging it up to drain. She'd press the remaining whey out by placing the bag between two round boards weighted with a heavy stone. We ate fresh "farmer's cheese", but my favorite was the cheese she hung in a bag nailed to the woodshed wall, where it was exposed to all kinds of weather. After a month or two, the cheese got rock hard, taking on a cheddar cheese flavor that was a delight to chew. Ma would rest the blade of a butcher knife on the cheese and hit the back of it with a hammer to whack off a chunk. Bam and a hunk of cheese would come loose. Carrying a chunk in my pocket was insurance against going hungry when I knew I'd be gone from home all day. I could gnaw on a small piece for hours, keeping hunger pangs away.

To separate cream from milk, we had a tall can with a glass window, about a half inch wide, going up the side. The glass had cracked, somehow, but Pa sealed it with window putty.

After the milk sat a while, the cream would rise to the top. To separate the milk we simply opened the spigot at the bottom and drained the milk down to the cream line. We had to guess a little because the putty blocked our view.

Sometimes we'd use some of the cream, after it soured, to make cream soups—beet borscht, kielbasa soup, or cream soups using sauerkraut liquid, or vegetable greens. Ma made a delicious cream soup with pig weed, until I told her the English name for it. She never made it again and denied ever making it. Ma used all manner of herbs in cooking and making teas. She even used the tendrils of grape vines for a distinctive sour taste in her cooking or canning. When there didn't seem to be anything to eat, she'd dice salt pork, fry it crisp, stir it into mashed potatoes and add sour cream, garnishing it with fresh parsley. I loved it. But, we saved most of our cream in our Daisy butter churn, letting it sour. The butter churn had a square glass container that held about a gallon. A crank and gears sat on top of the cover. Four canted wooden paddles, attached to the shaft, beat the cream as we turned the crank. Pa gave us strict orders to turn the crank slowly. Turning it fast would only whip the cream and it would never turn to butter, he said.

Sometimes in hot weather the butterfat would not gather, especially if the cream was not very rich. After I spent hours and hours of tedious slow churning, Pa would become irritated when I complained and tell me, "Don't be so lazy; just keep cranking."

One day when he was away, I poked a hole down through the floating soured cream with a long butcher knife, and poured off the whey collected at the bottom. I cranked the handle as fast as I could spin it. The paddles whipped the cream into froth. I became worried, but it was now too late to quit. I kept whirling the paddles.

"You're going to get it good when Pa comes home and sees the cream all whipped," my sisters warned.

But I wasn't to be deterred, and made the gears sing, beating at an even higher speed. Soon tiny nuggets of butter appeared. I added a glass of cold water to help congeal the butter fat. The churn handle turned harder and harder. I slowed to let the paddles pat the nuggets into a ball of golden butter.

The next time Ma gave me the job of churning butter, I, again, drained the whey and churned like mad despite her threat to tell Pa. A ball of butter began bobbing in the churn in minutes instead of hours.

When Pa came home and heard of my disobedience, he frowned at me. "Leave it to Joe to find a lazy way."

In the heat and humidity of summer, sour cream was apt to grow a thick black mold with blue and orange edges. It made interesting patterns but gave the butter a musty taste. I chanced upon a solution when Irene and I carried Emaline's lunch to Clapp's farm where she worked picking strawberries.

Ma had packed a quart of fresh milk with Emmy's lunch, adding a generous portion of sweet cream. The rich milk sloshed back and forth as we hiked over the trail through the woods. At the farm, we put the jar of milk to cool in the spring-fed water trough, and left. When Emaline came home from work, she wondered why we'd brought her buttermilk. It then dawned on me that we'd churned the milk into bits of butter by sloshing the jar on the way over.

That set the wheels turning in my head. I reasoned that we could make sweet cream butter and eliminate the musty taste of rancid cream. Once again, I angered my parents when I began churning butter before the cream had soured. They reproached me, saying the sweet cream would never turn to butter.

"Why you be such a stubborn mischief-maker and not listen to me?" my father asked. "I old enough and smart enough to know how to do things right. But go ahead, be a dumb. You'll find out you can't make butter that way. Be a good lesson for you."

I kept cranking, hoping he wasn't right. My stomach tightened, and I prayed the butter would gather. I was overjoyed to see gold flecks appearing even as Pa continued his harangue about me being so obstinate. I was saved— a big blob of butter bobbed merrily, as the paddles batted it about.

My mother wasn't easily mollified. She tasted the butter and declared it "niedobre", no good. "You lucky Pa doesn't hit you good, like you deserve— wasting good cream like that."

We kids all preferred the sweet cream butter, but that didn't sway our parents, any. The worse thing about milk production was herding the cows. If you think being a shepherd is romantic, you've never had to herd anything. We had cows, damn few fences, and lots of kids. It added up to "minding cows." I hated it. The only thing more boring, than watching grass grow, is watching grass being eaten. As long as you kept your eyes on the cows, they would not stray. But if you looked away, or tried to read a book or magazine, the cows would get into our corn or the neighbor's.

Our respite was going to school. Miss Pogoda was quick to praise, and it got us away from minding cows. If we were good, the teacher let us stay after school. Wiping the blackboard with a damp cloth or clapping the chalk erasers clean of dust was a prized privilege, rewarded by words of praise. Pa liked Miss Pogoda, too. She let us come to school barefooted as far into fall as we could stand. Pa figured that even if we didn't learn much, it saved on shoe leather. The bigger boys in school vied to see who could go without shoes the latest into fall. One boy, "Doody," showed up barefooted one morning when there were traces of white frost on the ground. He was tough-- the unsurpassed champion.

We were far more afraid at home than at school. Both of our parents warned us not to tell them about being punished at school because we would be punished twice as bad at home. Her most effective weapons were a frown or the words, "I am disappointed in you."

We were all afraid of Pa, including Ma. A harsh word or angry look was enough to make us comply—we knew the strap was next. Sometimes, if Pa saw us playing stick ball or tag, he'd say, "Pull some weeds or hoe the garden if you have so much energy."

In summer there was no shortage of field work, and in winter we had to do barn chores and bring in firewood. In a way, it was a good thing. We appreciated anything we got and we learned to work hard. Everyone talks about "The cruel world out there." By the time we were ready to leave home, "The cruel world *out there*." looked pretty darned good.

Pa's answer to any complaint was, "If you don't like it; there's the door." Most of the kids exercised that option in their early teens. The only separation anxiety we had was hoping for an early departure. Pa was forever telling us what an expense we were to him. "Just figure up, at a penny a day, what it costs, just to feed you."

Both parents lamented the fact there were too many children. Before I found out where babies came from, I wondered if someone were dropping them off like unwanted kittens. At any age, it hurt us to hear my parent's refrain—"Too many children." Even worse were the taunts from other kids at school, "Why does your family have so many kids?"

There were enough kids in our family for a scout troop, attracting the interest of a scout leader, who urged me to join. "Roughing it, builds character," he said. The scout master went on to tell what fun camping was— plenty of hiking, sleeping all jammed together on hard beds, cooking over a wood fire, getting a good workout in the fresh air, away from the comforts of civilization, while being bitten by all manner of bugs. I didn't join. I had had enough of that at home. We didn't know it, but we were having fun.

Chapter 19: Cleaning the Outhouse

Pa considered the depression as a time of hardship and sacrifice for everyone, viewing his sad financial state as humiliating, but temporary. Later, when times got better and he managed to get out of debt, he didn't collect the children's pay. But the memory of him taking my meager pay one day forever sticks in my mind.

I had worked hard all day splitting and carrying wood, mowing the lawn, and cleaning out an outhouse for our distant neighbor Charlie Sheiding. The outhouse hadn't been cleaned for years. I dug a hole, about 50 feet away, to bury the accumulation. When I disturbed the heap of excrement, it seemed to release some sort of nausea gas. My eyes watered, my throat tightened up, and it was all I could do to keep from heaving. Old Charlie couldn't take the stink. He clomped away with his walking stick as fast as his unsteady legs would take him.

Charlie had a visitor that day. He and his guest looked on at a safe distance as I carried away shovelful after shovelful of the repulsive slime. When disturbing the stuff, I'd hold my breath as long as I could, but it was never long enough. I would have to walk away to get a breath of fresh air before I went back to the stomach-wrenching stench for another shovelful. Charlie paid me extra for that job, and praised me for sticking with it. To finish out the day, he asked me to fetch some water from a spring at the foot of his hill. His visitor also wanted some spring water to take home to the city. Charlie's well, at the top of the hill next to his house, was laid up with field stones with gaps that made it easy for bugs, mice, or snakes to fall in. The water had a terrible taste.

The spring at the foot of the hill bubbled with sweet-tasting water. A wooden barrel, sunk in the ground, served as a reservoir. Whenever I carried water from the spring, I first knelt to take a long drink of that cold refreshing water, especially after I'd been fighting thirst all that day, unable to bring myself to drink the brackish water from Charlie's well. I liked to pause there to rest a bit in the shade of trees growing in that quiet grove—no one to berate me or order me about. I enjoyed the peace and quiet, the bubbling spring, and the gentle breeze that always seemed to stir the leaves. Kneeling made me feel as though I were somehow praying to the creator for this wonderful spring bubbling miraculously up from out of the earth. A clump of water cress grew at the edge. The crystal clear water flowed in at the bottom of the spring through a thumb-sized hole in the earth. That resting spot always seemed like an oasis in time and place. I'd drink again for the pleasure of it—there being no better tasting water in the entire world. But, then, I had to hurry or Charlie would ask what had kept me.

The water pails were equipped with cooking pot covers to keep out seeds from plants and weeds crowding along the path. That summer, weeds had grown so high it was hard to keep seeds from falling in—even with the covers. Scheiding's visitor paid me an extra quarter to bring two more pails with no seeds at all.

The next trip I held the pails high above the weeds, arms trembling from the strain. Thinking about the bonus money which would bring my total up to more than I had ever earned at Scheiding's, I was not mindful of the approaching car. I mused that I would add my earnings to my secret hoard. I was happily thinking about what I could buy for myself—perhaps a pair of pants for school and maybe even a jack knife with two blades and all sorts of things like an awl, and a cork screw. And if there was money left, I could buy a mold to cast toy lead soldiers and... Too late, I saw it was my father's car. There was no time to duck or hide. The car stopped.

"Did you get paid, yet?"

"Yes," I said, setting down the pails beside the road. I dug the coins out of my pocket and handed them over, not able to raise my head from a sudden tiredness that seemed to settle over me. From seeing Helen handing him her pay on Sundays, I knew it was the thing to do. But, still, it seemed unfair and I couldn't rid myself of disappointment and discouragement. None of my classmates had to turn in money earned. Some even got allowances, and most of them didn't even have to work, at all. But we somehow lived under different rules—rules that seemed so unjust it made me seethe inside. The only good thing about these rules was that it sometimes brought Helen home on Sunday to hand her pay over to Pa.

Chapter 20: Helen and Hard Times

I was always glad to see Helen when she came to visit. When I was younger, she read me the funnies. While I could figure out Henry, because there was no writing, I really needed someone to read me my favorite, The Captain and the Kids, the strip of the two Katsenjammer Kids who got into all kinds of trouble and invariably were spanked by the Captain. I could readily identify with those two boys. The comic strip was supposed to be funny, but I always felt sorry for them and saw nothing to laugh at. My mother said I was as naughty as they were. My father also said I was bad—not bad enough to be labeled a black sheep, he said, but bad enough to qualify for a grey sheep label. Pa was right; I was always in trouble for something, real or imagined. His policy was to hit first, investigate later. Sometimes, punishment was a sharp word or a slap. Other times it was a lot worse. Often, I had no idea why I was being thrashed and would get hit again for "talking back" if I asked.

"Who else but Joe would do such a thing?" he'd say when he found something amiss. Sometimes my sisters were hit, too. Ma used her hand. What I hated most was getting slapped in the face. But Pa often used his belt, instead. He'd unbuckle it in a flash, pulling it off and whacking, all in one motion, as swiftly and painful as a striking snake. Then Pa found a better way. He'd bought a new double razor strap for sharpening his straight razor. Driving a nail in the kitchen wall, he hung the old single strap where it'd be handy, he said. "There'd be no misbehaving, now."

This was the era of the sage expression, "Spare the rod and spoil the child." And no one could accuse Pa of that.

"I won't have you kids growing up a disgrace. You are going to learn to behave. And if you don't, I'll beat you like an animal until you do."

I hated getting hit with the strap. It hurt outside and inside, too. Ma never tried to stop him. I felt that she had deserted me. She was intimidated by him, though he'd only struck her once. Emmy had picked up a chair—said she'd kill him if he ever did it again—and he never did. But we children were still fair game. Pa sometimes hit me until he got arm-weary, put his hand on his chest and groaned. Now, see what you've done, you've worn me out—not good for my heart."

I felt like I was in trouble most of the time, no matter what. It's true I was mischievous and felt I deserved the thrashings, but, still, they only filled me with resentment. I longed for the day I could leave home, like the others had, to escape his tyranny.

One day when Pa was away and Johnny was burning brush, I took the hated strap down, ran out and threw it in the fire. Emmy fished it out and brought it back to the house. "I know you hate the strap," Emmy said, "but if Pa found out you'd burned it up, you'd really get it." The fire shriveled the end of the strap just a bit, but Pa didn't seem to notice.

Some times, he was in a far better humor. He'd find a bargain at the grocery store and we'd have a feast. Once he bought pork chops—his favorite---for 5 cents a pound. When he paid off his bill with the bread man, the peddler rewarded us with a free gift of pastries. In good times, we saw pastries on a weekly basis, in bad times it was weeks and weeks before the bread man got his money and we got a prize.

Pa often spent his days at the Polish Club weathering the bad times. The club also served as a pipeline to news of call-backs. With no telephone at the farm, he often missed out on being called back to work after a lay-off. At the Polish Club he could at least catch a rumor and try to be one of the first to respond. Meanwhile, playing cards and having a few beers with other unemployed men offered some solace and the hope of winning some money. He was good at card playing and once won in a tournament.

Chapter 21: Moonshine and Home Brew

During prohibition, Pa bought whiskey from people who operated moonshine stills, and began picking up spent mash to feed our farm animals. Still operators fermented a mixture of corn, grain and yeast to produced alcohol. After collecting the alcohol through distillation, the spent mash was of no use to them, and they were more than happy to get rid of the incriminating evidence. There was some residual alcohol in the spent grain. After feasting on this treat, our chickens and geese wobbled around for a while before passing out. The first time I saw our geese passed out, I thought they'd died. Mama told me to lay them in a cool place to rest. Their necks hung down like ropes as I carried them to a shady spot under the lilac bush behind the house. When I laid their necks out straight, they honked weakly, seeming quite content. The geese were regular lushes, ready to give the moonshine mash another go, as soon as they could navigate again.

With work at the mill slack during the Depression, and seeing some of his friends prospering from moonshine stills, Pa thought he'd like to earn some of that easy money. The remote farm, being situated on a back road, made it an ideal location for a moonshine operation. With animals on the farm, buying corn and grain wouldn't attract attention, not that most grain dealers cared. They were glad to sell grain to anyone who had the money; the more, the better. If my father got into producing moonshine, the animals would eat the spent mash, getting rid of the evidence and providing feed for them at the same time. It seemed like the perfect setup.

Pa bought a still, fermented a batch of mash for a few days, filled the still, lit the kerosene burner and began distilling. He never quite grasped the process of distillation and overfilled the still, figuring it worked like a coffee percolator—which, in this case, it did. First steam, then grain, corn, and all, percolated through the coil. The stuff coming out of the end of the coil was substantially the same product going in. Soon, the coils plugged. Pa was sure he had been stuck with a faulty still.

Phony "government agents" got wind of his operation and came to pay a call, to try to shake him down for a bribe. One man approached Pa as he was splitting wood in the yard. The other man stayed in the car with the motor running. The car was a huge monster with big disc wheels. I suspect it was a Packard or Pierce Arrow. The "agent", announcing he was from the "guvmint", flashed a badge that looked an awful lot like the Dick Tracy badges we got with a couple of box tops and twenty five cents for postage and handling.

Pa pulled the ax out of the chopping block and headed for the man. The phony agent broke into a run toward the car. Pa was right on his heels. The driver began backing the big ark out of the yard before his cohort got in the car. The "agent" ran and jumped on the running board, as the car roared off down the road, raising a cloud of dust, with the agent standing on the running board, trying to get inside.

After they left, Pa smashed the still to bits and buried the whole mess in the woods. He was so irate at the attempted shakedown that he reported the phony agents to the authorities. Big mistake--real government agents then showed up. They wore dark suits, shiny black shoes and had real badges. In searching the house, the agents found a bottle capper and a big box of caps. One of them demanded to know what we were doing with the bottling apparatus.

"Ketchup; we bottle ketchup," Mama answered.

"Looks like you folks are planning on eating a lot of ketchup," the G-man said.

"Well, we got a lot of kids."

Actually, the bottling apparatus was for bottling home-brewed beer, which Pa had been planning to try next. In fact, the hops were growing like grape vines out behind the hen coops the very day the G-men poked around the cellar. Up close, hops hanging from the vines look like tiny concertinas. There were some tense moments as the search continued. Fortunately, the G-men didn't get a close look at what was growing on the "grape vines" out by the hen coops, visible from the house.

Making homebrew also resulted in disaster. The beer fermented in the bottles to the point where most of the beer ended up on the kitchen ceiling when Pa tried opening the first bottle. Soon, bottles stored in the cellar began exploding. They sounded like a shotgun going off. No one dared open the cellar door to look. From time to time, explosions sounded, day and night, until every last bottle of beer shattered into smithereens. Pa waited a few days after the last detonation before risking a look.

Beer soaked the cellar walls, floor and ceiling. The house reeked like a brewery for months after. Ma worried that the G-men would return before the smell of beer faded. Whenever a strange car turned down our road, Ma would get all nerved up. She just knew the agents would be back, and she was convinced that only her prayers would stave off the time before they did. I'm sure she offered up a special prayer of thanks the day prohibition ended.

With the prohibition over, Pa's chance to regain his position of relative wealth evaporated. His luck with horses did not turn out to be much better than his attempt to cash in on prohibition.

Chapter 22: Horses

Prince the family horse, died not long after moving to Gill. Poor Prince was more pauper than prince. Pa bought him when the family sharecropped onions in Montage before moving to Gill. Pa bought horses from jockeys. These jockeys were not those who rode race horses. These were smooth talking horse traders who were skillful at concealing defects in horses.

When I was quite young, Pa took me and my godfather, Mr. Cislo, to places that had long sheds filled with horses tied up in stalls, open at the rear. Some horses were sturdy, well- groomed muscular steeds, and others, old nags one stop from the glue factory, sway backed, hooves overgrown, teeth worn down or missing, watery eyes, some so skinny their ribs stood out like a xylophone lay under their ratty coats. Pa wanted to replace poor old Prince, now lying buried in a field at home.

My brother Stanley was 13 when he had hauled coal, from Cold Brook Farm in Montague with Prince hitched to a wagon. It was about ten miles to our farm in Gill.

"The horse was big like the Clydesdales that haul the Budweiser beer wagon," Stanley said. "He had big feet like them, with white stockings but he didn't have no shoes, and the hard road hurt his feet, so he couldn't go very fast. He just plugged along."

Stanley set out early each morning and got back late afternoon, taking the entire day to make one trip.

"The steep hill going down into Turners Falls scared me just to look at it," Stanley said. "I was just a kid and scared to go down; afraid the wagon would get away and tip over and wreck. But I was more afraid of Pa. So, I stuck a big stick though the spokes like I seen him do, and let the wheel skid down the hill, hoping the stick didn't break. Who-ee, what a ride! It scared me every time."

Later, when Prince died, Stanley said he felt terrible because he was sure he'd worked the poor horse to death. Pa had given Stanley orders to harrow a field while he was working at the paper mill. Stanley harnessed up Prince, and hooked him to the harrow.

"The horse was old, and he acted sick," Stanley said. "He'd pull the harrow a little way and stop. I'd whip him and he'd pull the harrow a little way and stop again."

After a while, Prince barely moved when Stanley whipped him. Stanley figured, at that rate, he was never going to get the field harrowed before Pa got home. Afraid Pa would thrash him. Stanley reasoned he had to get that field harrowed, one way or another. Pa didn't ever want to hear excuses; he just wanted to see the work done.

"I cut a branch from a thorn tree growing on the edge of the field. The thorns were big and sharp, an inch or two long. When I whipped the horse with the thorn branch, he really jumped and dragged the harrow a ways before he stopped. Each time I whipped the horse he'd jump and go a little way less, and stop. I whipped him, again and again, over and over. And I kept on whipping him with that thorn branch until the field was harrowed."

Next morning, when Stanley went out to the barn, Prince was lying in his stall, dead.

"I could see the thorns stuck in his back—broken off where I'd been hitting him. It was awful—I'll never forget it."

* * *

Stanley had left home when Pa bought an unbroken young mare. I don't know where he bought her, but he was quite proud of her and let me choose a name. I picked "Maggie" from Maggie & Jiggs in the comic strip <u>Bringing Up Father</u>. I thought Maggie was a classy name. The mare's build was not as heavy as that of the plodding Prince. Her steps were light and prancing, and she was the best horse Pa ever owned.

Pa's friend Mr. Cislo said he'd help break Maggie. He was a grinder in a cutlery shop and fancied himself a horse expert, managing to doctor a fair number of healthy horses to death.

We spotted Mr. Cislo coming down the road with his horse hitched to a two wheeled sulky. When the horse got to the bridge, he came to a dead stop, and turned his head to eye the patched bridge. The town road crew had nailed new planks down in the wheel tracks across the old half rotten bridge planks. That was fine for the wheels of cars or the sulky, but the middle of the bridge was rotten. The horse wouldn't budge. Mr. Cislo slapped him with the reins and urged him on. The horse stood like a statue, head cocked to one side, eyeing the bridge.

We all gathered at the windows, watching as Cislo tried leading the horse across. The horse would not set foot on the bridge. Mr. Cislo turned back.

"He's going to go way around and try to come in the back way," Pa said. But Mr. Cislo turned the horse around a good distance from the bridge, and whipped him into a gallop. The horse came thundering across the bridge. One leg crashed through the rotten planks between the strips of new planking. The horse fell, hitting his nose. The horse was resting on his belly with one front leg down through the planks, nose cut and bleeding, eyes wild, thrashing to get up.

"Quick, get a saw," Mr. Cislo said. He held the horse's bridle, talking in soothing tones to quiet the horse until we got a saw and cut the planks back enough so the horse could pull his leg out and continue over the bridge. After that, I knew what people meant when they spoke of "horse sense."

Mr. Cislo did not try to break Maggie that day, and he always took the long way around after that. When he came to break Maggie, Pa and Mr. Cislo harnessed her to the sulky and ran her around the tobacco field until she was exhausted. This all happened before Arnold Studer bought the land. Pa didn't ask permission to use the tobacco field to break Maggie. He reasoned that he'd spoken for the land, making it as good as his, with only the payment to be made and the papers signed.

At first, Maggie didn't seem to know what the bit in her mouth was for and galloped around like a run-a-way. They yanked her head from side to side until she got the idea that it was to steer her in the direction they yanked. Soon, her mouth was dripping blood and foam. Her eyes rolled wildly in her head. I wanted to tell them to stop hurting her. For most of the day, they ran her around the field. When she became exhausted and slowed to a walk, they considered her broken. By then, she was wet with sweat and trembled all over. With a good horse, and the tobacco land nearly within his grasp, Pa figured his was on his way to put his share cropping days behind him and was sure to rise to prosperity as other Polish immigrants in the area had done.

Chapter 23: Dynamite

Polish immigrants generated a fair amount of resentment by living frugally, stuffing their savings into the mattress, and then hauling out the stash when banks failed and farmers couldn't pay their mortgage or taxes. Starting off as employees or sharecroppers, they often bought land or the entire farm of their host. Pa followed that formula at Cold Brook Farm, before moving to Gill. He worked in the paper mill while Ma and the kids worked in the onion fields. He joined them when he could.

After his move to Gill, Pa asked a family friend, Mr. Civic—a grocery store owner who lent money—to loan him money for the coveted tobacco land. Civic advised Pa to pay off the farm, first, or at least get another nest egg together. "Bide your time, pay your debts and save your money," He said. "You'll see, times are bad; the owner will drop his price."

With his mill work spotty and no sharecropping income, it was all Pa could do to feed his sizable family. Saving money was nigh impossible. Pa could have rented the tobacco barn and land for a nominal fee and raised tobacco, but he feared it would drive the price up if he showed too much interest. Instead, he continued to clear the run-down farm he'd bought. "We didn't have proper tools," Walter later recalled. "Just axes to cut the brush and a two-man cross-cut saw for the trees."

On a hill at the back of the lot, brush and trees had overgrown an orchard. They cut the trees for firewood. The brush, they stacked and burned. Pausing to rest, Pa stood surveying the neighboring farms.

"Boys, next, we'll buy the tobacco land, then one day, all these surrounding farms will be ours," he said, waving his arm in a grand gesture.

But the boys knew Pa was set in his ways. If they were going to farm with Pa, they wanted to see tractors and machinery.

"Tractors and machinery are expensive," Pa said, "takes gasoline to run, and that costs money, too. If you work by hand, you get the job done and you save the money. Save. Save. Save all you can. That's the way."

The boys weren't impressed. They had little enthusiasm for the day he would buy the tobacco land and barn. It only meant more hard labor. Though tobacco was a profitable crop, the boys knew they wouldn't get to share much, if any at all, if Pa's past performance was any indication. He was often scornful of families who paid their kids to work.

"Pay your own kids to work?!" he said with contempt. "How stupid can you get?!"

The tobacco field was about the size of our farm, except that it was largely dry and tillable. A tobacco barn stood on the far end of the land. Pa had his eye on the land when he bought the farm. It was level and fertile as the Nile river valley, able to grow real money crops. With productive land, the tobacco barn and enough kids to tend the labor intensive crop, Pa was confident that he would soon be as prosperous as the other Polish farmers that settled in the Connecticut valley.

Once the family cleared the orchard and pruned the apple trees, Pa showed Stanley and Walter how to graft scions of one variety onto trees of another variety. I don't know where Pa learned to graft, but he was able to successfully grow a variety of apples on the same tree. He was quite proud of his skill, but the lessons were not appreciated.

"While I show them how to graft, they are watching the neighbor plow with a new tractor. Everything has to be fast and easy, I tell them. They don't want to work; just want to do everything the lazy way."

They were able to plow brush stubble under with horse and plow, but tree stumps and boulders presented a problem. By the time Pa got to dealing with the stumps, the older kids had all left home. A good natured Italian, Mr. DeGrano, came to the rescue. He was a short jolly fellow who worked at Mass Broken Stone Quarry as a blaster.

On 4th of July weekend, Mr. DeGrano showed up with a case of dynamite, a box of blasting caps and a coil of fuse. He poked holes under the stumps, stuffed them with dynamite, and blew the stumps sky high with magnificent explosions of dirt and dust, leaving only the distinctive smell of explosives in the air. When he tucked enough dynamite under boulders, they shattered into crushed rock, seconds after he touched off the fuse, leaving a crater in its place. Shards of rock peppered the apple trees. It took the trees years to recover from the trauma and to bear a decent crop of apples.

Seeing the explosive force of the dynamite, I couldn't believe my ears when Mr. DeGrano asked me if I wanted to light a fuse, the very first day. Though he cut the fuse a bit longer than usual, I ran for my life as soon as I touched a match to the fuse and it began its ominous sizzle. My blast seemed bigger and louder than any of the others. It was the most glorious 4th, ever. Later, I bragged shamelessly to my friends about lighting the biggest firecracker of all and showed them the craters as proof.

"Put the rest of the dynamite in a safe-a place until I come back again to blast," Mr. DeGrano said at the end of the day.

Pa slid the half case of dynamite, coil of fuse and box of copper caps under his bed for safe keeping. When Mr. DeGrano came back to continue blasting , and learned of Pa's choice of a storage place, he told Pa the box of caps, alone, would have blown him to smithereens, never mind the dynamite.

"There be just a beeg hole where house was, if it go off."

The next time Mr. Degrano came to the farm, he came out to the hayfield, very agitated. "Bad news," he said, "war starts." Pa and Ma looked startled. Without a radio, telephone or newspapers we often did not know what was going on in the world until Pa got a weekly newspaper. "Terrible, terrible," Pa said.

"What is war?" I asked Mr. Degrano.

"That is when men fight with guns, and shoot each other on the battlefield," Mr. Degrano said.

"What is a battlefield?"

"It is a field like this."

I got scared. "Will they come here?" I asked, looking to see if anyone was coming, wondering where we could run and hide.

"No, the battlefield is far away," he said. But it was not reassuring to me. Why do they do that?"

"People go crazy and just begin to shoot each other and blow each other up with bombs that explode like the dynamite."

"If they came here, I would go upstairs with my gun and shoot them," Pa said. "They might kill me but I would kill some of them."

The whole idea of war was terrifying, and every time we blasted a stump or boulder, I thought about people going crazy and killing other people with explosions.

It must have been the beginning of WWII when Hitler's army invaded Poland or when Mussolini invaded Ethiopia. It may have been the latter, because Mr. Degrano was far more distressed than Pa and Ma. He used up the dynamite and did not come to the farm, again. Pa told me to throw the fuses and blasting caps in a pond in the woods. I missed Mr. Degrano; he was a kind and gentle man. I didn't think he would ever go crazy and want to kill people. I wished that he would come back to see us, but he never did.

Chapter 24: Tobacco Land Sold

After Johnny came home from the CCC, he couldn't find a job. One day, a Ford pickup turned into the driveway of the tobacco land, followed by a big flatbed truck, loaded with lumber. The big truck sank into the soft ground and got stuck. Johnny went out with a shovel and helped them get the truck going again. Ma spread a blanket on the lawn under the cherry tree. She said I could watch if I stayed on the blanket.

After they got the truck unstuck, the new owner of the land, Arnold Studer, asked Johnny if he would like to help unload the lumber. From there, Johnny went to work helping build a shanty and a big two story chicken coop. John moved into the shanty with Studer. I liked to hang around the shanty on Sundays or rainy days when they did not work. The shanty was about ten feet wide and twelve feet long. It was a great place. They joked and laughed a lot, and no one got mad or hollered at me.

A mahogany colored wall cabinet had a door hinged on the bottom, about four feet off the floor. When the cabinet door was opened, a leg dropped down to prop up the end, making the door a table. Shelves in the cabinet held dishes, silverware, food and spices. When the meal was over, they cleared the table, and up it went, out of the way. The table was now the door to the cabinet, again. I loved the way it worked, making everything neat and orderly. They had two bunk beds made out of 2X4's at the rear of the shanty. They drove nails into the 2x4 wall studs to hang their clothes. Neither of them had much in the way of clothes, so that worked just fine.

One rainy day, I slipped away from home and headed for the shanty. Johnny and Arnold decided to take a break that day. Arnold began cooking stew on the little wood stove. The rain came down harder. Each tried to get the other to go out to the garden to get some onions for the stew. Neither one wanted to get soaked in the pouring rain. Arnold offered me a quarter if I would run out and pull a couple onions. I would have done it for nothing. To get a whole quarter for just a couple minutes out in the rain sounded great. The cold rain came down in torrents and soaked me to the skin. I got back with the onions and stood by the stove. Water dripping from my clothes made a puddle. I shivered, turning to dry one side and then the other by the stove. When Arnold took the cover off the pot, the aroma of the stew made me hungry. Seeing he had paid me to get the onion I did not feel right about staying for dinner, but they set an extra bowl at the end of table, and invited me to eat. That was the best stew I had ever had. They talked and joked while we ate. It seemed good to relax while eating in that cozy shanty. Someday, I decided, I was going to have a shanty like that for my very own.

Arnold began raising chickens so he could sell eggs. It took about four months before the chickens began laying eggs. Arnold bought chicken feed from Potter Grain Company on credit. For food money, he sold the empty grain bags to the bag man who came around about once a week. He paid them a nickel a bag, enough to buy food for the two of them. Arnold said he would settle Johnny's wages when they sold the eggs in the fall. But Arnold was an impatient man and sometimes had a quick temper. Eggs needed to be gathered, often, during the day, cleaned and weighed—every one—pea wee, small, medium, large, extra large and jumbo, and then put into boxes, and the boxes into crates. .Arnold hated doing all that tedious work with the eggs. The Depression dragged on, and when the government began buying eggs from big producers and giving them away to folks out of work, the price of eggs dropped.

One day, Studer let out a loud curse and hurled a bushel basket of eggs against the wall in a blind rage. He sold all the hens to a poultry dealer and switched to raising turkeys. Turkeys also laid eggs—big ones, but they weren't very tasty, and no one ate them except when baked in a cake or in some kind of cooking. The turkeys were raised for meat. Since turkeys are subject to catching all manner of disease, especially from chickens, Arnold painted the floors and the walls four feet up, with Black Flag. It was made from coal tar and stunk something fierce. Turkeys take about six months or more to grow big enough to butcher. Arnold and Johnny were back to selling grain bags for food money.

Pa was incensed that Studer had bought the land from under his nose when he had made it known he planned to buy the property. "Niemiec!" Pa spit out the word like an expletive—German, age-old enemy of Poland, destroying his dream. He ranted on about how the Germans had driven the Poles off their land and shipped them off to America where they had to work off their passage like indentured slaves. He went back to clearing and draining his land, more bitter than ever at the continued bad luck that seemed to dog him at every turn. Johnny divided his time between working for Arnold, raising turkeys, and delivering grain for Potter Grain Company with their Mack truck. Potter Grain paid weekly.

Chapter 25: Struggle for Survival

Long before Arnold Studer bought the tobacco land, Walter left the abandoned tobacco barn where he had been hiding after running away from home. Walter, 13, went to look for his 15 year old brother Stanley. He found Stanley living with a farmer.

The farmer had inherited three farms from various relatives who'd died, most likely during the influenza pandemic. The farmer had given up farming to celebrate his new found wealth, and was known to take a sip or two. His wife left him, and he lived alone on his isolated farm.

Stanley was a welcome sight to the lonely old farmer. He took Stanley in to live with him to keep him company. Later, when Walter showed up, the farmer fed him and they chatted for a while. When the farmer went out to the barn to milk his one remaining cow, Stanley unveiled a plan.

"Come back after dark and I'll get up and unlock the door when he goes to sleep."

That night, as soon as the farmer began snoring, Stanley unlocked the door. Walter was waiting outside in the cold. Stanley got him something to eat, and brought Walter to his room to share his bed. In the morning, while the farmer was out milking and feeding his cow, Walter bolted a quick breakfast and left to look for work. For several nights Stanley unlocked the door for Walter, who soon found the first of a succession of temporary farm jobs.

The farmer's son, who lived on the other side of town, was happy to have Stanley around to keep an eye on his father and to keep him company. But Stanley said he felt like a free-loader and was uncomfortable staying at the farm. Finding a job that included room and board, Stanley went to inform the farmer's son that he was leaving the old man. When he got back to the farm, the house was dark.

"Things didn't look right with the lamps not lit," Stanley said. "I was afraid of what I'd find."

He stumbled over the farmer's body, lying on the kitchen floor, already cold. Stanley hurried back to the son's home.

"I felt bad that he died," Stanley said. "He took me in and fed me when I didn't have anywhere to go."

Both Stanley and Walter found a series of short term farm jobs as "hired man" with the customary room and board and a small stipend. The two boys would often get together to hot wire Pa's Essex to go joy riding. They somehow managed to break a rear axle when they were about 10 or 12 miles from Turners Falls where Pa garaged his car when at work at the mill. They were in a panic, knowing Pa would get out of work soon. While trying to determine what to do next, a car stopped and the driver asked if they wanted a push to get started.

In those days, bumpers were sturdy and flat; ideal for pushing another car. The man pushed them for a couple of miles before figuring out that their car was never going to start. He drove on. The boys got out to wait for another car, and another push. After a number of pushes they eventually got the car back to the house in Turners Falls.

Pa told us how Mr. Civic, the storekeeper who owned the garage, raised the window in his apartment above the store when Pa came to get his car after work. "Don't bother trying to start your car," Mr. Civic said. "Your boys pushed it into the garage."

With the fall harvest done, the farmer who employed Walter sent him on his way. There were no jobs to be had. Walter asked family friends, the Makers to take him in, rather than come home to face Pa. He went out looking for work each day. And each day, found none.

Bitter cold soon froze the Connecticut River solid and C.A. Davis Ice Company in Turners Falls prepared to harvest ice. The company stored blocks of ice in their ice house to sell customers for use in ice boxes and mixed drinks, even though the river was a repository for sewers. Once the ice on the Connecticut River got a foot thick, C.A. Davis began harvesting. Signs went up in town advertising for help. Men hoping for work gathered out on the ice. First, a few men were hired to drag a marker over the ice to scribe the ice into two foot squares. With large ice saws, workmen sawed down through the ice along the scribed lines, making blocks two feet square. Workmen lifted the floating blocks out of the river with tongs, each time slopping water onto the ice, making it slick. Often workmen slipped on the treacherous surface and injured themselves, or fell into the frigid water—or both. When that happened, the foreman ordered the crew to get the man out of the way. He chose a replacement from the knot of men who hung around hoping for just such an opportunity to get hired. The man, injured or wet, got home as best he could.

Walter stood shivering out on the ice, all one cold wintry day. Frigid winds swept across the expanse of ice. He stomped his feet—waiting and hoping. Each time it came to hire, the foreman looked past Walter to point to a grown man. At the end of that long day, Walter went home feeling half-frozen and discouraged. Next morning, he didn't feel well at all.

"My back hurt when I woke up. And I fell on my face when I got out of bed. My legs wouldn't move—they were paralyzed."

No one was sure what the problem was. Having no money, he didn't see a doctor. Polio was rampant at the time, and in any event, there was no cure. He stayed in bed in the attic until summer. Meanwhile, back at the farm in Gill, no one knew of Walter's problem. They had their own problems; Emaline had broken her arm.

Chapter 26: The Library Saves the Day

With Helen gone, Emaline had become Pa's favorite. She was spunky and had a sunny disposition. At the end of a long day haying the Sheiding homestead, a half mile away, Pa unhooked our horse from the mowing machine and hoisted Emmy onto the old mare for a ride home. Emmy liked the idea of holding onto the brass knobs of the horse's harness hames, riding horse back like a Wild West cowboy. But just as she was ready to leave, the midwife came waddling out, hooting for Emmy to stop. She handed Emmy two jars of pickles.

"Now don't forget to return the jars," the mid-wife said, "and don't drop them,"

With a jar of pickles in each hand, Emmy had no way of hanging on. The horse realized the day was over, and eager to go home to be fed, he bolted down the steep hill towards home. Emmy tried to hang on with her knees but soon fell off, holding the two jars of pickles safe from harm.

Pa saw, from the odd angle of Emmy's arm, that her arm was broken. He took her to a doctor who splinted her arm, more or less straight, and sent her home. It healed, after a fashion, but bothered her forever after. With her arm in a sling, Emmy did not have to work in the fields and spent time reading.

She got books at the Slate Memorial Library in Gill Center. One of the books was a Western Romance novel. I began reading it. But just as I got to the exciting part where the Indians were getting ready to attack the circled wagons, and the heroine was in the arms of a cowboy guarding the wagons, and they were engaged in some heavy duty snuggling in the dark under the wagon, Emmy caught me reading it. "You wouldn't understand it," she said.

"If I don't understand it, what's to hurt me reading it?" But she did not let me find out what happened to the heavy breathing pair. When I tried to borrow the book from the library, the librarian would not let me check it out. I guess, she too, did not want to corrupt me. Despite my disappointment, with no television or radio, the library was our salvation. The books that lined the walls offered solace and a refuge from the oppression we felt at home. The library was open on Friday afternoons and evenings. It was only a mile or so from home. Library day was the highlight of our week. We'd hike there, together. But we'd have to slip away, one by one, so as to not attract Pa's attention.

"Do you all have to go? Pa would demand. "Can't one of you go and get the books instead of all of you wearing out shoe leather?

We slipped away from the house, one at a time, to hide and wait to gather together for our joyful jaunt to the library, talking and singing along the way as though we were walking down a yellow brick road.

The librarian maintained an air of reverence. We tiptoed inside and barely dared uttered a word in this hallowed place. Mrs. Blake whispered to us and we answered in whispers or a nod. If anyone began a conversation, even in whispers, she'd clear her throat and admonish us with a stern look and a finger across her lips.

In winter, Mrs. Blake kept a cheerful fire blazing in the fireplace. Sitting on the fireplace benches by the comforting fire, as we browsed through books, created an escape from the world.

Irene found a bonanza in library books. We always needed paper for homework. And the school did not supply paper for that. One day, Irene noticed that there was a blank fly leaf in most books. Using a razor-sharp knife, she'd neatly remove the page, with no one but her, and her conscience, the wiser, until she confessed the dark deed to me. She hoped Mrs. Blake wouldn't notice. She didn't, and after that, we had a supply of paper for homework, but never took more than we needed, though our conscience never ceased to nag us.

Browsing through the library, reading magazines and luxuriating in the quiet atmosphere, amidst the enchanting smell of books and the open fireplace, was a pleasure we could not convey to Pa. Communication with him was difficult at any level. And what made it more difficult was that we were not allowed to speak anything but Polish at home. Ma would let us speak to her in English if Pa wasn't home, but he took it as an affront.

Pa seemed to fear we'd learn too much from reading books. He often informed us that since he was older than we were, and since wisdom came from age, he would always have superior wisdom—because he would always be ahead of us in years. To his credit, though he had little formal education, he did learn to read Polish and was an avid reader of Polish newspapers. He reversed his dim view of the library when we brought home a Polish book left by the Bookmobile. When he found we could get Polish books at the library, Friday library nights became as important an event for him as it was for us and he didn't object to the waste of shoe leather when we left in a group.

Chapter 27: Pa Mellows

During all this time, we had no idea what had happened to Stanley and Walter. They made themselves scarce, figuring Pa was still angry with them for hot wiring the Essex and breaking an axle while joy riding. We did not know Walter became paralyzed while living with the Maker family.

One stifling hot day, the grandmother applied a hen manure poultice to his paralyzed legs. "The hot stuffy attic was bad, enough." Walter said. "With the hen manure heating my legs, I couldn't stand it another minute. Somehow I got downstairs and dragged myself around hanging onto things."

Gradually, Walter regained the use of his legs. The Maker family got Walter a job running a moon shine still in Gardner. Walter had considerably better success at distilling than Pa. "That was the best job I ever had," Walter said. "The work was easy, I didn't have to do much walking, the job was steady, and the pay was good."

A former chicken coop next to the railroad tracks served as the base of operations. After mixing a batch of corn and grain in barrels, Walter waited for the mash to ferment, giving it an occasional stir.

"The worst part, of the job, was tasting the stuff to see if it was ready. After a while, just the smell of whiskey made me feel sick."

The moonshine operation was no great secret. Often, railroad men, switching rail cars, would stop by to chat as steam rose from the still.

"Keeping them chickens nice and warm, ain't cha?" one of the men said one hot summer day. They'd talk and joke, and sometimes buy a pint or two. Prohibition was not always strictly enforced. One of Walter's best customers was a police chief. The still owner delivered booze to hotels and speakeasies quite openly, which led Walter to suspect the owner was making political contributions. I suspect he gave the police chief a break on the price of his moonshine.

Walter urged Stanley to move to Gardner where there were more job opportunities. Stanley got a job in a junkyard smashing apart engine blocks with a sledge hammer for 35 cents apiece. One day a sliver of steel flew deep into his eye. Pa did not learn of Stanley's eye accident until after he lost the eye.

Meanwhile, Pa's heart condition improved and the mill kept Pa working on a more regular basis. He mellowed and forgave the boys for joy riding in the Essex and breaking the axle. He even began laughing about it when he told someone the story. To my great joy, he began taking me fishing on the Connecticut River.

A fellow worker at the paper mill let Pa use his boat. I liked being with Pa, just the two of us, alone. I did not speak unless spoken to and sometimes not even then. I just watched and listened. Once we were out on the water, Pa uttered not a word—not even a whisper. In absolute silence, he put a worm on the hook at the end of a fish line tied to a long slim maple pole. He even set the can of worms down ever so quietly. Everything felt serene, calm and peaceful, with only the sound of water gently slapping the sides of the boat. The faint odor of fish, drifting over the water, was enticing. Occasionally, fish jumped out of the water to snatch hovering insects. Seeing that there were fish nearby and that they were hungry got me excited. But Pa never got into fly fishing. He just used worms, with a bobber on the line. I'd want to shout when the cork bobbed and went under. Pa raised the pole and hauled the fish, splashing and wiggling, out of the water. I wanted to take a turn with the fish pole but didn't dare ask. And, he never offered.

One day while rowing out into the cove, an oar-lock broke. Pa examined the break. He took dirt from the floor of the boat and rubbed it on the break. He saw me watching, and grinned in embarrassment.

"It was an old break that finally let go, just now," he said. "My friend will expect me to buy him a new one if he thinks I broke it." I don't know what his friend said or whether Pa bought a new oarlock, but we never used the boat, again.

I felt close to my father during the time he was employed, and I missed going on those fishing trips. Perhaps if the mill had kept Pa employed more steadily, he would have had a better relationship with Walter and Stanley. During the first few years after Stanley left home, the family seldom saw him and had no idea he had injured his eye, or even knew where he was living, or what he was doing.

After the steel flew into his eye, the junk yard company owner sent him to a doctor who examined Stanley's eye. "I see a hole in the eyelid," the doctor said, "but I can't see anything in the eye—it must have fallen out. Go on home; you'll be O.K."

A few days later, Walter found Stanley in bed, his eye painfully swollen the size of a golf ball. Walter took him to the Gardner hospital for treatment. The infected eye got no better after several days. Helen arranged to have Stanley admitted to a Springfield hospital. From there, he went to Massachusetts General Hospital in Boston. By then, Stanley had a headache of major proportions. Two days later, doctors decided to remove his eye. By now, Stanley didn't care—he just wanted relief from the pain.

Because he was, then, blind in one eye, Stanley dared not apply for a driver's license. But that didn't keep him from driving. He and Walter were on their way to Springfield to see Helen, one Sunday. Stanley was driving—fast—as usual. A policeman stopped him. Stanley blurted out the truth about not having a license. Tears came to his eyes, and he began to cry as he told the policeman he was on his way to see his sister whom he hadn't seen for a long time. The policeman let him go, on the condition that he got a license.

Stanley passed the license eye exam by peeking through his fingers with his good eye when told to read with the blind eye. For many years, he drove cars, trucks, and motorcycles. He successfully operated a taxi business, though his schooling had ended when he failed to enroll in grammar school at the red brick school house when the family first moved to Gill.

Chapter 28: The Old Green Car Destroyed

Mama was always happy when we kids went off to school in the fall. So were we. Some of the happiest days of my life took place in that one room brick school house---and some of the worst. School was wonderful for the first three years. Our teacher, Miss Pogoda, was young and petite. She had a ready smile, dark flashing eyes, and long brown hair, falling in soft waves. There was something more, something indefinable—an aura, of sorts. We couldn't help but love her, and we felt loved by her.

Miss Pogoda had only two years of college. She may have still been a teenager. During the depression, college students could teach in lieu of taking teacher training classes. What she lacked in training, she made up in enthusiasm. There was no better teacher in the universe as far as we were concerned. Gill students attended Turners Falls High School after graduation. A teacher, who kept records, found that Gill students from our one-room school did much better than students who had graduated from the nice new Turners Falls grammar school.

Miss Pogoda praised us at every turn. Even on the playground when we played baseball, she marveled at how far we could bat the ball and how fast we ran the bases. For kids who heard only criticism, backed up by the strap, those words of praise were gold.

"You're so smart," she often told me. "You catch on so quickly."

That kind of praise surprised me, having been told so many times how bad and how stupid I was. Then when she asked me to help my fellow first grader, my ego swelled. I loved school and couldn't wait to get there in the morning.

One day when I came home from school, I found Pa dismantling our beautiful old green car. For years, the car stood parked out behind the barn. Now, he'd already ripped out the luxuriant mohair upholstery and had bagged it for sale to the rag man. He was in the process of dismantling the back of the car with a crow bar and an axe. He smashed and beat and tore at the car.

"What are you doing to our car?" I asked, panic and depression gripping me. I felt I was losing something much more than an old broken down car. This had been our passport to worlds beyond---our escape from grim reality to pure pleasure and countless hours of happiness. This island of make-believe was being destroyed. I felt panic and tried to hold back the tears, but it was too late to stop him even if I could. The car was half gone. Seeing Pa wrecking the car brought back all the good times we had playing in it. I was heartbroken. Now I could never buy an engine for the car and drive it all over as I'd always dreamed I would. He did not answer me. A lump came in my throat. I wiped away tears. He pried sheet metal loose from the rear of the car and lugged it to the swamp where other hunks of green tinwork lay. I wanted to beg him to stop, but it was too late. "Why are you doing this?" I asked, again.

"Should have done it long time ago," he said. "This Essex was a big thing for me when I buy it; now; time for it to go."

Pa then told me that buying the emerald Essex had ended one of the best arrangements he'd had in his entire life. It was after he had laid his wife to rest in an unmarked grave in Easthampton, and married Mama. He paused to explain it all to me.

"When I was a boy like you, the Russians came galloping into our village on horseback. Cossacks, they were, I am sure. They saw my Tata working on a roof and they took him to the railroad station and threw him in a box car with prisoners going to Siberia. They didn't let him come home to say goodbye to us, or to get warm clothing. My Matka doesn't know where he is or what has become of him. All she knows is what the villagers tell her. 'Russian soldiers take your man to the depot and put him in a box car.' My Matka was scared and crying. 'What will happen to him?' she said. Who will take care of us?'

"For three years we suffered. Your grandfather used to get potatoes, cabbages, meat, and things like that in trade for work, so we had just a small garden, and a cow for milk, and a horse to take us places and to haul lumber for the carpentry." Pa flattened the sheet metal in the swamp and shoveled muck onto it.

"I don't know how we lived," he said, pausing to rest. "We had no money, and there was my younger sister and a brother to feed. Like beggars, we lived." His voice showed his bitterness. "Neighbors feed us from what little they had. It was a time of such misery.

"After about three years, my Tata comes home, weak, skinny like a scarecrow, and in rags--very bitter. 'Poland is no place for you, as long as the Russians rule,' he says. 'Go to Germany and earn passage to America where Russian can't take you into the Army or send you to Siberia to work like a slave.'

"So, he gives me 50 cents and a new pair of shoes. I cut off the tops so they are not so heavy, gave them to a friend, and set out on foot. I do what Tata says. At day's end, I stop at a house and ask for food. There's a story in Poland that Christ will come to your door disguised as a stranger. No one refuses. They feed me and let me find a place to sleep. In Poland, only the parents slept in a bed. Children slept where they could. They would give me a little pile of straw to sleep on. I found out that I'd get fed better at a house where old people, with no children, lived. They'd be lonely and there wasn't a mob of kids grabbing the food before I could get to eat. The old people would pack me a lunch of black bread and cheese. I cannot read, so I have to ask the way. In Germany, I have trouble because I don't speak German. But I find a job on a big German farm where they feed me and let me sleep in a building with other workers. By and by, I earn enough to buy a ticket on a boat. I come to America in steerage, down in the lowest part of the ship. I find my way to my uncle in Easthampton, and work where I can find it. I start working for a man who hauls beer with a horse and wagon. When I get enough money, I buy a horse and wagon and begin hauling beer, myself."

Pa worked long hours, saved his money and bought the first truck in town. Delivering beer with the truck meant he could deliver to more businesses. He prospered, married, and bought a Maxwell, one of the first cars in town.

"On Saturdays people hire me and my Maxwell for weddings."

For a former penniless immigrant, it was a heady time.

"I somebody," Pa said, with pride.

His demeanor changed and he sounded angry as he told how his first wife, Rosalie, had begun getting drunk despite his best efforts to keep liquor away from her. He said she got to the point where she lost her mind from drinking, and he had to put her in a "crazy house." She died in the state insane asylum.

Years later, I called the state hospital where a clerk looked up Rosalie's records. In reality, the poor woman was suffering from renal disease. As her kidneys failed, her brain swelled. Staggering and dementia gave her the appearance of alcoholism and insanity. I do not believe Pa ever visited her before she died.

After her death, Pa said he went to church one Sunday to hear the parish priest putting his children up for adoption. Soon, Helen was in the process of adoption by one family. Stanley was placed with another. Walter stayed with family friends. With his home repossessed, truck seized by creditors, out of business and out of a job, Pa had little more than his Maxwell car and a little money. And that was dwindling fast. Pa never forgave Rosalie, believing she was responsible for his fall from prosperity and happiness.

The family that took Helen made her a makeshift bed of blankets behind the kitchen wood stove. Frightened and feeling abandoned, Helen couldn't sleep.

"The woman came so slowly and quietly into the kitchen carrying a lamp—without a word, "Helen said. "I was scared, not knowing what was going to happen. The woman raised the lamp to the ceiling. It was covered with bugs. She would lift the lamp up and they'd drop into the lamp. I didn't want to live there with all those bugs; I wanted to go home to my mother.

"One day someone told me my mother was coming home. I was happy to go home to see her."

When Helen saw her mother and touched her, she was terrified. "I began crying hysterically and they took me away. I had expected my mother to hug me and hold me. No one had explained that my mother had died. This wasn't my mother---this was someone else, cold and hard as a statue."

Pa was beside himself. He was now without a wife, without a mother for his children, without his children, without his truck, without a business, and soon to be without a home. Friends introduced him to Ma.

With no welfare or social security programs, Ma was desperate, struggling to survive. Trying to work and care for her two children and the new baby, she welcomed meeting a young man in a similar predicament. Pa proposed marriage on the first date and she accepted almost before he finished asking. It was not so much a marriage of convenience as one born of desperation. Little did she know that, ironically, one day she would have to support him and seven more children.

After their marriage, Pa rounded up his kids on the ruse of a final farewell. The boys were happy to go with him, but Helen had grown attached to the woman who wanted to adopt her and went with some reluctance.

"When I asked her if she wanted to go back where she'd been living," Pa said, "or stay with us, she said, 'I didn't want to come, but now that I'm here with my brothers, I'll stay.'

Pa piled them into the Maxwell and fled in the dead of night. They stayed with friends of Ma in Housatonic. After the couple married, the newly joined family came to Turners Falls, where Pa went to work for the Keith Paper Company. Soon, Pa got the deal of a lifetime. Fred Field, who operated Cold Brook Farm, was looking for someone to sign on as a sharecropper to grow onions. In the sharecropping deal, Field provided the family with a house, a pail of milk a day, and garden space. The family arrived at Cold Brook with what little they could carry in the Maxwell touring car. The Field family's 120 acre Cold Brook Farm was more plantation, or small village, than farm, with endless fields of produce, a dairy, beef cattle operation, steam boat landing, water powered saw mill and cider mill. The farm even sported its own hydro-electric plant, long before electricity blessed the surrounding area. Cold Brook Farm swarmed with the activity of an ant colony. Several barns housed dairy cattle, hogs, beef cattle and horses. Long tobacco barns served to dry and process the lucrative money crop. Forty acres of asparagus and endless onion fields brought in money for both the farm owner and sharecroppers, alike.

Twenty six rooms in the farmhouse accommodated city folks taking summer vacations in the country. There were cottages for hired help, including a Negro couple. Constant activity was the norm, raising produce, tobacco, beef, hogs, chickens, and dairy cattle. The labor force raised and processed commodities for market, shipping produce, cider, and vinegar to Boston markets by the train carload, and delivering milk on a local home delivery route. The Fields urged their farm help to cater to the whims of the vacationing city folks for fear they'd get bored by idleness and not return. While the rich city folks lounged about, waiting to be served and entertained, Ma and the kids slaved in the onion fields under the hot sun.

Ma was grateful the family had chanced upon such a wonderful situation; the family had plenty to eat all summer, with surplus to store for the winter. The potato bin was filled each fall. They prepared a barrel of sauerkraut from cabbage raised on their garden plot. Miscellaneous root vegetables crowded the cellar. A small flock of chickens supplied eggs and chicken for Sunday dinner. Coal for winter heat could be picked up along the railroad track when it fell from coal trains passing through. If a train happened to pass by while the kids were out picking up coal, the fireman on the locomotive would sometimes shovel coal out for them. Rows of canned preserves crowded shelves in the cellar. On top of all that, at harvest time when onions were sent to the Boston Market, Field presented them with their share of the profit. In short, they had found their Promise Land.

Then the Maxwell broke down. Pa had to walk the eight miles round trip to work each day. Not only was the daily hike tiring, but it cut into the time he could spend in the onion fields. It was also a blow to his pride to be on foot. He had a horse but had nowhere to stable it while he worked at the mill.

By scrimping and saving and pooling their earnings, the family accumulated a nest egg of $1,000---the equivalent of two years wages at the mill. They hid it in the pages of a Sears & Roebuck catalog under the mattress.

Pa began making plans to buy a farm of his own. But he felt he first needed a car. On his way to work each day he trudged past the local Ford agency where Model T's were on display. The Model T's were all painted black, didn't have a bit of nickel trim and for over nineteen years of manufacture, all looked alike. A brand new touring model (with a canvas top) sold for $265-- a good used Ford, looking like brand new, went for $50, and a clunker could be had for $5 or $10.

Cassidy's garage held a franchise for luxurious Essex automobiles, available in a variety of colors. Pa often paused to admire a gleaming emerald beauty displayed in the showroom window. Pa hadn't planned on buying an

Essex. On the day he went shopping with the $1,000 nest egg in his pocket, his intention was to buy a good used car—maybe one of the used Model T open touring cars on sale at the Ford agency for $50. The nest egg in his pocket was there to help him make a decision. He often said, "A man without money is a man without reason."

He asked the Ford salesman for a demonstration drive.

"When the salesman starts cranking," Pa said. "The Model T moves ahead, so he calls another salesman over."

"Hey, come here and hold this thing so it don't move."

"What I going to do when I start it by myself—tie the car to tree?" Pa asked.

"The clutch bands is new," the salesman said. "Once they get wore in, it won't move on you."

But the "Tin Lizzie's" strange transmission with three pedals and only two speeds didn't impress Pa. The rigid seat on top of the gas tank had no adjustments for driver size. Only the seats were upholstered, the rest of the interior was metal painted black.

The car wasn't overpowered, either. The Model T couldn't climb most hills in high and barely crawled along in low while the motor roared.

Pa described how he trudged over to Cassidy's garage after the Model T test drive. He gazed in admiration at the fancy closed car glistening with nickel plated trim. Best of all it had a six cylinder engine and a conventional three speed transmission.

The Essex had features still not available on some automobiles seventy years later. An automatic system lubricated the chassis so that it never needed greasing. The engine had rollers on the valve tappets, adjustable radiator shutters, automatic spark advance, aluminum transmission case, and adjustable front seats. A six cylinder engine featuring aluminum alloy pistons for fast acceleration and smooth operation supplied ample power. The car, in essence, was a fine piece of motoring machinery, well advanced for the time.

On impulse, Pa blew the entire $1,000 nest egg on the grand looking Essex. Years later we found out the selling price was $650, but Pa never knew he might have been scammed.

"I think to myself a fine automobile get me back to riches," Pa said, leaning on his shovel in the swamp where he was burying the Essex's tin work. "When I work for a man driving a team of horses and wagon, I am nobody. But when I buy the first truck in Easthampton, I somebody—business goes like crazy and I make money, lots of money."

The haggardness seemed to leave his face and he smiled as he reminisced.

"I make three, four, trips a day, instead of one. I carry bigger loads, and best of all, I somebody. I leave my village in Poland for Germany on foot, a boy, with a new pair of shoes and fifty cents. In Germany I work on big farm all summer to buy a ticket to Ameryka.

"I have only one day of school in Poland. I do not know how to speak English when I get here. I a Greenord. Nobody knows me. But when they hear my truck backfire on the way down Mt Tom, everybody knows me, and they line the street to buy my beer. I'm 'the guy with the truck'."

He paused. His eyes lost their lively look.

"I thought it would happen again when I buy this Essex." He shook his head. "But it did not go that way."

When he'd come sweeping into Cold Brook Farm with that grand looking emerald beauty on the proud day he bought the Essex, Pa relished the surprised look on farm owner Field's face. But soon after that, Field told Pa the family would have to go because onion thrips were invading the farm. But Pa knew it was really the Essex that had soured the deal. And, sure enough, before Pa finished moving out, a new family of sharecroppers took their place in the cottage. Pa bought the farm in Gill.

"I wanted to buy the tobacco barn and land, too, but before I can, the German bought it. So that's the way it is."

He plopped another shovelful of muck on the piece of tin holding a plate glass window now broken. A window shade lay torn and muddy. Pa covered those pieces of the beautiful emerald Essex with mud, burying our magic chariot and our world of dreams, and maybe his, too.

Chapter 29: Life Gets Better

Not long after Pa buried the old green car, the Keith Paper Mill began providing him with fairly steady work. With the girls handing over their pay from their housekeeping jobs and the farm providing much of the family's food, Pa had a fair amount of income. He even patched the roof and remodeled the back shed into a kitchen. A fellow worker from the mill helped him.

The shed floor sloped, so Pa and his helper sloped the ceiling to match. Ma nearly burst with pride when anyone admired her new kitchen with wainscoting installed on the lower portion of the wall. A chair rail ran around the top. Pa and his helper put up sheetrock above the chair rail.

They used the wrong kind of nails on the sheetrock walls and ceiling. Paint wouldn't stick to them. They compounded the error by countersinking the nails too far. Pa's helper suggested using roofing tar to fill the holes. The tar bled through the paint, despite repeated painting. They next tried window putty, and eventually got the paint to stick. The countersunk nails didn't hold and the ceiling began to come down. They next nailed strips of lath over the joints to keep the ceiling from collapsing. A breech baby would have been a far lesser ordeal.

Pa built a pantry on the North end of the kitchen and installed a pitcher pump and sink. Ma was delighted to be able to draw water right there in the pantry without having to go outside to fetch water. We were glad to see the kitchen built, because it got rid of the dark and spooky shed with boxes and barrels half hidden in the shadows where there was no telling what danger lurked. Ma was happy to have the kitchen but we were even happier to have windows bringing daylight into that scary place.

Pa converted the former kitchen to a bedroom, so he and Ma could move out of the dining room. He never got around to fixing the two bedrooms upstairs and seldom went upstairs except to whack us with the strap if we were not quiet at bedtime. Girls slept in one room, boys in the other. When our parents invited people to stay over, the guests slept in our beds and we slept outdoors or in the barn. Pa had a lot of friends who visited back and forth. Often they held lawn parties at the farm, eating and drinking, talking and laughing.

One day I asked Pa why we couldn't have a picnic for just the family. Pa said we would. And true to his word, when we dug new potatoes late in the summer, he built a big bonfire in the field by our house. When the fire died down, he buried a dozen or more potatoes in the glowing coals. When they were done, the baked potatoes looked like charred oversized lumps of charcoal briquettes. He scooped them into a burlap bag, took one end and Ma held the other end. They shook the potatoes back and forth to knock loose charcoal off. When they opened the bag, the potatoes were still black.

"Eat. Eat," Pa said.

To wash them down, Ma had prepared a kind of "lemonade" made with water, onions, salt and pepper. That was our picnic. Pa was quite pleased with the results and often repeated the ritual. We didn't dare suggest hot dogs, marshmallows or root beer. To our surprise, the potatoes were quite good. The charcoal made them taste salty. Still, hot dogs, marshmallows and root beer would have been nice.

The autumn harvest of potatoes was marked by a falling water table. At summer's end, the well often got low. Pa would put a ladder down and send someone to clean it out. When the older kids had all left, it came my turn to descend into that deep forbidding place.

My hands shook as I climbed down, down, down, into that fearful dark hole in the ground. I always fought claustrophobia in the cold dampness at the bottom. It got worse when Pa hauled the ladder out. I looked up. The opening looked small and far away. My bare legs felt like they were freezing in the icy water. The air became ever harder to breathe as I worked to scoop clay into a bucket with an old kettle. Steam from my breath hung in the air.

My imagination ran wild thinking the tiles would crack and break, or that I would dig too deep and cause the tiles to drop and tip, trapping me in that chilly tomb. I struggled to keep from yelling in panic for Pa to put the ladder back. I scooped clay from the bottom of the well, pouring off water before dumping it into the bucket he'd lowered on a rope. When the bucket was nearly full, I'd stand against the wall and hold my hands over my head in case the rope let go. Sometimes bits of clay fell from the bucket, hitting me on the head or shoulder, giving me a start, thinking that the rope had broken or come loose and the bucket was coming down to crash into my head.

Then Pa lowered the bucket, and I crouched down again in that cramped place to scoop more clay. Stories of tiles that had been undermined and dropped went through my mind—tiles turning sideways to trap the person in the well. The thoughts filled my brain and made the possibility seem ever more certain

"Dig deeper," Pa said, looking small up there so high in the world above. His words echoed off the cold wet walls. "Not much water coming, yet."

My body began to shake from cold, from fatigue, and from nervousness. Each time I straightened up, my feet would be sunk deeper in the clay, now more like quicksand, and it became harder and harder to pull free. I dug some more. Water rose until my butt was wet. My breath formed a cloud of fog in the cold and airless place.

At long last, he sent the ladder back down. I worked to get my feet free from the suction of the clay that seemed to want to claim me for its own. I climbed the ladder quickly as I dared, feet slipping on the rungs slippery with clay. I hurried in near panic to reach sunshine and air to breathe. I did what Pa told me to do because I was afraid of him, afraid of the razor strap that he had hanging in the kitchen. I am sure he felt that I deserved a spanking, but I could seldom remember what I'd done to warrant it. I only remember the sudden sting of the strap and the anger and resentment that welled up inside me. I may have gotten into mischief, or maybe he may have been irritable. He would hit me until I cried, then say, "Go outside and pee, so the pee doesn't come out your eyes."

After a while, I quit crying. I don't know why. Maybe it was because he'd teased me about peeing out of my eyes. Maybe I was damned if I would give him the satisfaction of seeing me cry. Then, later, I couldn't cry. Sometimes in frustration, Pa thrashed me good. I just covered my head with my arms and curled up on the floor until he wearied of hitting me.

His double razor strap had a metal buckle that held two strips of leather, bolted together with an eye to hang it. He used the double strap for sharpening his straight razor. When he was really angry, he'd hit me with that. The leather was thicker and heavier than the single strap he used for everyday thrashings. While flogging me with the double razor strap, one day, he grew weary of trying to make me cry.

"This kid doesn't seem to feel any pain," he said. "Let's see what he thinks of the other end," and hit me with the buckle end. I jumped up, ran off, and hid in the woods.

Along about supper time, I got cold and hungry and began watching the house. Johnny came by after work, but didn't stay. That meant Pa was still home. I figured Johnny must have gone home to Studer's shanty across the tobacco field, because he didn't spend any more time at home than he had to, when Pa was home.

As I hid in the woods, I thought about the stew Arnold and Johnny had shared with me that rainy day I spent in the snug cabin. And I began to feel more, and more, hungry, not so much for stew but for the feeling of friendship and acceptance, and maybe even love that I felt the day they shared their stew with me.

The Essex backing out of the driveway brought me back to reality. There were no kids outside after the car left. That meant Pa had taken everyone with him. My stomach seemed to gnaw on itself with hunger as I watched the car drive away. I started sneaking home to get something to eat and some warm clothes. I didn't know where I was going or what I was going to do, but I knew I was leaving. I had to cross an open hayfield, and started running, crouched down, when a loud whistle stopped me in my tracks. It was Johnny, out looking for me. He took me home to feed me the supper Ma had left warming on the back of the kitchen stove.

Johnny talked to me for a long time, that day. He told me he knew how tough it was, but there really wasn't anything else I could do, right at that time.

"Keep out of the way, Joey, keep quiet, and do what he tells you."

Johnny never called him Tata or Pa--- just "he" or "him".

"Try not to get him mad," Johnny said. "Study hard in school. Learn all you can for yourself. Don't study hard for your mother, or him, or for the teacher—do it for yourself."

After that, when Johnny stopped by in the evening with Potter's Mack truck, I was always happy to see him. I could tell he really liked me. Sometimes he'd give me a choice of a nickel or five pennies to go do some chores, like throwing hay down from the hay mow, or to go gather eggs in the hen house. I always chose the pennies, figuring that if I lost one, I'd still have four left.

One evening, Johnny left the truck's parking lights on. He told me to figure out how to shut them off. Pa always said, "Don't touch anything," whenever he left me alone in the car. I was glad Johnny trusted me to flick the truck switches all I wanted. The leather truck seat was up high and the big wooden steering wheel had smooth rounded notches on the inside to fit your fingers. Two shifting levers stuck up out of the floor almost as high as the steering wheel. An emergency brake handle next to them stood as tall as the shifting levers. The long hood stretched out to a nickel plated radiator cap with a wire retaining clip over the top. There were rows and rows of little toggle switches on the varnished wood dashboard. Some switches were in the up position and some down. None were labeled. I had fun seeing what each switch turned a light on. It took quite a while to try all the switches because I had to get out, look at the lights, and then, climb back up the high step to the cab, again.

The next time Johnny came and left the parking lights on, I shut them off right away. I ran into the house to tell him, and watched to see the surprise on his face at how fast I'd done it. Mama and Johnny stopped talking when I came in and didn't look at all happy I was back in the house so soon.

"Go outside and find something to do," Johnny said. I felt unwanted and my spirits fell.

From then on, when I shut the parking lights off, I would not go in the house to tell them. I would just sit behind the wheel and pretend I was driving the truck. I would move the gear shift levers and turn the steering wheel from side to side. One evening, after Johnny talked with Mama, he came out looking angry.

"Why do you make Irene do all the chores, and not help her?"

I tried to tell him that Irene and I always got along good and did chores together. And when she got a chance to work at Studer's turkey farm, picking turkeys, like this day, I did all her chores, alone. He acted as though he did not believe me.

"Ask Irene yourself, if you don't believe me," I said. "She's picking turkeys at Arnold's, right now."

The accusation made me feel depressed and frustrated because Irene and I got along great. Though she was only two years older, Irene looked out for me. And I tried to make life easier for her. I'm sure she got this across to Johnny, because the next time he came to visit, he tried to make up for bawling me out, but it was never the same, again. I don't think Johnny ever knew how close Irene and I were, and what she did for me one day when we were haying.

We all admired a Polish family whose loads of hay always looked as neat as a loaf of bread. We didn't groom our load with that much fanaticism, but we did try to build the load well. A neighboring family never did master the art and endured the embarrassment of often losing most of their sloppily built loads in a comical avalanche of hay on the way to the barn. We'd laugh our heads off.

One day during haying season, Irene and Louis were up on the hay wagon. Irene could distribute hay and build a load, looked neat and square, while Louis tramped the hay down so it'd stay in place and not come tumbling down. We were short of hay forks, so Irene took the forkfuls of hay with her hands as we pitched it up to her. Pa had given me a short handled manure fork to use. It worked all right when the load was small, but as the load grew higher I had trouble getting the hay up high enough for Irene to grab. Once, I shoved the fork up towards her outstretched hands and the fork left my hand. To my horror, I saw it dangling from her hand. I'd driven one of the prongs all the way through her palm!

Irene didn't cry out. Without a word, she yanked the fork loose and tossed it back to me. She wrapped her handkerchief around her hand to stop the blood, and kept on working so I'd escape Pa's wrath. I never forgot her doing that for me, especially since she was a little squeamish about blood—even that drawn by bedbugs.

91

Chapter 30: Bedbugs and Peddlers

Our farmhouse was infested with bed bugs when the family moved there. They looked like little flat brown lady bugs. After feeding on your scalp they'd swell up with blood and take on a reddish color. They secreted a substance that numbed the skin so that it didn't hurt when they bit, similar to what leeches do when they suck blood. But, in the morning the sore would hurt and itch when the effects of the secretion worn off. Those miserable bugs came back to feed on our scalps, night after night. We hated those bedbugs and were afraid someone would find out we had an infestation of them. Having bedbugs was a major disgrace.

From time to time, Ma tore the beds apart and rubbed the crevices of the mattress with a rag soaked in kerosene. To get bedbugs hiding in the coils of the bedsprings, Ma held a rag under the springs and poured kerosene onto the springs from the spout of a small kerosene can. Bedbugs would come running out. They'd fall to the floor and wave their legs for a few seconds before they died. She'd stamp them dead, giving a little grunt, as if to say, "There, you little bastards, die," even though they were dying, or dead, already. Sometimes their bellies popped with a little splotch of blood. I didn't feel very sorry for the bugs, seeing it was my blood that made their bellies bulge.

Our beds stunk of kerosene for weeks, and fumes stung our eyes until the kerosene evaporated. It kept the bugs away for a while, but soon, more came out from under the wallpaper to chew spots on our scalps as we slept, making sores that never seemed to heal. We tore off the wallpaper, but they hid behind the plaster laths where the horsehair plaster had fallen away, or from between the cracks on walls covered with boards.

In the end it was the Raleigh man who saved us from the bed bugs. He sold Ma some insecticide. And by spraying every crack and crevice we could find, the hated bedbugs were, at long last, gone for good. The Raleigh man came by the farm about once a month peddling patent medicines, household supplies, spices and miscellaneous extracts. Ma was not supposed to have any money. Pa doled it out when she went into a store to shop, and he'd have his hand out for the change when she got back to the car. But she'd short-change him, secretly holding back a little change so she'd have a stash of spending money. When she was short of cash, the Raleigh man took eggs in payment.

Ma always bought a squat round bottle of orange drink concentrate and root beer flavoring. One day, the Raleigh man held out a big bottle of vanilla. "This is a very good vanilla," he said with a knowing look. "It's very popular-- 90 proof."

I told Ma we still had a small bottle full of vanilla in the cupboard. She got red in the face and tried to suppress a smile. The Raleigh man smiled, broadly. Ma bought the big bottle, but I never saw it in the cupboard.

After the Raleigh Man left, she packed us a lunch with orange drink and told us to go out into the woods for a picnic, or at least out behind the garage in the shade of some trees. When we got back she seemed calm and rested with the smell of vanilla about her.

Sometimes when we pestered her to make root beer, she'd tell us she had to get the house clean and the barn chores done first. We worked like driven slaves in our hurry to make the root beer. I rounded up all the bottles I could find, filled them with soapy water and added a few pebbles, and shook the mixture to scour the bottle clean. After filling them with root beer, the worst part was waiting for the fermenting yeast to give the root beer some fizz. It seemed to take forever. Sometimes we just could not wait, and Ma would let us open a bottle when it was still flat. We really appreciated Ma taking the time and energy to make that delicious treat, and it made us feel good to know that she loved us.

The Raleigh man wasn't the only peddler who came around. A man driving a truck marked DRY GOODS used to come bursting out of the woods on the little used dirt road, and tear by the house at a high rate of speed. Only a few foolhardy people braved the road beyond our house and then only in the summer when it was passable, but barely, making his whirlwind appearance all the more surprising.

"Why does he go by so fast?" I asked my older sister Gladys.

"He does that to raise a lot of dust to get back at Ma for not buying any dry goods from him when he stopped one day."

"What are dry goods, anyway?"

"They're dried up old stale bread and rolls and bakery stuff."

It wasn't until years later that I found out he sold clothing.

A couple of Greeks also came around selling groceries, fruit and vegetables. Business was good, but they were always arguing. Soon they broke up, and each had their own truck. They continued to cover the same area, each trying to undersell the other.

"Just tell me what he charges and I'll sell for less," one of them once said. From then on, customers only had to say the other guy's item was cheaper and they sold it for less---and less. Prices went down, down, down, until they put themselves both out of business.

One day some swarthy men came around selling rolls of linoleum. When my father said he didn't have any money, the peddler asked, "You have wedding rings, watches, jewelry? I buy. Geef you good price."

Pa brought out his gold watch and two wedding rings linked by a safety pin. Ma said she'd rather not sell the rings, so Pa asked the peddler to tell him what he would give for the watch. It was the last vestige of his days of prosperity.

The peddler took the watch and looked it over, briefly.

"Four dollars," he announced.

"No, I've had it for a long time and can't sell it for that; it's worth a lot more. That's a good watch; it has a jeweled movement".

"I don't care about the insides," the peddler said, smashing the face of the watch on the post of the baby crib. Glass, cogs, and wheels flew over the floor. "I'm just interested in the case,"

Pa opened his mouth but no sound came out. He looked like someone had hit him in the stomach. The peddler opened his money bag and handed Pa four dollars. Pa looked at the glass and cogs on the floor, shook his head in dismay and accepted the money. He looked sick.

One day, nature proved as tricky as the peddler. After a summer storm, we kids all went down to the brook to swim while the water was high. Louis was just a toddler. My sisters sat him on a wooden Kraft cheese box in the shallows and took turns watching him. The water was the color of coffee because of the storm, but we didn't mind. We had fun swimming and cavorted like dolphins. Soon, someone yelled in alarm, "Where's Louis?"

There was no sign of him. The Kraft cheese box was floating down the muddy stream. We frantically felt for him in the water. He was nowhere to be found. We searched more desperately. We dared not run home to tell Ma. She couldn't telephone anyone for help, anyway; we had no phone. We lived too far away to use a neighbor's telephone. Besides, there was no one to call. Our town had no police force or fire department. All we could do was to keep searching—keep feeling with our hands, searching—feeling nothing but the bottom of the brook. We were scared. The girls began crying. After what seemed an eternity, someone found him. He was limp and lifeless.

We didn't know anything about resuscitation or CPR. The girls laid him on the bank of the brook, face down, and began pressing on his back. Muddy water spouted out of his mouth—more pressing, more spouting. After a while he began to cry and cough up more water. We never told Ma, and definitely not Pa. Louis was tougher than we thought, and did not seem the worse for his near drowning.

During dry spells, the brook would diminish to a trickle. We tried building a dam of dirt and sod, but the rising water soon cut a path through the top, or washed the dam out at the bottom. Pa saw our futile efforts and brought down some 2 x 4 studs and wide boards. He drove the posts into the brook bed and nailed the boards across them. The rising water, now two or three feet deep, spilled over the top of the boards. We were a little taken back, but grateful for his kindness and wisdom. We splashed and frolicked in the deeper water the rest of the day keeping a sharp eye on Louis.

Next morning, the water was back to a small stream. The dam had washed out underneath the boards. We tried filling the washout with dirt and sod, but the current swept it away. Pa saw that his dam had failed but he said nothing. He took the dam apart and lugged the lumber home. He looked sad, and I felt sorry for him.

Chapter 31: Waterhole

A water hole next to the brook was full of eels, snakes and lizards, but we only used it for fishing. A WPA crew had dug the hole and lined it with stones to serve as a fire pond. WPA stood for Work Projects Administration, one of many make-work agencies formed by President Franklin Delano Roosevelt during the Great Depression to give unemployed people jobs in order to get the economy going.

The crew fenced the water hole with four sturdy posts and hog wire, as a safety measure. We never dreamed that the fire pond would ever be needed to fight a fire. The water hole was just a good place to fish. We perched on the fence until it sagged flat to the ground, giving us easy access to the little pond.

During the summer, we liked to fish late into the evening when the fish were biting best. The air got chilly next to the brook, so we came prepared with sheepskin coats. I don't know where they came from, but Ma said they were like the sheepskin coats that her father sewed. As nightfall came on and temperatures fell, we'd huddle under the coats, trying to cover our bare feet to keep them warm.

When our can of worms ran low, we'd cut down to a single pole. The fish poles were thin maple saplings with a piece of fish line tied to the end. We took turns holding the pole. The others gave instructions---lots of instructions.

My younger sister Lora sometimes went wild with excitement when her turn came. Irene and I took up stations on opposite sides of Lora, peering into the twilight to catch the reflection of the water. We relayed instructions to her.

"A touch," we'd whisper

"Another touch."

"A nibble."

"A bite!"

The cork bobbed, way under.

"You got a good bite! Pull the pole, Lora! Pull the pole. Give it a yank!"

Lora yanked the pole with all her strength. The fish went flying up out of the water in an arc, high into the air, off the hook and far out into the pasture on the other side of the road.

Everyone went looking. We could faintly hear the fish flopping. It never dawned on us to simply catch another fish and forget about searching for the one flipping around in the dark. But we found the bull head and somehow got it into a pail without getting stuck by the horns.

I loved living on the farm. It was quiet and peaceful in the broad valley with the brook running through it. I knew all the pools where fish liked to stay.

Deer sometimes fed in the meadow. White button mushrooms popped up in the pasture after a summer rain. All sorts of birds flew about. I loved the barn swallows for their grace and verve. We heard the whip poor wills on summer nights, and sand pipers took up residence one summer. In winter we skated and went sliding on crisp cold nights.

While we were engaged in all these things, it seemed that those days would never end—that life would go on the same forever.

But life did change in a surprising way. Family friend, Annie, divorced her husband, and soon found a drinking buddy, a small- time politician, who was now a minor WPA executive. Annie came to the house to ask Ma if she wanted a job. Ma's eyes sparkled at the prospect of getting out of the house and going to work. She looked over at Pa to see if he would object, but he just sat with his head down, studying his hands.

Next day, a man came with a pickup to move Ma's Betsy Ross treadle sewing machine to the town hall. Annie arrived in her 1934 Ford sedan. Few women drove, back then, and even fewer owned their own car. But Annie was a liberated woman. She came into the house to oversee the sewing machine move.

"We need her home," Pa protested. "Who's going to cook, and clean, and can?"

"You are," Annie said. "You ain't working."

Pa did not like that idea, at all. The moving man seemed oblivious to the argument, calmly going about the business of moving the machine out to his pickup, probably having been through similar scenes, before.

"Come on, Mary," Annie said to my mother, heading out to her car. "We're going to work." Ma beamed. She whipped off her apron and hurried after Annie.

Ma's Betsy Ross joined several other sewing machines in the town hall, set up in a row to resemble a factory. Local women, including the WPA executive's friend Annie, began sewing clothing for distribution to the needy. The politician left Annie in charge, though she had already taken charge--long before he gave her the official nod.

Since the clothes were destined for the needy, Annie reasoned the women should sew clothes for their own families, first. "Goddammit, Annie said, "they wouldn't be here sewing if they wasn't needy. No sense in sewing clothes and sending them to the damn distribution center and then having everyone go down and get the stuff to bring it home. This way, they can sew what they need, and take it directly home without all this damned fool nonsense of sending it and then going to get it to bring it back home."

The politician caved in, apparently not wanting to argue with Annie and jeopardize their cozy relationship. Annie sewed a jumper from curtain material for Louis, as a lark. It was cool and Louis loved it. He wore the dress most of that summer with nothing on underneath, being too young to realize there was anything wrong with being a semi-nudist. When company came, Ma, or the older girls, would quickly dress him in something less revealing, over his objections.

Ma was sad when the WPA sewing project ended, but the boost to her self-esteem stayed with her. She often stood up to Pa, and he seemed to respect her more. It was during the period when Ma was sewing for the WPA that I got my first glimpse of Mount Hermon School for Boys.

As we rode past the rear entrance to the school, one day, I looked out at hundreds of pigs rooted in a fenced piggery on one side of the road while a herd of cattle grazed in a pasture on the other. A little further on, flocks of chickens roamed on a fenced range.

"What are all these animals here for?" I asked.

"This is a school where boys learn to farm."

"Will I be able to go there, some day?"

"Oh, no; you have to be rich and very smart to go here."

Like my older brothers, Pa had pretty much cured me of farming. I wondered why a rich boy would need to learn how to shovel manure. And if he were smart, it seemed that he'd find something better to do. I wished that I were rich, or at least smart.

In truth Mount Hermon is a college prep school. The pigs, roaming the piggery and feeding on garbage from the dining hall, would end up as pork on the table. The cattle produced milk, butter, and beef for the students. Chickens produced eggs and meat. Though the school work program required boys to work ten hours a week, farming was usually the furthest thing from their goals. In reality, the hard work may have also cured them of ever entertaining the idea of farming for a living, and made them study harder.

The next time we visited the school, we drove to the Mt. Hermon school dump with our two-man crosscut saw in the back of the Essex where the cushions had been removed. We didn't own a wood lot and Pa struggled to find wood to fill the wood shed each winter. Pa bought or begged wood where he could. We were at the dump to salvage elm wood, discarded by the school maintenance crew. I felt good about to be chosen to go with my parents. In reality I was the only one left at home to partner on the two-man saw. The back and forth action on the saw was too taxing for Pa's heart condition. Ma and I teamed up well.

We lugged the near-useless elm wood home in the back seat of the Essex, Pa's pride and joy, now tainted with the smell of burning garbage. The only good part was that, with the rear cushion removed and the back loaded to the ceiling with wood, I got to ride in the front seat between Ma and Pa. Elm wood does not throw much heat, but we needed firewood. We probably generated more heat cutting and stacking the elm than the wood produced when we burned it in the stove that winter.

One evening, as we were sawing away, the Mount Hermon farm manager drove down the road to the dump.

"Someone's coming," Pa said. "I wonder if we'll get in trouble for taking the wood."

Pa and Ma knew the manager because he was also the town tax collector. They smiled nervously, and waved. He made a U-turn and left without waving back. Maybe he did not see us wave, and meant no offense, but Pa left with the load of elm wood, and we never went back. I felt Pa's shame and embarrassment at the snub. No one talked on the way home. I wished that we had a wood lot, or money to buy wood or a load of coal. I wished we didn't have to pick wood out of the dump.

Pa eventually purchased a wood lot when both he and Ma were working and piling up the money. Owning a wood lot restored his dignity, but it still took a fair amount of time and energy to cut, haul, split, saw and stack wood in the woodshed. We originally used a "one-lunger" single cylinder gasoline engine. Sometimes, on the way home from school, I could hear the "putt-putt" of the engine and the scream of the circular saw tearing its way though a log, long before the saw was in sight.

When I was about ten years old, Pa put me to work taking wood away from the saw. I'd hold onto the end of a log, just inches away from the whirling blade, fearful that the saw would bind and pull my hand into it. Doing such dangerous work boosted my self-esteem. Long after the screaming saw was silenced, the sound continued to roar in my ears. The act of preparing for the long cold winter appealed to me. Maybe it was from reading the ant-and-grasshopper story, or maybe I just wanted to be warm.

Pa replaced the one lunger with a 1927 Dodge car engine and eliminated the belt drive. The belt had served as a safety factor, falling off if the saw jammed. He now had the saw arbor welded solid to the car drive shaft. The six cylinder engine was far more powerful than the single cylinder putt-putt engine, making it a treacherous set-up. I dared not mention it to Pa, but someone who saw the lethal solid connection had warned him. Pa ran the engine at a lower speed, after that, and fortunately, no one was maimed before he gave up cutting wood. I missed the hustle and bustle of sawing the winter's wood. I always liked doing a man's job even though I was just a kid. I would casually mention to other boys about taking wood away from the saw, operating the mowing machine, working as a teamster or driving a farm tractor, when many of them were not allowed to so much as open a can of beans for fear the can opener would maim them for life.

Chapter 32: Government Business

One day our luck changed for the better after that humiliating day at the dump. A big van truck turned onto the dirt road leading to our farm, trailing a cloud of dust.

"Pa! Pa! Someone's coming," I yelled.

Skippy, our dog, came to life. He hadn't had anything to bark at, for a while, and was making the most of the opportunity. Pa came out of the house, just as the truck swerved into our driveway. Dust swirled around us as the truck skidded to a halt. Pa raised his hand to shield his eyes from dust and the noonday sun. He squinted to make out the man sitting in the truck.

"Charlie? That you?" he asked.

The truck door opened and the squat driver lowered his considerable bulk to the ground, holding onto the door for support. He turned, and stuck out his hand.

"Hello, Joe, you old son-of-a-gun."

"What you doing driving that nice new truck?"

"Because I own it, that's why," Charlie said, with a chuckle. "Me and the bank. I traded in that old junk of a Model A when I got this guvmint contract to deliver surplus food. This here truck's got one of them new V-8's. Powerful. Goes like Hell. Only thing is; the payments. But that don't worry me none. I make more money, now, than I ever did before the depression hit. And I still get to do some of my regular trucking, nights and weekends. Yessiree, this depression's the best damn thing that ever happened to the country, far as I'm concerned."

Skippy quit barking and begin sniffing and making his mark on each tire. He stopped to sniff the front tire next to Charlie. Skippy raised his leg to make a mark.

"Get outta' here! Don't be pissin' on them tires!" Charlie yelled. He kicked at the dog. "Them tires cost pret' near a hundred dollars, just for the four rear ones. Imagine that? A hundred dollars. A guy working in a shop would have to work months for that. Course, for a guy making the dough I make, it ain't hardly nothing a' tall. Trouble is; I could cut a tire, right today, and get a blow out—just like that. I hold my breath when I think about delivering up on Pisgy Mountain Road. Guy living up there, all alone, and I gotta' deliver him his little dab of stuff," he said, shaking his head.

"Homer ain't even home; working at Modern Laundry over in Greenfield. But I still gotta deliver it. This here's guvmint business and guvmint business has got to be done eg-zackly as they got it wrote down on the paper." .

They got some plenty smart guys working for the guvmint to figure all this out, I can tell ya. This here list, tells me who gets what, when, and how much. See there?" pointing with his pencil, "Now, Homer, he gets one can of corned beef, one dozen eggs, and one can of grapefruit juice. You could deliver that much with a goddam bicycle. But the guvmint don't care if you cut a tire on them ledges sticking up like they do on that cow path of a road. They just want it done just eg-zactly like they got it on the paper—period."

Charlie turned to my father to ask, "How're things going with you, Joe?"

"Not so good Charlie, my heart not too good and I got the lay-off at the mill. My wife, she got a WPA job, sewing. We selling a few eggs, but now the government gives them away; and we don't sell so many."

"Yah, I know. The guvmint'll buy them goddam white eggs from some big chicken ranch out West from some guy who knows a politician and they don't give a hoot if they put the little guy out a' business. The state rep', who got me this job, told me all about politics. There ought to be a law against it. 'Course, in my case it worked out pretty good. Can't complain, really."

Charlie moved around to the back of the van, saying, "Look, Joe, I'd like to stay and gab some, but I'm a very busy man, and this bein' Friday, I gotta' get all this stuff delivered clean out of the truck. Got a moving job for a nice widder woman."

He looked at the clipboard. "Let's see, now. You got six grapefruit, two canned meat, three cans of grapefruit juice, and three dozen eggs."

"Eggs?!! Charlie, for chrissakes. I got eggs. I got eggs up the dupa, I can't sell now. Please give me something else. Something we can use; some that corned beef, or flour, maybe. Let somebody else have the eggs. I even give you some my eggs to give to peoples."

"Look, Joe. Let's get something straight, right now. See this here list? This is guvmint. What it says; goes. I can't go changing things, willy nilly. Now, lemme get your stuff unloaded, and get the hell outta' here. I can't be hanging around chewing the fat all day."

With a frown, he heaved his body up into the van body and began stacking items on the tailgate, carefully checking off each item. When done, he sat down on the tailgate with his feet dangling. He drew a line through the items next to my father's name.

"Thank you, Charlie. Thank you very much. Can I offer you something to eat? Some eggs, maybe?"

"No, no. I just et. I'm getting so damn fat, now, I can't hardly move. Besides, I gotta get going. I ain't got time."

"Well, how about one for the road. I got a quart of whiskey for my heart. A shot every day, the doctor says."

"Well, now, a drink don't sound like too bad an idea. I like to take a drink now and then, myself. A fellah needs something to cut the dust in his throat from all these dirt roads."

Pa hurried into the house.

"Get two shot glasses out of the cupboard," Pa said, reaching for the bottle. "Hurry."

Outside, Charlie watched him pour. He licked his lips. Pa didn't completely fill the glass closest to him.

"I already had my dose this morning," Pa said, not looking at Charlie. They held up their glasses to toast each other, "Good luck," and downed the drinks.

Charlie set his glass down. Pa refilled it. Charlie downed it, and set it down, again. Pa had the cork close enough for Charlie to reach. But Charlie didn't look like he was in any hurry to reach for the cork. Pa poured, again.

Charlie drew a cigar from his shirt pocket. He took a few puffs and studied the clipboard. He reached for the pencil stuck up under his cap, and drew a line across the page.

"Well, Joe, you're got yourself a little extry meat. Homer's got a good job, let him buy his own goddam corned beef."

He picked up the shot of whiskey and swigged it down for emphasis.

Pa hurried to pour him another shot. Charlie studied the clipboard, again, tilting his head so the cigar smoke didn't get in his eyes. After a few thoughtful puffs, he drew another line across the page.

"Them two is both working," he said, his words a little slurred. "They don't need no surplus food. Let them buy their own damn food. If the guvmint keeps giving stuff away, who's going to buy any? No wonder the country's going to hell. That's the trouble with them assholes running the guvmint. They never think about practical stuff."

Pa just kept pouring. Charlie found a reason to scratch every name he came to.

By now, afternoon shadows were beginning to fall across the truck. Charlie hauled out case after case of all manner of food—grapefruit, oranges, fruit juice, corned beef, bags of flour, and several crates of eggs.

"Charlie, for chrissake. No eggs!"

"Well, you're getting 'em, whether you want them or not."

"What I do with eggs? I got eggs I can't sell, now. These are white eggs. Nobody wants white eggs. They not fresh".

"You ain't telling me nothin'. I been hauling them eggs around in this truck all week. Another day riding around in the hot sun and I'll be delivering baby chicks. Them eggs has gotta go. I got to move that widder woman's furniture, tonight. Got a little bonus promised, iffen I don't charge too much," Charlie said with a wink.

He stacked the food on the lawn. I could hear the eggs cracking as he plopped the crates down. He sat on an egg crate to rest, wheezing and coughing, as he mopped his face. The egg crate creaked. I waited for the crate to collapse into a giant omelet, but it held.

Pa gathered up the glasses with one hand and bottle in the other. He pointed at Charlie with the uncorked bottle and gave him a questioning look.

"Don't mind if I do. One for the road, I always says"

After downing another drink, Charlie hauled his bulk up into the truck cab. He started the engine, and grinned. He gunned the engine a few times so we could appreciate the powerful sound of the V-8.

Charlie backed out of the driveway with a roar. He backed a little too far, and one pair of duals dropped into the ditch. He shifted into first gear and raced the engine wide open. The tires smoked and shrieked as they churned their way out of the ditch, hurling out a hail of mud and stones. Charlie honked the horn as he roared off down the road, leaving the smell of burning rubber in the air. The brake lights winked on as he slowed to line his truck up with the narrow bridge. The truck sailed over the planks, one dual coming perilously close to the edge. Soon the truck was nearly hidden by dust as the truck picked up speed. The brake lights came on, again, as he turned the corner. The truck tipped to one side, settled back, then picked up speed, again, and was soon gone from sight.

Pa held the whiskey bottle up to the light to see what precious little was left. He then looked at the food stacked high, and smiled.

"I don't know what we going do with all them eggs, but we having corned beef and cabbage for supper."

Chapter 33: Fun at the Park

With Ma working at her WPA sewing job and the family getting surplus food from the government, Pa was in a better mood. One Sunday he took us all to the public park playground in Turners Falls to play on the slides and swings. Ordinarily, it would have been a rare treat, but this day I was sick with some sort of stomach upset. Pa coaxed me to come along.

"Playing in the fresh air would make you feel better."

He parked near the park, next to a café, and sent us off to play. Every few minutes I'd make a trip from the park to the bathroom at the cafe. One man sat at a table with his head, face down, on his folded arms.

"What's the matter with him?" I asked.

"He's sick."

I hoped he didn't have what I had, and would be too sick to make a trip to the bathroom if the need arose. Worse than that, I hoped he wouldn't be using the bathroom when I needed it. After a half dozen trips, Pa told me to use the toilet in the park maintenance building, because I was not only embarrassing him but stinking up the place, as well. Besides, people would get the idea I was sick or something, he said, and it wouldn't look right.

By then it was getting late in the day, I hadn't eaten much and I was getting weak, so I sat on the toilet in the shed, resting, for a fair spell, and making sure I wouldn't have another eruption.

When I got back to the swings, it was quiet. No kids hollering, nor any squeaking of swings. The place was deserted. I looked around and called out for my brother and sisters. There was no answer. I was all alone.

I hurried over to the café. The Essex was gone. I went inside to see if anyone was waiting for me. Neither Ma nor Pa were there. The bartender came out from behind the bar with a piece of rubber hose. He smacked the hose on the table where the sick man sat resting his head. The man hardly moved. He began poking the man with the hose.

"Closing time! Wake up. Get out. Goddem bum. Get out." He hit him over the head and shoulders, as he pushed the man toward the door. The man staggered out, waving one arm for balance, and holding the other over his head, trying to ward off blows.

The bartender scared me half to death. I was afraid to ask him about Ma and Pa, afraid he might figure I was sick, too, and let me have it with the hose. I went out into the street.

I went to another tavern, not far away, thinking my parents might have gone there. The booths were crowded with people talking and laughing. The men were red-faced and sweaty. The women's hair looked frazzled. The place smelled of stale beer, the air thick with cigarette smoke. I went from booth to booth, hoping to find them. People stared at me, glassy-eyed.

I couldn't believe my father had just driven off and left me, knowing I was sick. They probably went to get me some medicine at the drug store or at a grocery store a few streets away. I hurried there. But the stores were dark—closed---every one. It was getting dark, outside. I tried to think of what to do. The streets were deserted. Lights began coming on in apartments. Everyone seemed to have gone home for supper. I wished that I were home, too. The night air began to turn chilly. Shadows began forming in alley ways, making them dark and scary. A shiver went down my back. I don't know if it was because I was cold, sick, or hungry but I shook all over.

Trying to keep warm, I kept walking. Pretty soon, I saw a square backed car in the distance. It looked something like the Essex. I hurried closer. I knew right away it wasn't the right car. But, maybe, with it getting dark and all, I just maybe wasn't seeing well, I hoped. The car was more rounded in back, more like a Buick, but I walked toward it, anyway, just to be sure. I prayed it would be our car. But it turned out to be the wrong car.

Maybe Pa was mad at me for embarrassing him by running to the toilet in the cafe in front of all his friends. If he would only come back to get me I would promise to be better and not be so much trouble.

I walked back to the cafe and sat on the curb to wait under the street light. The light hummed, and bugs clustered around it. Away from the circle of light there were shadows where bad guys could easily hide. My older sisters had warned me about bad guys. "Don't talk to strangers." But what do you do if a bad person jumps out of the dark and grabs you? I tried not to think about that, and wished I were home in my bed.

At last, I saw car headlights coming. I didn't dare hope it was Pa. I didn't want to be disappointed. The car lights drew nearer, blinding me. Then, the rear door opened and there was my sister, Irene.

"I bet you were plenty scared we not come get you, weren't you?" Pa said. He laughed.

"I wasn't scared," I said, blinking back the tears, happy to be with my sisters and brother, but sad, knowing that Pa had so little regard for me and my safety. Irene told me that they had gone home to eat supper and do the milking, and said she worried about me.

Chapter 34: Bad Times and Bitterness

After the abandonment incident at the park, Pa was laid off, yet again. We were grocery shopping one evening when Pa stopped at the Polish Club. He heard about a call-back at the paper mill, and drove over to the superintendent's house. The super's wife told Pa he was at his club. At the club, the bartender said the super had just gone out the back door. The bartender told Pa where the super was headed. When Pa got to that destination, he was again told that the super had just left.

"Just missed him, again," Pa said. "I run after him and holler but he no can hear me; just drive away, very fast."

I wished Pa didn't have to chase after the super and pester him for a job. Pa spotted the super's car and tailed him to his home. We caught bits and snatches of the conversation.

"For chrissakes...no money...kids to feed..."

The super relented and Pa was jubilant to be working again.

Sometimes when Pa was working steady, he'd buy us a treat. A big neon sign hung outside the tiny shop—McCann's Ice Cream, 10 cents a Pint.

Most of the time, it seemed that Pa was either laid off when he was well, or sick when there was work. Meanwhile, other Polish families who settled in Gill seemed to be prospering. Many of them kept dairy cattle, sold milk, and raised tobacco, in addition to having the income of the father working in a shop. Most of these families paid their kids a share of the tobacco check for working on the farm.

Pa ridiculed the families who paid their own kids to work. He said the kids should be paying the family for raising them. He figured he, too, should have been well off with all the free labor he had.

"Fate just wasn't with me," he said. "Besides, when I show Stanley and Walter how to graft apple trees, they are looking at the neighbor plowing with a new farm tractor. They don't want to work by hand. They want to do everything by the machine, quick and easy. Layzors--that's what."

Pa was still angry with Stanley and Walter for deserting him. And though Johnny wasn't his son, Pa felt he'd betrayed him by helping Studer succeed on the tobacco land. With all his free labor gone, Pa no longer talked of prospering and buying up all the surrounding farms. Those dreams were dead. He scowled a lot and was quick with the strap. That Christmas, he hit bottom.

Chapter 35: Christmas

Christmas was a bright spot in our lives. Miss Pogoda put on a Christmas play, giving everyone a part. I had only to read the play a few times to learn most of the lines, in addition to my own. If someone was out sick during rehearsal, I knew their part and filled in. A couple of days before Christmas, Miss Pogoda sent the boys out to find a Christmas tree. We'd long since picked one out during the summer, but we weren't about to give up our holiday from classes. While we roamed freely through the woods, happy to have a day off, the girls made popcorn to string. They also cut and pasted colored strips of construction paper to form chains, and made angels, bells, and other decorations to hang on the tree. About an hour before the school day ended, we showed up with the tree, a hemlock, which became a thing of beauty with the ornaments the girls made.

The Christmas play crowned the grandeur of the Christmas pageant. Our parents came to watch. Every student had their moment of glory with a speaking part, from the youngest to the oldest.

Irene got to play Mary. Miss Pogoda asked her to bring a doll to use as baby Jesus. After school, Irene confessed that she had only a rag doll Ma had fashioned out of a stocking. Miss Pogoda told Irene not to worry because she would bring a doll she'd saved from childhood.

The doll had silky blond hair and was beautifully dressed. For the play, Irene removed the dress and wrapped the baby in a blanket. At the end of each day, she dressed the doll and put it back in the box. Miss Pogoda allowed Irene to take the doll home each night, impressing on Irene that this was a favorite doll from childhood and wanted Irene to take good care of it. The real baby Jesus would not have received better care.

For Pa, this was his worst Christmas. He had little hope of going back to work soon, there were bills to pay, I'm sure the mortgage was in arrears, and Ma was barely supporting us with her WPA sewing job. Still, it wasn't all that bad. Ma was working steady, the kitchen was warm, there was food on the table, Ma was happy to be getting out of the house and being the breadwinner. While she prepared food for Wigilia, the traditional Polish Christmas eve dinner, we got ready to go to the school play for our moment of glory--the highlight of the year.

The house bustled with preparations. We took turns using the mirror hanging on the kitchen wall. Pa sat at the table with a necktie on and his hair slicked down, ready to go to the play.

Ma began humming Christmas carols. She liked to sing, Dzisaj w Betlam, Today in Bethlehem. Pa sang a verse. She answered with the next; then, they both sang the chorus together. The spirit of Christmas filled the kitchen. I felt warm and secure in the presence of this love and harmony.

Emmy was standing in front of the mirror combing her hair when someone knocked. She opened the door. A wintry blast blew in. A fellow member of the Saint Stanislaus Society stood there, grinning. He held a food basket wrapped in cellophane with a big red bow on the handle.

The Saint Stanislaus Society offered insurance at reasonable rates, marched in processions to the church on holidays, threw a Christmas party for member's kids and gave baskets to the poor. Pa was always quite proud of his involvement with Saint Stan's and the giving of charitable gifts to the poor at Christmas.

At first we thought the man from the Society might have stopped to get directions to a poor family's home. Then we realized that we were the recipients. The bustling stopped. Pa looked mortified. The man stood in the doorway grinning like a fool.

"Come in," Pa said.

The man stepped inside and closed the door. He held the basket in front of him. No one came to take it. After a long silence, the man stepped forward to set the basket on the table. He stepped back, still grinning. He waited for a response. None came.

"Merry Christmas," he said, lamely, as though he didn't know what else to say.

"Thank you," Pa replied.

The man stood, shifting his weight from foot to foot.

"Well, I got to get going. Got more baskets to give to the...." And he was gone.

Cooled by the blast of frigid air, the kitchen felt chilly. The lamp that had cast such a cheerful glow now seemed dull. The room looked drab. Black patches showed where the linoleum had worn through. Clothes drying on a line strung by the wood stove now hung like dingy rags. Even the mirror looked shabby with the silver backing peeling away in one corner and its glass wavy with imperfections. The girls stopped primping. Pa got up, went into his bedroom and closed the door. We tromped somberly to the school. Miss Pogoda didn't ask why Ma or Pa hadn't come to the play.

That evening, when the play was over, Irene lovingly dressed Miss Pogoda's doll for the last time, put it back in the box and closed the cover. It was getting late and Irene was keeping Miss Pogoda from leaving. At last, Irene handed her the doll.

"Merry Christmas Irene, you've taken such good care of the doll, you may keep it." Irene was dumbfounded and could only hold it close.

Chapter 36: Maggie, Duke and Misery

Work at the mill continued intermittent. And Pa was still short of money. One day, a man in the next town saw our horse, Maggie. Though she was high spirited, she was easy to handle. The man was smitten with her and offered to pay a good price. Pa took it. I was heartbroken. Since he had allowed me to name her, I'd assumed she was mine and I had expected her stay with us permanently.

A couple of years later, as we were driving on a country road to pick blueberries, I spotted Maggie plowing a field in team with another horse. I begged Pa to stop, and ran out to see her. The farmer brought the team to a halt, and let the horses rest. I called her name. Maggie pricked up her ears.

Maggie's coat was dull and ratty. She didn't hold her head high the way she used to. I talked to her for a while. She shook her head up and down a couple of times as if to let me know she remembered me.

When the farmer said, "Giddy up", she put her head down and threw her weight into the harness and the team went back to plowing the land. I never saw her again, and I always felt emptiness when I thought about her.

After Pa had sold Maggie, he bought Duke, a strong healthy horse that had been mistreated and turned mean. He tried to kick or bite whenever he got the chance. Pa warned everyone to be careful around him.

While bringing our cows in from the pasture, one evening, I tried to drive Duke in, too. He was grazing and wasn't about to leave. The stick I carried was short. I was afraid to get close to Duke, so I tossed the stick at his rump. It just bounced off.

With nothing in my hand, Duke came charging at me, ears laid back, teeth bared. I ran for the fence. Duke was right behind me. I stumbled and fell— turned to look to see Duke's front hooves high in the air, ready to crash down. I closed my eyes and turned my head away, waiting for the hooves to hit me. The hooves crashed down next to me. Ma had been watching from the kitchen window, and had run out, flapping her apron to divert him.

When Pa got home, Ma told him that Duke had to go. PA listened to her, for a change. I'd hoped he'd buy Maggie back. Instead, he bought a swaybacked old mare that was ready for the glue factory. Her hooves were diseased, and hadn't been trimmed in years. Her feet were so big she looked like she was wearing snowshoes.

Mr. Cislo trimmed her hooves back until they showed pink. But they were still so long she stepped on my heels when I led her. But, I could walk on ahead of her without holding onto her bridle, and she followed me like a dog.

Pa laughed at her sad condition and named her Biala Bieda, which, strictly interpreted, means White Misery, but actually has the connotation of "sad sack". But we all loved her and she became a pet.

One afternoon my sister Irene came to grief when we began feeding White Misery grass in her stall. We brought handfuls of grass into the stall from the rear. If White Misery was standing too close to the side of the stall, we'd nudge her hind leg and she'd move over. She really liked the fresh grass. But on one trip, I got some nettles mixed in with the grass. It must have stung her tongue, because she spit them out, moved over, and blocked our way.

Irene arrived with a handful of grass and nudged Misery's leg. The mare wouldn't move. Irene got more persistent and nudged her leg harder. Misery lifted up her hoof and kicked. It didn't seem like a strong kick but it caught Irene in the stomach and sent her flying. She lay still on the barn floor.

I ran to the house and told Ma the story from the very beginning. Ma was busy and only half listened. When I got to the punch line, "Irene's laying on the floor and she won't get up," Ma dropped what she was doing and ran to the barn.

She carried Irene into the house and laid her on her bed. Irene woke up after a while, but kept moaning. When Pa came home, Ma told him what had happened and asked him to take Irene to a doctor.

"She's not bleeding," he said, "What's a doctor going to do?"

It took years for Irene to recover.

Poverty slept standing up, as horses usually do. Horses have the ability to lock their legs and stand even when sleeping. But one morning we found Misery down in her stall, unable to get up.

"Someone must have fed her too much corn. Too much corn will cripple, every time," Pa said.

That evening, after work, Johnny came to the farm and helped dig a grave for the mare in a field away from the house. The adults were secretive about what was about to happen and Ma told all of us to stay in the house. We heard a loud gunshot. Johnny had shot Misery in the head. He dragged her body to the grave with Studer's home made tractor. I guess that's when Pa got the idea that a tractor made sense. He later bought a tractor made from a cut down Reo truck. He figured a tractor would last longer than another worn-out horse and he wouldn't have to feed it when it wasn't working, nor bury it when it needed to be killed.

Pa gave me the job of cleaning out the barn. Congealed blood lay six inches deep in the gutter. It was then that I realized that a farm was an awful bloody place and not at all the happy scene depicted in children's books like <u>Rebecca</u>

of <u>Sunnybrook Farm</u>, as Irene repeatedly tried to tell me. Everything that had happened to poor Misery got me depressed. The only bright spot in my life was our teacher Miss Pogoda.

Chapter 37: Immunity and Self Esteem

Miss Pogoda could make a person feel good even when reprimanding.

"You boys look so nice;" she said one day as she looked out at her classroom of grungy looking boys. "I wonder if we could start school with a nice clean shirt each Monday."

The boys were apt to wear the same shirt to school until the sleeves took on the sheen of leather. Pants were changed with the seasons, but she let that go. Girls were no problem because they usually wore clean dresses and did not get them dirty the way the boys were apt to do. Though often, the girls had but one good dress to wear all year.

Even in High School, my sisters wore their one good dress all year washing it on weekends. My sister Irene always remembered the embarrassment of seeing other girls sporting a different outfit each day. But she kept her dress clean and it proved no deterrent to friendship.

Miss Pogoda allowed the boys to come to school barefoot after the first of May. But she would not tolerate dirty feet. Since there was no plumbing at the school, we washed our feet in a nearby brook if we got them dirty walking on the dirt roads. It would have been good if we'd drawn our drinking water from the brook, too.

The teacher rewarded boys by choosing among the best behaved to fetch the water from an old bachelor's dilapidated house diagonally across from the school. The slate roofed house was collapsing around him. A school committee member had the water tested and found it highly polluted. From then on, we carried water from a farm farther away.

The farm water ran by gravity, through a lead pipe, a fair distance from up in a cow pasture dotted with meadow muffins. We dipped water out of the farm watering trough with a galvanized pail. The pupils all drank from the pail using the same dipper. The student body, on the whole, was remarkably healthy. Perhaps the constant exposure to a variety of germs served to build immunity. The school doctor put our little inoculation program in jeopardy by mandating that each student bring in his own drinking glass.

On a shelf by the water pail, we lined up an assortment of glasses and jelly jars, each labeled with the student's name on a piece of adhesive tape. The jars sat gathering dust while the students continued taking turns drinking from the dipper.

Miss Pogoda never learned of our arrangement because she never drank from the pail, that was in the back hall out of her sight In fact, other than drinking what she carried in a small thermos bottle, the sip or two of soup was the only thing we ever saw her eat or drink. The soup was part of our Hot Soup Program--2 cans of Campbell's Alphabet Vegetable Soup and 4 cans of water heated on a hot plate. At about a quarter to twelve, our teacher sent a couple of girls into the back hall to prepare the soup. Soon the mouth-watering aroma of vegetable soup drifted into the classroom, making my stomach rumble. I don't know why it was always alphabet soup. Perhaps the school committee felt it would be more educational. They were right, because we did try to arrange letters to spell out words. Though the soup was thin, it was hot and delicious compared to the jam or mustard sandwiches we brought from home.

The girls gave our teacher less soup stock, but extra vegetables and letters. Not completely selfless, they took turns polishing off Miss Pogoda's uneaten portion, out of sight in the back room where they washed dishes in a basin.

Since Miss Pogoda was completing her teacher training by internship rather than attending classes at Fitchburg State College, she needed to report there from time to time. She always brought back sorely needed school supplies. She departed the school Friday noon, leaving us on our honor, she said. No one uttered a word to breech the code of honor. We'd sit quietly doing our school work until the end of the school day, lock the door, and leave.

The school committee heard rumors that Miss Pogoda was leaving the school unattended for half a day at a time, and decided to investigate and see, for themselves, what havoc we were creating. We spotted the group parking their car some distance away from the school and watched them out of the corners of our eyes as they crept up to listen at the window. The school room was as quiet as a cloistered convent. The school committee members looked in on a room full of silent kids bent over their work. They trudged back to their car, shoulders slumped in disappointment.

Soon after that, the school committee sent Miss Pogoda a problem kid from another school. The petite Miss Pogoda possessed a benevolent power to tame the most unruly child. Tommy was a product of a troubled home. Under Miss Pogoda's loving care, he strived to please her and soon excelled.

When I'd first started grade school with her, I spoke more Polish than English, because only Polish was to be spoken at home. But it didn't take me long to learn English. Later, she asked me to help an English speaking kid, which made me feel proud and happy. Miss Pogoda had no idea I was a bad boy and I felt a little guilty whenever she praised me. She even praised me for day dreaming—said I had a great imagination. She told me I was smart and caught on to reading easily. When I was in the fourth grade, Miss Pogoda announced she was getting married. Teachers could not marry if they wanted to teach, but love won out. We were ever so sad to see her go.

She said she left word for the new teacher to let me skip the fifth grade because I got good grades and knew the fifth grade work. With all eight grades in the same room hearing the lessons recited and watching the blackboard made it easy to learn ahead. We loved Miss Pogoda but never knew how good she was to us until we got the new teacher.

Chapter 38: Pets and Death

It was shortly after Miss Pogoda got married that our red cow, Bruncha, went lame and couldn't get up one morning. Her hind quarters were paralyzed.

"Someone must have fed her too much corn," Pa said. "Too much corn will cripple, every time." I think he would have said that if an animal had broken a leg.

Bruncha was pregnant and Pa said he hated to lose both her and her unborn calf. He dragged her into the hay barn. She pulled herself along with her front feet, while Pa hauled her paralyzed legs along with a pulley block and tackle. Once he got her into the hay barn, he rigged up two slings to support her body. He attached the pulley block to an overhead barn beam, and hoisted her up so that her feet rested lightly on the floor. With the weight of her body off her legs, he hoped she'd begin using them again.

In a few days, it became obvious that the slings were cutting into her body, causing her pain and swelling. Pa lowered her. Bruncha's hind legs crumpled and she lay on her right side, from then on. Hay stacked against the barn windows blocked the light and made the interior of the hay barn dark and gloomy when the door was closed. She dragged herself around in a big circle.

Ma saved potato peels, bits of cabbage leaves, and other vegetable greens to vary Bruncha's diet of dry hay. When I opened the barn door, she turned to face me. She seemed happy to see me. While she ate her treat, I'd talk to her and pet her. She seemed to listen as she munched her goodies in that dim light. When I went out the door she'd turn her head to watch me leave.

"Goodbye Bruncha; see you tomorrow," I'd say, and close the door, shutting out the light.

When the day came for Bruncha her to give birth, the calf's forefeet came out just a bit. She couldn't push them any farther, no matter how hard she tried. When the legs stuck out for several hours of labor, it became obvious Bruncha was never going to give birth by herself. Pa summoned a couple of neighbors to help. He let me stay to watch.

"The boy will learn a bit of what life's about," one of the men said, making me feel grown up. I felt indebted to Pa for allowing me to stay. He wrapped a rag around the calf's legs and tied a rope in a slip-knot over the rag. The men lined up, holding the rope. Each time Bruncha pushed, they pulled. At long last, the calf came sliding out, to lie there in a wet heap.

Bruncha turned her head and made little nickering sounds, "mmmf, mmmf." She scrambled to reach her calf, trying to drag her useless hind quarters, front feet slipping on the barn floor.

"See? She wants to see him," Pa said. He showed me how to rub the calf dry with hay. He then picked the calf up in his arms and carried him within Bruncha's reach. She sniffed and nuzzled the calf, licking him, and making more sounds, "mmmmf, mmmf".

The calf was as anxious to see his mother, as she was to see him. He stood up on wobbly legs and staggered towards Bruncha's udder, swollen with milk. He tried to suckle but raised his head each time.

"He wants to pick his head up to reach her tits because the cow should be standing up," one of the men said. "Better take him to feed off another cow."

Pa tied a rope around the calf's neck and led him wobbling into the cow stable where the calf could nurse on a milking cow. Bruncha began to bellow. When Pa came back into the barn, he lowered the pulley block. I figured he was going to hoist Bruncha up with the sling so the calf could suckle. Instead, Pa set a whiffle tree next to Bruncha. He picked up a sledge hammer and swung it; "Bam," hitting Bruncha between the eyes. Her front legs collapsed and her head fell to the floor.

Pa stabbed a hole at each heel of her crippled hind legs with a knife, pushed the hooks of the whiffle tree in to catch her heel cords and attached the pulley block to the center loop of the whiffle tree.

The men grabbed the rope to help Pa hoist Bruncha up until her head was off the floor, hind legs spread wide by the whiffle tree. Her right hindquarter looked like polished leather where it had was worn smooth from dragging herself around on the floor. She looked dazed. Pa grabbed one of her horns to hold her head steady and swiftly slit her throat with a razor sharp knife. Blood poured out on the floor. I headed for the house.

I wished she didn't have to die. I wished I had not gone out to watch. I wished I'd never brought her treats, or petted her, or talked to her, or got to know her. Tears stung my eyes.

Seeing Bruncha die in such a brutal way depressed me. I really loved that cow, and I knew she loved me. Irene tried to console me. "You've got to remember that, sooner or later, almost everything around here is going to be killed. You've got to stop naming calves, or chickens, or pigs or anything else. And don't go making pets out of the new calf."

But I couldn't resist the baby calf with the pretty blue eyes and the wavy hair on his brow, and I began calling him "Brownie", not having a lot of imagination when it came to names. I fantasized that he'd somehow be spared. But, in the fall Pa opened the hay barn door and hung up the pulley block. "Bring the calf, here," he said. I dreaded what was coming next.

"Hold him steady."

The big hammer struck a stunning blow to that forehead of wavy hair, sending him to his knees. His beautiful blue eyes with the curved lashes looked dazed. Pa slit his throat. Blood spilled out in a torrent. It all seemed familiar, yet unreal—like a bad dream that keeps coming back. A stab at each heel made a hole for the hooks of the whiffle tree. And Brownie was hoisted aloft with his life's blood draining out on the hay barn floor and on out the door, already stained red from previous butchering.

A while after that the rabbits I thought had considered my pets, met the same fate.

"Bring me a rabbit."

Pa struck a blow with a knife handle at the base of the rabbit's skull. The rabbit stiffened and quivered. Pa cut the rabbit's head off, and sliced open the stomach. The rabbit's guts spilled out. Pa laughed as he held up a long intestine with pellets of droppings. "Want some peanuts?"

I could hardly see through the tears.

Pa enjoyed slaughtering. He apparently felt he was fulfilling his role as provider, furnishing food for the family. His efforts to teach me about life only served to confuse me and make me increasingly frightened of him. He tried his best to toughen me, but I was a poor candidate. And there was no longer any Miss Pogoda to lift my spirits.

Chapter 39: A New Teacher

When a new teacher began teaching at our red brick school that fall, the first thing she did was join us at play. The field across the road from the school belonged to a weekend farmer who did not object to us using it as a playground. We loved to play baseball and thought our new teacher had come to admire how well we played, the way Miss Pogoda had. We waited for her to express surprise at how far the boys could bat the ball. To our surprise, the new teacher picked up the bat and socked the ball farther than anyone had ever socked a ball before—for a home run. I'm sure she wanted to show that she was "one of us" but she took all the fun out of it. No one felt like playing baseball after that.

The teacher started me in fourth grade. I told her that Miss Pogoda was going to skip me into fifth grade.

"Well, I'm running things now. When I get through with you, you'll be lucky to get through the fifth grade, never mind skipping it."

I'm sure she'd grown sick of hearing about our great Miss Pogoda. As for my performance that year---she was absolutely right. I made all kinds of careless mistakes, could not memorize anything, began chewing my nails and stuttering. Life at home only compounded the problem. Pa was still not working steady, and money always seemed in short supply. I still didn't have enough sense to keep quiet, giving Pa an excuse to vent his frustrations. Whereas school had once been a haven, it now became a continuation of stress.

When the new teacher cast the Christmas play, I didn't get a part, no doubt because of my stuttering. My stomach began to hurt, and I started wetting the bed. I hadn't done that since I was little. Pa teased me about the skunk coming at night to pee in my bed, perhaps thinking he'd shame me into self-control. I was ashamed all right; I was so ashamed I wanted to die. Sometimes, no matter how many times I got up at night to make a trip to the outhouse, or to pee over the back porch railing, by morning I'd wet the bed. We didn't have pajamas and, in winter, I slept in my long underwear. My long johns didn't get changed but once, all winter. I knew I stunk, and the other kids in school were sure to remind me, just in case I didn't know.

The new teacher liked to sneak up behind students who were fooling around, or looking out the window. Despite her full figure, she'd stalk the offender with the stealth of a leopard and give them a chop on the knuckles with a metal edged ruler. She caught me gazing out the window every time.

Both my parents warned me, "Don't ever come home and tell us your teacher hit you because you'll get hit twice as bad at home."

On day, during lunch hour, the teacher checked the gas gauge on her car. The needle lay on "empty". She lit a match to look in the gas tank. I knew a nearly empty tank was far more dangerous than a full one, because of the larger volume of explosive fumes. "Don't put the match near the tank; it'll blow up!" I warned. "Use a stick to measure.

"Mind your own business. I don't need a smart Alec like you telling me what to do."

Why the tank didn't blow up is a mystery to me.

I began having nightmares and walking in my sleep. One morning after a bad night, my sister, Emmy said she was afraid I was going to step out the upstairs window and get killed. Right about then, that didn't sound like too bad of an idea.

One day when I was looking through a humor magazine, I found an entire page picturing various ways to commit suicide. One guy was drinking from a bottle labeled with skull and crossbones. Another one had cut his stomach open and was snipping his guts with a big pair of scissors. An old bearded man held a pistol to his head. Other pictures showed people drowning, hanging, and killing themselves in interesting ways. It was comforting to know there was a way out.

Hanging sounded pretty good. My sisters used to sing, I Died For Love—a song about a girl who committed suicide. The words of the song, telling how her father found her, stuck in my mind—"He went upstairs, the door he broke, and found me hanging by a rope."

It sounded like a good way to go. My stomach hurt enough without drinking poison, and cutting up your guts with scissors didn't sound like anything I wanted to do, either. Emmy caught me studying the magazine. I told her about my troubles at school and about being sick of being a bad boy all the time. She comforted me and ordered me never to read that magazine, again. She stopped singing I Died for Love, and said things would get better. They didn't. They only got worse.

121

Chapter 40: My Friends in the Pigeon Loft

In the fifth grade, my grades were so bad, the teacher passed me "on trial". My parents bawled me out.

"How can you bring home such a bad report card? You always brought home a report card with A's, before. You have to study better."

And this was the very grade that Miss Pogoda said I could skip. A knot grew in my stomach. The teacher and Pa were right—I wasn't smart, after all. Life didn't seem worth living. I sneaked a look at the magazine with the various ways of killing yourself. It seemed like the best way out of this mess.

Soon after receiving the bad report card, one of Pa's friends came to the farm with a box with about eight pigeons. He had spoken of them, previously. Now they were here. When he asked me if I wanted them, I got excited.

"Can I have them, PA?

He smiled and nodded.

There was an empty pigeon loft in the barn with little arched doorways cut through the wall to a landing that ran along in front of the holes. Everything seemed to be perfect—too easy. My suspicions should have been aroused, especially when Pa agreed so quickly. But the thoughts of owning those sleek feathered beauties distracted me. The man told me to block the pigeon holes for a couple of weeks.

"If you don't do that," he said, "they'll be back at my loft before I get home. In a couple of weeks, the pigeons will come to accept the new loft as their home and they will stay there."

Each day, I fed the pigeons, and carried them water. When I fed them, they cooed as they crowded around me, bobbing their neat little heads. I petted their soft silken heads and talked to them for hours. After a while, they got tame enough so that I could pick them up and hold them in my lap. I forgot all about the bad report card. All I could think of was the pigeons, my friends.

Pa bought more pigeon feed when the small bag, that the man had given me, ran out. Pa did not buy dog food or cat food for our dog and cats, and here he was buying feed for my pets. I felt that I'd misjudged Pa, unfairly. I had assumed that I would feed them chicken feed which wasn't expensive. The pigeon feed contained pellets the size of peas. The feed looked expensive with the round pellets, smooth and white as pearls. No one could tell me what they were. I had no idea if they were seeds of some sort or manufactured pellets. I asked Pa.

"You ask too many questions," Pa said.

In the beginning all the pigeons looked alike, but each one had slightly different markings, and each one had a different personality. Some were shy, and others bold. But they were all especially affectionate when I fed them. They cooed and crowded around my feet, bobbing their heads as they padded about. I was happy that they were my pets, and mine alone. I loved them, and named them all. Irene was forever warning me not name animals, knowing I would be upset when they were butchered. But, these were pets, and they were special; it was O.K. to name them, I said.

As the time came to release them from their confinement, I grew increasingly nervous and questions arose in my mind. What if they flew away and never came back? Should I wait longer? Will keeping them cooped up too long, weaken them and keep them from flying, or leave them too tired to fly back to the loft?

At last, I took away the boards blocking the exits and watched as they ducked out of the opening. They walked back and forth on the landing, cooing away. Soon, as if by some signal, they all took off together in a flutter of wings. They flew high into the sky and circled around a few times before landing on the roof of the tobacco barn, far across the field. They seemed to hold a conference on the roof. Soon, they took off into the air, again, circled in a wide arc away from me, and flew out of sight. Depression and panic came over me. They were headed back home to their old loft. I knew it. The man said they would. I should have waited longer. Maybe if I had petted them more and told them how much I loved them, they would have stayed.

I was crestfallen. My beloved pigeons had left me. They were gone. My eyes blurred and a lump came in my throat. Why hadn't I waited longer before letting them out?

Long after I had given up on them, tiny black specks appeared in the sky. The specks grew larger and larger. My friends were coming back! I could not believe my eyes—they were coming back. Joy filled my heart as they flew closer. My depression evaporated. I wanted to cheer. My friends swooped down to land, and strut on the landing in front of the pigeon holes. They'd come back----every one of them! They loved me, after all. I stayed in the pigeon loft a long time that day, feeding, talking, and petting them. They cooed to me, bobbing their heads and milling around my feet, pecking at the feed with the smooth white pearls. Each day, the pigeons seemed to grow bigger and bigger. I couldn't wait until they began laying eggs in the nesting boxes, and hatching out babies.

Late one afternoon after I'd been away all day, and felt starved. I got home just in time for supper. My mother brought a heaping platter to the table.

123

"What's that?" I asked.

"Chicken."

"Those look like awful tiny chickens."

My father grinned. I looked to my mother for an explanation. She tried to suppress a smile. I looked out at the pigeon loft. Empty—not a pigeon in sight. My father laughed. Tears blinded me as I ran from the house. I felt as though something had been torn out of my chest. I ran to the woods behind our house and sat leaning against a big pine tree, overcome with sadness. I stayed until dark, when I knew my father would be in bed. I didn't feel like eating anything that night. And I cursed myself for being so dumb. Irene was right; I couldn't learn. I deserved that failing report card.

Chapter 41: Circus Pigs

Pa did not stop in the yard when he came home one day. He drove the tan Essex out past the barn by the old green car. We ran out to see what was going on. Pa had two pigs in a burlap bag in the back seat. He hauled them out and dumped them into the pig pen. They seemed ordinary enough.

"Go get them something to eat," my father said, his eyes twinkling.

We got some garbage and milk from Ma. He poured the slop into the pig's trough and commanded, "Pray."

The pigs put their front hooves together as if in prayer. The pigs could understand our language but we couldn't understand theirs. Maybe pigs are smarter than we are, I thought.

"O.K., eat."

The pigs began to eat.

The pigs were Hans and Fritz. I figured their previous owner Fred Kerslake had named them after a couple of mischievous comic strip characters who were always getting into trouble. The pigs were well named. Since they were trained to climb a ladder, climbing the side of the pen was no problem, and they were soon getting out of the pen. In their circus act, the pigs pulled their owner on a cart, walked a narrow board to simulate a tight rope act, climbed a ladder and slid down a slide, worked a teeter-totter and performed other tricks. Catching them at our farm when they got out of the pen was easy. They came when called by name and went back into the pen when commanded, especially when tempted with food.

I believe these pigs were from the last pigs trained by Fred Kerslake. He had inherited the act from his father Seabourne Frederique Kerslake who much preferred the nickname "Lil" to the moniker "Seabourne." Lil's father raised pigs and when a brood sow died, Lil raised her piglets by feeding them with a spoon. They followed him around like puppies. He found that they caught on quickly and that he could easily train all of them. He began taking the trained pig act to county fairs, and soon began touring with Ringling Brothers, Barnum & Bailey, and the B.F. Keith vaudeville circuit, in addition to the fairs. His pigs even toured Europe and performed for heads of State.

The pigs grew too big over the winter, so Lil kept one pig to train the new troupe each spring. When he retired, his son S. Fred Kerslake took over the act. He did not have the patience his father Lil had, and he tired of continually training a new troupe. He figured dogs would not outgrow the act and he began training terriers. But he found that they were not as smart as pigs. They did not catch on quickly, and he went back to training pigs.

Lacking his father's patience, he used a whip to hasten their learning. The whip was on the end of a long thin stick, which he used to tap the pigs to prompt them. The SPCA did not take kindly to his training methods and kept after him until he grew tired of the whole thing and sold the pigs. I have no idea how Pa found out they were for sale, but he bought Hans and Fritz, much to our utter delight.

After the pigs were at the farm for a time, they went off their feed. Pa was worried that they were sick. At dusk one evening, we heard a commotion. Chickens were cackling and squawking. They had taken to roosting on the top railing of the pig pen. Hans & Fritz regarded this as their own little KFC fast food outlet and were apparently enjoying a snack each evening. We locked the rest of the chickens in the hen house, and Hans & Fritz went back to the hog trough for food.

Being isolated on the farm made the occasional visitor a special treat. When word spread about our circus pigs, people began showing up. We delighted in showing company our pigs. Often, Hans & Fritz would run around and perform all manner of antics, running and jumping over each other, or whirling around in place. We learned later that the pigs performed a spontaneous "free-for-all" at the end of each performance when they were on tour. It was not anything they had been trained to do. They just loved to show off and hear us applaud. We thought of the pigs as pets, bought for our amusement, not realizing what would eventually happen to them. We couldn't wait to show them to Helen.

Chapter 42: Mood Changes

The family that employed Helen in Greenfield, allowed her to attend night school. But she didn't let Pa know. He didn't think much of education, especially for girls, even if it was free.

Helen's employer temporarily moved to Springfield, more than 40 miles away. When the employer and his family moved back to Greenfield, Helen stayed. A couple of college professors hired her. She still visited, occasionally, arriving on foot, rather than spending money on trolley fare to Turners Falls. She'd accept rides with motorists who stopped to offer, but she never put out her thumb.

Helen's visits became few and far between. Quite small and slight of build, she feared who might pick her up. She was shy, never even dating a boy until she began college.

The day that sticks in my memory was the Sunday she arrived at the farm about noon. As usual, she passed over of her hard earned money—every cent—in the customary handshake. They spoke for a few minutes before Pa turned and went into his bedroom without a word of thanks. Helen stayed to talk to us kids for a just few more minutes. We begged her to stay longer. It'd been quite some time since we'd seen her and we hated to see her go.

"I have to get going; I don't want to get caught out on the road after dark."

I wondered why Pa wouldn't give Helen a ride, at least to a traveled highway, but that apparently never entered his mind.

Helen will always live in my mind's eye, as this slight figure walking down the dirt road that chilly fall day, coat billowing in the wind, her figure growing smaller and smaller in the distance. We watched until she was gone, hidden by trees at a bend in the road.

Helen continued to visit home and give Pa the golden handshake. She wore cast off clothing and did without. She adored Pa and he loved her, especially since she was such a dutiful daughter.

Helen rated high with Pa as long as the money kept coming, but when she wrote him the good news that she had been accepted at American International College, and would need money for clothes and college. He dictated a letter that read—"You are no longer a daughter of mine."

, but refused to pass up the opportunity to fulfill her dream of going to college. There she met Ludovico Magrini, an immigrant from Italy. He enunciated in excellent but accented English. Pa didn't like Magrini and tried to discourage Helen from marrying him, but she eloped. Pa liked Magrini even less when he began putting ideas about education into my head. He urged me to apply for admission to Mount Hermon School.

I don't think that Helen ever got to see the circus pigs before Pa's butcher friend arrived with a .22 rifle and a satchel of knives. He got out of his car and headed for the pig pen.

"What's he doing with the rifle?" I asked in alarm. "He's not going to shoot the pigs, is he?"

"Of course, he is. But it will be interesting," a visiting neighbor boy said. "When they cut the pig open, the heart and all the insides will move and tick, like a clock. It'll be fun to watch."

The butcher, confident in his marksmanship, brought only two bullets. Pa called Hans. He trotted up to face them. The butcher held the rifle close, and shot Hans between the eyes. Hans fell over as if in sleep. It didn't seem anywhere as gruesome as I'd expected.

Fritz began racing around the pig pen. The butcher tried to draw a bead on him as he passed by. A second shot rang out. But it didn't hit a vital spot and Fritz kept running. The butcher leaped into the pen with a dagger-shaped "pig sticker". He grabbed Fritz by the ear, threw him on his side, and began sawing on his neck with the knife. Fritz began screaming. I covered my ears and ran for the house. The last words I heard were those of my father, hollering—"Fritz! Shut up!" Fritz stopped screaming, immediately.

That evening when the butchering was done, my mother served up a platter heaped with fried pork chops. The butcher helped himself to a pork chop, marveling at how well the pigs behaved. He ate with great gusto.

"What a strange thing; that pig just wouldn't die," he said with a smile. "I kept shoving the knife down his throat, but it wasn't until I held the end of the knife by my very finger tips and shoved hard, right into his heart, that I finally killed him." He demonstrated, holding a dinner knife with the tips of his fingers and thrusting it. "And all that time, he kept quiet and never squealed after you told him to shut up."

"Eat. Eat, Jozek," my mother said. But my stomach hurt and I couldn't eat. Forever after, whenever I tried so much as a morsel of pork, my stomach knotted up.

Chapter 43: A Bike of My Own

When I was 12 years old, I thought I was the only boy in school who didn't have a bike—maybe the only one in the country. No one in our family had one.

A janitor at Mount Hermon School cleaned out the bicycle room at the school dormitories when the boys graduated. He kept the bikes they left behind, and sold them for a dollar or two dollars, prior to WWII. We bought the first bike with money we earned doing chores for neighbors and picking up soda bottles along the road. Pa went with us and bargained the janitor down from $4 to $3.50. The bike had cord tires. There was no tube. If a tire went flat, you needed to buy a new tire. I had to share the bike with my sisters, and that caused friction. Then the front tire went flat. I filled it with milk. It soured and plugged the leak, for a while, but then the hole got bigger and the milk all sprayed out.

With WWII on, there were no cord tires in the stores. I put a tricycle wheel with a solid rubber tire in place of the front wheel. It worked, but the other kids in school laughed at me riding the bike with the much smaller wheel in front. I endured it, but my heart was set on a balloon-tired bike with tubes in the tires.

I went back to see the janitor. He told me the boys were taking their bikes with them when they left. He had only one bike, and it was a beauty.

"Twenty five dollars," he said, eyeing me with my tongue hanging out. "And I could get more," he added to make me think it was a bargain, even though it probably did not cost that much new.

All I had was five dollars. When Ma asked me why I was looking so glum, I told her of my problem, never expecting she could help me. But she dug $20 out of her stash. I never forgot it, and paid her back many times over in later years, long after the event was lost in her failing memory.

With my own set of wheels, I now could join the guys who hung around D.O. Paul's general store. It felt good having a bike, to be one of the guys.

Mr. Paul's first name was Dorilla, but everyone called him D.O. Kids sometimes called him Dorilla the Gorilla, though not to his face. He was anything but a gorilla—slight of build, weighing about 125 pounds with his overcoat on, and not much over 5 feet tall. He had a mild manner—except when it came to politics. Herbert Hoover was his man; Roosevelt, he hated with a passion. But kids he tolerated, and maybe even liked, though it was hard to tell.

D.O. stocked canned goods, ice cream and soda, and other convenience store items. Best of all he had penny candy—a whole row of clear glass jars filled with candy. The decorative square jars had ground glass covers that fit snugly. But they couldn't contain that wonderful aroma of the penny candy they held.

When a kid came in with a few pennies to buy candy, the transaction would take forever.

"How much are the root beer barrels?"

"Two for a penny."

"How much for the green Gummy Leaves?"

"Six for a penny?"

The buyer would ask the prices of one candy after the other—chocolate babies, Maryjanes, licorice, orange sections, butterscotch drops, bubble gum and Red Hots—then ask him to repeat the prices, over and over.

D.O. would stand peering through his owlish glasses with infinite patience, repeating the prices, again and again, until the pennies clutched in the sweaty little paw would finally be exchanged for the little brown bag filled with delicious treasures. D.O. lost an eye somehow—no one ever wanted to ask—and it was sometimes disconcerting to have one eye fixed on you while the other one wandered about a bit. I could never figure out which eye was real and which was glass.

Each summer D.O. closed the store for a month and took to the road in his Buick to tour the country. He ceased his cross-country trips when his eyesight failed to the point that he could not read the numbers on pumps when dispensing gasoline. He continued to terrorize local motorists on his occasional forays into town He had once chauffeured a limousine in Washington, D.C. and liked to reminisce about the time he drove the Ambassador of China to Kitty Hawk, to witness Wilbur and Orville Wright's first engine powered flight. I listened to his stories in rapture.

Kids were his soft spot. He never once scolded a kid for running a bike over the hose that lay across the approach to the gas pumps. It sounded a bell inside the store, annoying his wife, Edna, no end. He'd gaze out the window and tune out her sputtering.

One day, after I'd ridden my bike down to the store, I bought some candy and came out to join the group. We all sat on our bikes bantering back and forth. In a little while, they began to leave.

"We're all going over to see Sonny," someone said, as he ran his bike over the bell hose. "Wanna' come?" Neither Sonny nor his folks had ever invited me to visit. There was a fair amount of resentment of the influx of Polish immigrants. "They come here with nothing and before you know it, they own the place," was a common complaint. They referred to families who lived frugally and squirreled their money in the mattress. When hard times came, the immigrants hauled out their stash and bought the foreclosed property. To the old time residents, it somehow seemed unfair.

The other boys lived in the neighborhood. Sonny's mother greeted them warmly. Soon, she brought out a dish of ice cream and called to Sonny to come up on the porch. She called another boy, then another, and another, until all the boys were up on the porch, talking and laughing as they ate their ice cream. I waited for her to call me. But she never did. When it became obvious that she had no intention of extending the invitation to me, I hopped on my bike and rode away.

Not long after that, our entire family was hard at work in the field. Pa planned to hill up our potatoes using our homemade tractor. He tried teaching Ma to drive it, but she got all nerved up, stepped on the gas instead of the brake, and the tractor lurched into a deep ditch. We spent hours getting it out.

Next, Pa tried having me drive, but I put the tractor gear shift into third speed instead of first and stalled the engine. He wouldn't give me another chance, parked the tractor, and began pushing the plow in short thrusts. I tied a rope to the plow and began helping by pulling the plow. That worked pretty well, so Pa sent me home for more rope.

He made up several slings of various lengths and soon had everyone, including Ma, ready to pull. His mood had turned lighter, and when we were all hooked up and pulling the plow, he yelled "giddy up!", pretending to be stern. Just then, Sonny came riding by with his Daddy. Their heads turned and their eyes bugged out at the sight of us pulling the plow like Roman slaves. After they went on by we stopped and had a good laugh before going back to pulling the plow.

A few days later, Pa was tipped off that Adelaide Hood, from the Society for the Prevention of Cruelty to Children, was going to pay a visit.

"I bet Lambert reports us," Pa said. "When the woman comes, say nothing."

In reality, Lambert lived a half mile away and would have had to use binoculars to see us in the field if he could have seen through the trees and brush, had he been inclined to look. The diminutive but tough Miss Hood was kindly enough, but our lips were sealed. Pa had warned us that it was all a trick to get us put away in some terrible place where all we'd have to eat was stale bread and water. After Miss Hood's visit, Pa changed his ways. After that, if he had us pull the plow, we did it in the early morning when the fog hung low, so Lambert wouldn't see us.

Chapter 44: Baked Goods and Dentists

Pa failed the paper mill physical again because of his heart condition. Seeing his friends become prosperous, embittered Pa. He lashed out in anger at minor things. Earlier when he'd come home from work, my younger sister Lora and I would run out to open the garage doors. Pa would beam, and let us carry his woven birch lunch basket into the house.

We'd open the basket tainted with the smell of caustic paper mill chemicals. His sandwiches tasted different, despite having been made with the same rye bread as our sandwiches at home. The rye bread we found in Pa's lunch basket was no longer the bread he brought home from the bakery. Maybe it was the paper mill smell or the bread having had the crust cut off. But the bread seemed to have transformed in his lunch basket like the bread and wine at Holy Communion. Though the bread didn't taste very good with the paper mill taste, we still wanted to partake of it.

Ma cut the hard crust off the rye bread when she made his lunch because Pa had only a few teeth left. He pulled his own teeth, one by one, as they decayed. Pa loved sour dough rye bread, especially when it was fresh and easy to chew. He bought it from a Polish immigrant who operated a bakery in the Polish settlement called "The Patch" in Turners Falls. Rye bread was common in much of Poland because rye would mature in the country's short growing season when wheat would not. The crusty bread had caraway seeds, throughout, with a few extra sprinkled on top.

When Pa worked the graveyard shift, he'd stop at the bakery on his way home to bring us bread for our breakfast, still warm from the oven. The baker sometimes gave Pa stale bakery goods to feed to the pigs. Ma made them into bread pudding. I discovered that heating the rock hard crescent rolls made them soft again. They were delicious with a pat of butter.

"Leave it to Joe to find it out," Pa said with a smile. It felt good to get praised, for a change.

One day, I brought a cupcake to school in my lunch bag. It looked delicious, frosted in pink icing and topped with a maraschino cherry. Unknown to my envious classmates, it was as hard as plaster. I ate the cherry and the frosting with great gusto. Then, as the others turned to walk back to the schoolhouse, I pitched the stone hard cupcake into the bushes.

I don't know if eating bakery sweets was responsible, but I got a toothache, and made the mistake of complaining to Pa. I should have known better, knowing he'd pulled his own teeth.

Too late. He sent me get his pliers out of his toolbox, and warmed them on the stove. Wiping off dirt and grease with a rag, he put the pliers into my mouth to clamp on the aching tooth. With one quick twisting yank, it was out. The smell and taste of grease and the anxiety of the ordeal was nearly as bad as having the tooth pulled.

"Dentists charge too much," Pa said. "See? That wasn't so bad. And we saved the cost of the dentist."

I wasn't nearly as joyful over this kind of thrift as he was, leaving me wondering if a dentist could have saved the tooth. When the next toothache struck, I kept quiet. Emmy showed me how to soak a bit of cotton in Pain-Expeller and put it in the cavity to dull the pain.

Pa rarely showed his two remaining teeth, except when he laughed loud when he'd been drinking. Seeing those two lower teeth was frightening. But soon they, too, met the grease encrusted pliers from his tool box. His dentistry wasn't nearly as bad as what we experienced with a real dentist, fresh out of college.

The recently graduated dentist came to the red brick schoolhouse with a great bargain. He examined our teeth, free, filling out a card with two horse shoe shaped diagrams with boxes representing our upper and lower teeth. A diagonal slash indicated a needed filling and an occasional X indicated an extraction. The rate for either filling or pulling was the same reasonable rate of 60 cents each.

We had yet to visit a dentist and Ma figured it was a good opportunity to insure we'd keep our teeth and not end up toothless like our father. She never suspected what would happen. She signed the exam card and sent in the money from her secret stash.

The dentist arrived at the town hall in a tiny Crosley. The sub-compact car didn't look much bigger than a toy pedal car. But, somehow, the dentist managed to cram in all his equipment, including a folding chair and an electric dental drill. When he unloaded the tiny Crosley, it looked like a circus act where a dozen clowns and a donkey climb out of a car.

The dentist's shapely assistant pumped water from the kitchen hand pump into a dish pan to heat on a hot plate. She wagged her rump along with the pump handle. The town hall had only a hand pump for the shallow well. There wasn't any flush toilet—just an outhouse. The "nurse", wearing a skimpy skintight uniform, sterilized instruments between patients with a quick swish in the hot water and a little waggle of her behind.

The dentist shot all of the patients full of Novocain and began taking us alphabetically. The A's got their teeth filled with considerable care. As the day wore on, fillings proceeded at an increasingly faster rate. He hadn't got down to the P's when the great healer looked at his watch.

He turned to Daisy Mae, saying, "Honey, we gotta' be in Keene by six tonight. Why don't you just draw another line across the rest of the boxes."

The slashes in the boxes became X s and that was the end of fillings for the day. Our good dentist set aside the drill and took up his pliers. He began yanking teeth no matter how small the cavity. I don't recall him pausing to rinse the pliers from one patient to the next. His well stacked assistant packed our mouths with rolls of cotton to stem the flow of blood, and sent us on our way.

All my lower molars ended up in the growing pile of teeth in the basin. My sisters' back teeth met the same fate. Apparently, fearful of parental wrath, the dentist let front teeth stay. Judging by the teeth in the basin, he had a profitable day.

We had to walk more than a mile home—spitting blood all the way. We stayed in bed a couple of days. Lora was a bleeder and her gums didn't want to stop bleeding. We thought she would bleed to death. She stayed in bed long after we recovered.

With the extracted teeth gone, and the signed cards with X's in his possession, there wasn't much parents could do. Pa may have been right about steering clear of dentists—at least, that one.

Chapter 45: Paper Mill Tour

Not long after our ill-fated encounter with the traveling dentist, Pa took me to see where he worked --The Keith Paper mill. He was quite proud of his employment there and wanted me to see how he spent his work day in the beater room. I think he hoped to inspire me to get a job there, too.

Crossing the footbridge over the canal and down the stairs to the mill was like crossing the river Styx to the lower world. The dark water, rushing far below the bridge, was dizzying. As we entered the mill, the noise and vibration of heavy machinery seemed to hit us like an assault. The entire building reverberated with a din of pulsing, pounding, howling, clattering racket that penetrated every cell in my body. I did not know how Pa could stand it all day long.

He took me onto a freight elevator and lowered the safety gate. The elevator started with a lurch, and we drifted down into the bowels of this howling paper making monster to Pa's workplace—the beater room. Water stood in puddles on the concrete floor; dampness and caustic chemical odors filled the air.

Pa tried to avoid the puddles. He said that he went barefoot when he worked the graveyard shift and the super wasn't around. He added that his feet were wet all night, anyway, and wearing shoes only held the wetness in. Going barefoot allowed his feet to dry, occasionally, so they wouldn't rot. Spared his shoes, too, he said. He showed me the gigantic oval tubs filled with chemicals and bleach where huge paddles beat floating rags and wood pulp into shredded fiber called "stock", as the material went around and around.

The beater room seemed more like a torture chamber than a place of employment. Pa seemed oblivious to it all. He beamed and waved greetings to fellow workers who smiled and waved back in an air of camaraderie. Their faces had a prison pallor, as though being confined in this sunless atmosphere of chemicals had bleached their skin to resemble that of cadavers. We followed the paper making process from soggy stock to finished paper. Pa shouted explanations over the din, as we went along. To see sodden fibers flow onto wide blanket-like belts, then between rollers, and emerge miraculously as a continuous sheet of paper fascinated me. We met the "color man" who concocted dyes with scales and beakers to produce the specified tint.

We continued along the path of the paper making process. Damp paper passed over and under whirling cylinders in the adjoining air dryer where an inferno of hot air blasted the paper dry. Whirring winding machinery made paper rolls as wide as a room and taller than my head.

Other machines unrolled the paper and chopped it into four foot squares, stacking it on pallets to be trimmed on noisy vibrating trimmers and sometimes embossed or cut into smaller sizes. And always the noise and vibrations of these machines, sometimes louder and sometimes blending into the overall din. I went home half-deafened, ears ringing, head aching, and with a new appreciation of what Pa had to endure to feed the family.

On the way home, he stopped at the Essex dealership, Cassidy's Garage, to buy gas. Pa could have bought gas cheaper at another station, but everyone treated him so well at Cassidy's he liked trading there. The manager greeted Pa like a long lost brother. He fawned over him, suggesting Pa try out one of the new cars displayed in the show room. Pa seemed rather flattered by all the attention.

Chapter 46: Depression Deepens

As the depression deepened, work at the paper mill was sporadic at best and Pa was often laid off. As time went on he longed to trade the boxy Essex for a more streamlined car. Pa could not even afford to buy a newer used car. He decided that if he couldn't buy a new car, he'd make the old one look new by painting it a new color. He bought a can of red enamel, and a paint brush, at Aubuchon hardware. After giving the car a good washing, he decided to give it a proper preparation by removing wax from the old finish with kerosene.

The paint took a while to dry because of the kerosene, but when it dried, the Essex looked rather grand with its shiny new fire-engine paint job—for a while, at least. At first, people thought Pa had purchased a new car, making him proud and happy, but not for long.

Paint doesn't adhere well to oily surfaces. In a few weeks, the new paint began to crack and peel in strips. The paint lost its luster and turned the color of dried blood. Hairy strips of peeling paint made the car look like a molting mastodon as it went down the road, paint strips fluttering in the breeze. The paint kept peeling until the increasingly tattered Essex appeared to have succumbed to a devastating skin disease.

One day, Pa drove the molting Essex to Cassidy's garage where he'd once been a valued customer. Needing a hair cut and shave, and dressed in clothes nearly matching the shabby Essex, he pulled up to the gas pumps. Like most gas stations during those dismal days, a sign read---"Six gallons for $1."

The lift, given the economy by Roosevelt's New Deal, petered out in the mid thirties. Everyone's spirits sagged as the depression ground on. Lay-offs were increasingly common. With few customers with money to buy gasoline, Cassidy let the gas pump attendant go.

Pa hesitated a moment, as if to get up his courage, then walked into the car agency with a box of eggs in his hand. I followed, waiting for Pa to tell me to get back in the car. But he seemed preoccupied and didn't appear to notice. I tagged along, trying to remain inconspicuous.

Cassidy's garage had always held a fascination for me. I loved the atmosphere, charged with the smell of new paint, tires, grease, oil and exhaust. Mechanics busying themselves with the mysterious innards of automobiles, friendly gas attendants, and smiling salesmen with pencil mustaches and slicked down hair, exuding friendship and opulence, all added up to a congenial atmosphere.

In the past, when we came in to get gas, the manager would say, "Take a look at one of these new models, Joe. Time you was moving up in the world."

You'd think Pa was the manager's best friend. This time the manager sat leaning back in his office chair with his feet up on the desk, cleaning his nails with a pocket knife. A candle stick telephone sat ready at his elbow extended from the wall on a lattice work extension rack. He pointedly ignored Pa. The smell of grease and oil and car exhaust was still there, but the gas pump attendant and salesman were missing, and shop sounds were muted. Two used cars sat where new models customarily stood.

A salesman was demonstrating a tire re-groover. The gadget had a cord that plugged into an outlet. When the little U shaped blade heated up, the blade slid through the bald tire he held, cutting grooves to resemble good tread.

"Look at that—just like new," he said. "Now, that'll make a car sell."

"Won't that make the tire weaker so it'll blow out?" the manager asked.

"Maybe so, but I figure re-grooving a bald tire will make it easier to stop and be safer," the salesman replied. "And if a tire does blow, you can always sell them a new one."

The manager agreed to take one, on trial, still ignoring us. Pa shifted from one foot to the other. He cleared his throat.

"I need some gas."

The manager continued working on the dirt under his nails, seeming not to have heard.

"I almost out the gas."

The manager looked bored and turned without meeting Pa's gaze.   "Got any money?"

"I got a dozen eggs."

"Can't pay my bills with eggs."

"Come on, I been a good customer long time. For chrissakes I almost out the gas."

Pa hung his head. I wished I'd stayed in the car. I wished Pa had money and didn't have to be humiliated by this dirty little man. I wished Pa had a lot of money so he could buy a brand new car and his gasoline somewhere else. I was ashamed to see Pa reduced to begging.

The manager took the carton of eggs, opened the cover and took out an egg. "They's kinda small."

Pa's head came up, his face flushed, eyes flashing. He growled.

"Give me what you will, and go to Hell."

A mechanic came in asking what to do next.

"Go out and pump him a gallon of regular."

After the mechanic pumped the gasoline and hung up the nozzle, Pa sped off with a roar. He looked fierce, "Rotten bastid," spat out.

Chapter 47: New Shoes

The one place Pa could trade eggs, or other farm products, was with his friend, the cobbler. Pa had traded him for a stand and a set of various steel lasts so that he could resole our shoes at home, since leather wore out fast.

I liked to watch Pa re-sole shoes. He'd select a last, put it on the stand, and slip a shoe over it. Then he'd select a piece of leather of the appropriate thickness—thick for work boots, medium for men's dress shoes and thin for women's shoes. With a special hammer with a wide flat face, he tapped little nails through the leather into the sole, driving the nails through to strike the steel last where the nails headed over. With a sharp jackknife, he'd cut the leather sheet away from the sole with a "crrrk crrrk" protest from the leather. After a final fine trimming, he'd feel around inside the shoe for nails that stuck up, and give the whole row of nails a sound hammering with special emphasis on any offender that stuck up. Since there was a great deal of tapping in the process, resoling shoes was called "tapping."

The occasional nail that stuck up reminded me of Irene's warning to keep quiet and to remember what happens to the nail that sticks up. Pa seemed quite happy as he went about renewing shoes and maybe even hammering down the nail that stuck up. I'd always attributed it to his pleasure in saving money. But when I got older I tapped my own shoes, finding a feeling of accomplishment and satisfaction in self-sufficiency I hadn't anticipated.

Women's shoes are hard to tap. The construction is of thinner leather and the nails would stick up too much, making walking in them a torture. That summer, before school started, my sisters had been putting cardboard in their shoes to cover holes where the sole had worn through. Pa was aware of their need of new shoes. With money scarce, the only hope lay in our family friend, the cobbler, who often bought odd lots of shoes.

The cobbler was a dandy of sorts. Even when repairing shoes, he wore a suit and tie, and he kept his hair and moustache neatly trimmed. On warm summer days, he wore a shirt and tie, with garters on his shirt sleeves to hold them from interfering with his work. Because people could not afford new shoes, his business boomed.

Shoe stores often failed, and the cobbler attended the liquidation auctions where he bought large quantities of shoes at a fraction of their cost. Not only did he sell these shoes at bargain prices, but he was willing to swap for anything of value. Though he prospered, his entrepreneurship was not without peril. He'd once purchased thousands of beautifully crafted shoe samples from a shoe salesman, only to discover that few had mates. Almost all were shoes for the right foot. There was hardly a pair in the whole mess.

On one visit to the cobbler in quest of shoes, the cobbler led us to the back room where he picked up two shoes that seemed to be mates. He held them up to show us that each was a slightly different size. The cobbler hurled the shoes against the far wall with a vengeance. He cursed the salesman, the salesman's company and the salesman's mother for having borne such a son. I was impressed by his command of profanity, his vocabulary of oaths and his creative combinations.

The cobbler later hunted down the salesman's home office and went there to demonstrate his mastery of profanity. He raised such a ruckus that they refunded him his money, and told him to keep the shoes. The sample debacle dampened the cobbler's enthusiasm for bargains and his shoe inventory sank to a low level, not counting the back room full of mismatched samples. The prospect of new shoes dimmed. Pa attempted to resole the girls' shoes, but their shoes were beyond repair.

My sisters were not entirely unhappy; they would have preferred to continue to placing cardboard in their shoes rather than clump along with the thick leather soles my father would have applied; to say nothing of the nails sticking into their feet. First day of school loomed closer and closer, and still no new shoes. My sisters dared not remind Pa of the need.

Then, one day he came home, jubilant. He had new shoes—bushels of them. The entire back seat of the car was loaded with bushel baskets full of new shoes. My father knew a good deal when he saw it, and had traded something, for an entire lot of high quality women's' shoes—first making sure they were matching pairs. He proudly announced that, never again, would a female member of the family need to buy new shoes.

The girls were thrilled at the prospect of new shoes. That was, until they got a closer look. The shoes were high button, hopelessly out of style, with Cuban heels and mostly in colors of deep purple and ghastly green. My sisters looked like they wanted to die, right there, in their old shoes. Up to then, I'd never seen any shoes other than the traditional white, brown, or black.

My sister Emmy picked out a pair with the most normal looking heels she could find. She sniffled as she cut the high tops off and tried to make the shoes presentable with shoe polish, hoping no one at school would notice.

My sister Gladys, who read a lot, had a fertile imagination. She took a different tack. She picked out a purple pair with heels a flamenco dancer would have killed for.

On opening day, she strutted into school, showing off her new shoes, proclaiming them the latest fashion. The shoes were an instant hit. The other girls clamored to learn where she'd got them. Being of such a recent style and scarce commodity, she said she would obtain the shoes for them.

I don't know how much she charged, but she'd get the sizes from the kids and bring these hard-to-find shoes to school in a day or two, never letting on that we had bushels of them stacked in the shed attached to the barn. Soon, every girl in school was strutting about in heel-tapping grandeur. Miss Pogoda, whom I'm sure knew what was going on, put up with the tap-tapping of all those high heels; bless her soul.

My father never learned of the craze he'd spawned, limited as it was. The shoes we sold, or gave away, hardly made a dent in the supply. With what seemed a nearly infinite supply of shoes on hand, my father took considerable comfort in knowing that he'd never have to worry about buying shoes for the girls, again. He seemed pleased with his sense of style when he saw my sisters' classmates wearing identical shoes.

My sister Elizabeth, who we all called "Bessie", got teased when she wore those ghastly shoes to high school. She scuffed the tip of her shoes on the way to and from school, until the sole began coming loose. She then managed to work the sole from the shoe with her fingers. She hoped to go through all the shoes in her size so she could convince Pa the bargain shoes were of poor quality and that she needed a pair from a store.

She didn't get her store-bought shoes. She couldn't take the five mile hike to high school in winter over snow covered roads in the bitter cold. She quit school to go to work as a nanny.

Chapter 48: Hurricane

Winter weather was not the only problem in our lives. We did not subscribe to a newspaper nor were there any weather forecasts that we could rely upon, except for what Pa saw in signs in dew, wind direction, and cloud formations. No one had any inkling that a hurricane of major proportions would hit our area in September of 1938.

First, heavy rain fell. Winds began to blow, harder and harder. Trees bent before the wind. The brook flooded and I got to see my first seagulls, blown there by the high winds. Two of our hen coops were lifted into the air, moved about 20 feet and dropped. The coops disintegrated into a tangle of boards and timbers. We watched as the roof of a neighbor's barn, a quarter mile away, lifted up into the air, intact, hovering for a moment before disintegrating in a flutter of slate, boards and timber, then crashed to the ground. The hurricane uprooted many trees, including huge pine trees in the woods behind our house.

One day a group of us hiked up Mason's Hill to get a view of the valley and a wider look at the hurricane's destruction. A boy in our gathering was the son of a family who sported a real bathtub with hot and cold running water. He had come uninvited to accompany us on our walk through the pasture up to the top of the hill.

Our family did not have a bathroom. Few folks in the country did. Most people had an outhouse. Bathing in a brook or river in summer was common; "cat baths," sponge baths out of a basin, the rest of the year, sufficed.

Bathing too often was considered unhealthy, especially in winter when a body could take a chill and catch a death of cold. The smell of cigars, whiskey, and sweat, either horse or human, was considered a manly smell. Manly smelling men were common, maybe even prevalent.

Our neighbors, the Lamberts, had their bath tub in the kitchen as was often the case—the kitchen being the warmest room of the house. The tub had a wooden cover and served as a low table or counter when not in use. The bather closed off the kitchen, usually late in the evening, and bathed in privacy. We had a midwinter bath in a washtub when we were little. As we got older, we took cat baths with a basin in the pantry.

Our self-invited hiker had running water at his house, and the luxury of hot water piped right to a real bathtub from a hot water tank heated by their kitchen wood stove. We joked and horsed around as we walked, occasionally scaling dried cow pies like frisbees, just enjoying each other's company. Then, our privileged neighbor threw a cow pie, hitting someone.

He was quite proud of his family having a real bathtub with hot and cold running water, rarely passing up an opportunity to remind us of his elevated station in life. He'd already mentioned, several times that day, about his present status of being freshly bathed with clean clothes—including the luxury of underwear—clean underwear, he stressed.

He laughed when the target of his cow pie complained, saying his aim was off and it was all an accident. We gave him the benefit of doubt. He then "accidentally" hit someone with one, again. The targeted kid picked up a pie to retaliate.

"Wait. Don't throw it. I just had a bath and I got all clean clothes on," the son of privilege said, pronouncing bath—"bawth."

We came to an area rich with cow pies. He scaled another pie, hitting another kid. This time, there was no mistaking that it was a deliberate hit. The boy picked up a pie.

"Wait. Wait. Don't throw it. I just had a bawth."

Everyone paused and we looked at one other. Almost as one, we let fly with dried cow pies. All his slights, and taunts that I was a Polak and sounded like a crow when I spoke Polish, that we had no electricity, too many kids, and his bragging of his family's wealth, fine clothes and "bawth" tub with hot and cold running water, boiled up in me. I hurled pie after pie at him with a soul satisfying vengeance.

When the supply of dried cow pies ran out, I hurled a soft centered one. The soft centered pie hit with a satisfying splat. The other kids followed my lead. He was soon covered with cow manure from his once freshly shampooed regal head to his now manure-splattered shoes. The sight of him standing stupefied, plastered with stinking manure, satiated my anger and resentment. "There--- now go home and take another ba-awth."

The others chimed in, "Yah—go home and take yourself another bawth—you stink."

Chapter 49: Education

About the time of the incident of the boy with the real bawth tub, Raymond came into my life. I was sitting in the back seat of our tan Essex parked in front of a café, one Sunday. A boy about my age came out of a door next to the entrance. He stood by a light pole looking at me.

"Hey kid, my name is Raymond; what's your name?"

"Joe."

"What are you doing sitting in the car?"

"Waiting for my father."

"Why don't you get out?"

"My father won't let me."

Raymond was dressed in Sunday clothes. He leaned against the pole, looking bored. "Your father won't know if you get out."

"He will if he catches me."

Raymond gave up and walked back to the doorway leading to the upstairs apartment. The next time I saw him was when my parents went to visit them in their new house. Raymond's father invited my parents to a picnic at the new house. It had an outdoor fireplace at the edge of woods where they had a cook-out, with hot dogs, hamburgers and beer. Everyone had a nice time with spirited conversation and laughter.

Raymond and I began exploring the many paths in the dense pine woods surrounding the house. We grew to be friends, and I began walking the three or four miles to his house to visit him. On occasion, he came to visit me, but he was petrified of Pa, and would head for home when he saw my father's car coming down the road to our house.

One day when I cleaned the gutter in the cow barn, Raymond tagged along. A cow raised her tail and spread her hind legs. A huge bowel movement came out, plopping into the gutter. She next produced a cascade of urine, lowered her tail and moved her feet back together. Ray stood observing the scene with keen interest.

"I've never seen a cow do that before."

"Trust me, it's nothing new."

Raymond studied the cow's rear end. "Aren't you going to wipe her with toilet paper?

"No. I don't think so. We don't even have toilet paper in the out house; just newspaper or pages from the catalog. And, I'm not about to wipe a cow's rear end, anyway."

"What is that slime hanging down?"

"Beats me. It's just something that oozes out."

"It doesn't look very sanitary."

I shook my head. This city guy has a lot to learn about farming, I thought. I pushed the cow flop down to the end of the gutter and shoveled it out the rear barn door onto the manure pile.

Raymond was close to graduating from grammar school. We talked about going to Mount Hermon School, at length. His parents were going to pay his way. A year older than me, he was admitted as a day student. If I qualified, I could go tuition-free, but I had to get money together for books, lab fees and lunch money. A suit coat and tie were mandatory for chapel and dining hall. Most of the boys came from affluent families. I had neither a suit coat, nor a decent looking pair of pants.

The other kids in grammar school weren't much better off than we were, so I felt like a big shot when I came to school sporting a pair of wing tip shoes that I had purchased with my own money. But I was far from getting together the amount of money I would need for Mount Hermon. I began to get discouraged, until I got a demonstration of determination from Helen's husband, Magrini

They had continued to urge me to get an education, with each visit. The idea took on more appeal after the paper mill tour. I think Pa sensed my attitude and took it as a rejection of his values. Though Helen's husband name was Ludovico Magrini, every called him "Magrini"—even Helen. My father didn't want Helen to marry Magrini because his right arm was gone—blown off when he had hammered on a live artillery shell that he and his friends had found on a World War I battle field in Italy. The exploding shell blew Magrini's arm off, and blinded a companion. Magrini was lucky to survive. He always wore long sleeved shirts to cover the artificial arm. Only a gloved hand showed.

Pa warned Helen about marrying him. "You'll end up on welfare with that one-armed cripple." The prediction turned out to be true. Ironically, Magrini's first job after graduating from college was administrating a welfare office.

When they came to visit, Magrini always came inside to greet the family, and after a little while, would excuse himself. As long as he was in the house with them, they'd struggle with English. They took no offense at his leaving and were undoubtedly relieved that they could then begin speaking freely in Polish.

Magrini talked to me, man to man. He continually encouraged me to get a good education, and go on to college. He had worked his way through college polishing furniture and assured me I could also find a way. I hated to tell him about getting such poor grades in school, that there was little chance of me ever attending Mt Hermon, much less college.

While outside, one day, I heard a tire hissing on his car. I pointed it out to him. He took the spare tire off the back of the car, jacked up the car, put on the spare tire, fixed the flat and put the wheel on the spare tire rack. The screw jack operated with a long handled crank designed to be used with both hands. The holes on the wheel were not easy to line up with the studs sticking out of the wheel hub, but Magrini did it with one hand while wearing a tie and long sleeved white shirt. After putting the spare on the car, Magrini proceeded to pry the flat tire off the rim. He held one tire iron down with his foot while he pried with the other. When he got enough tire pried off to get a hand hold, he planted his foot on the wheel and pulled the tire off the rim with his hand.

He removed the tube, patched it, put it back inside the tire, mounted the tire on the rim, pumped up the air pressure with a hand pump, and put the wheel on the spare rack. I couldn't believe he was able to accomplish all that in so short a time. But what impressed me, most, was that he kept his white shirt clean! I could get a white shirt dirty standing stock still out in the open. Just as he was securing the tire on the spare tire rack, the other members of the family came out. Someone asked what the problem was.

"No problem; just a flat tire."

"Why didn't you come in to get us? We'd have changed it for you."

"Why? I'm no cripple."

After that, whenever I was faced with difficulty, I thought of Magrini overcoming the loss of his right arm. Even when living alone, he dressed himself, lacing his shoes in such a way that he was able to pull one end to tighten the laces and somehow fasten the loose end all with one hand.

He learned to drive a standard shift car by sticking his left arm through the steering wheel and shifting the floor mounted gearshift lever while steering the car. He passed his driving test on the first try.

His dress and manners were that of a gentleman. In addition to his administrative job, he opened an insurance agency, and later, a monument business. The day Magrini fixed the flat tire he demonstrated the power of determination. He seemed to have a different prospective on life than Pa.

Chapter 50: Shotgun

Pa came home from an auction with a shotgun. He first tried it out by creeping up on the snake lying in the garden. At close range, he let loose a blast. When the dust had cleared, the snake was gone.

"How could he get away so quick?" Pa asked, shaking his head. I doubt the snake could have slithered away, and suspect he had blown the snake to smithereens. He next tried the shotgun when butchering.

A cow had given birth to a bull calf earlier that summer. Pa decided to castrate the calf and raise it for veal. He tied the calf's legs, together, cut open the bull's scrotum, cut out the testicles, and dumped salt brine into the wound. When he untied the struggling calf, the poor thing ran leaping and kicking in agony. My father laughed, "Stings some, I guess."

I had followed Irene's advice and did not name the calf. On the first frosty day of fall, Pa opened the hay barn doors and hung up the pulley block. He sent me to get the calf.

"I'm going to try something different," Pa said. He placed the muzzle of the shotgun on the young steer's forehead and fired. "Bang!" The calf's head swelled up and his eyes bulged. He fell to the barn floor, dead. The stench of gun smoke, scorched hair and smell of blood filled the air. Pa grinned. "Spoiled the head, I guess."

He hung the dead animal by the heal cords and slit its throat to drain the blood. These gruesome scenes had a traumatic effect on me. Pa figured that I would become hardened to these bloody scenes, but it only made me more sensitive.

After the calf was butchered, Pa spoke about looking forward to having some veal. At supper, that evening, Pa wondered why I did not want to eat meat from the calf, when it was so tender and tasty. That was fine with him; he said, it meant that he could present more veal to his friend, Mr. Taradana, who often came to visit. He worked in a dusty foundry and loved to come to the farm to work out in the fresh air and sunshine. He did not drive, but took a train to Greenfield where he hired a taxi to drive him to the farm. I was always happy to see him.

One day when Pa was yelling at me, Mr. Taradana said in a gruff voice, "Let him come to work out in the field with me—I'll handle him."

Ma packed us a lunch with a bottle of milk for me and a bottle of beer for him. In the field where we were going to lay drainage pipe, he had me put the bottles in the cool water of a spring we were draining. He praised me at every turn. He was a kindly man and it made me feel good when he said he always wanted a son like me. He had two oafish daughters who took after the sad spectacle of his wife. She had become pregnant by him, when he was young, and he felt duty bound to marry her. He never complained, but did not spend any more time with her than he had to.

He made me a cast iron bank at the foundry. It was a figure of a horse. I treasured that gift from this kind man, but somehow I lost it. Years later, I bought a replica and have kept it ever since.

Pa loved to drive around the countryside in first the emerald Essex and then the tan one. He especially liked to visit Mr. Taradana, who lived in Easthampton, the town Pa had left in the dead of the night when he was down and out. I think he wanted to show his old friends that he'd become prosperous, again.

Later, when Mr. Taradana moved to Hartford, Connecticut, Pa began driving down to see him, there, when the mill laid him off and when he was recovering from his heart problems. Sometimes, Ma and Pa would leave for a day's visit and stay a week, or two, leaving us alone to light kerosene lamps and start a fire in the wood stove to prepare our meals. Sometimes they would take one of the children with them. On one occasion, I was chosen, but I did not like the city and begged to go home. They did not take me again.

One day when we were home alone, Emmy poured kerosene on a smoldering fire. At first the kerosene hissed and smoked; before it exploded. The stove lids flew off. Fire singed her eyebrows and hair. Flames leaped up to the ceiling. Smoke filled the house. One lid was made up of a series of rings. The rings scattered over the stove and some fell to the floor. Meanwhile smoke poured into the kitchen and flames licked the ceiling. We hurried to get the hot lids back on before the house caught fire.

After Emmy left home, we were left alone when our parents went away. They left Irene in charge. She was twelve. With Emmy's experience with the stove fresh in our minds, she dared not build a fire to cook meals or even light the lamps. We sat waiting in the dark, late into the night one long day. It got later and later. We worried that the barn chores hadn't been done. Pa often said cows would dry up if not milked on schedule. But we were afraid to light a lantern to go out to the barn to try to do the chores. We sat huddled in the dark, cold and hungry with our stomachs growling, feeling abandoned.

They came home far into the night with heavy footfalls. For supper, we got leftover soup stored in the cellar and heated on the wood stove, once a fire was going. The barn chores got done after a fashion.

We had mixed feelings about our parents leaving us alone. Sometimes, when the older kids were still home, they'd dig out the ice cream churn, round up eggs, cream, ice, and make a batch of ice cream. For that, we had to enlist the aid of a neighbor boy who lived on his bachelor uncle's dairy farm. He brought ice from his uncle's ice house and additional cream to round out a batch. While we crushed ice to mix with rock salt for the churn, the girls cooked vanilla, sugar, eggs, and cream in an enameled kettle over the wood stove. We had to hurry to get the ingredients assembled, the mixture cooked and churned, the ice cream eaten, and everything cleaned up and put away before our parents got back.

Without a double boiler, the girls invariably scorched the mixture in their haste. Even with a lookout posted, we had more than one narrow escape when Ma and Pa came home early, and we had to scurry around concealing the evidence. I don't know if it was the scorched mix or the fact that it was forbidden fruit, but no other ice cream has ever equaled that homemade delight. But later, despite being free to do what we wanted to do—or dared to do, when our parents left us alone, we always felt uneasy. Sure, enough; disaster followed them home one night.

Chapter 51: The Barn Catches Fire

Late one night I was sound asleep when Ma and Pa came home. Something woke me. An eerie red light bathed the entire bedroom. Shouts came from outside the window. I could see that the yard was lit up, but I couldn't figure out the source of the light. I could only hear shouts—desperate shouts.

I ran downstairs and stood in the open kitchen doorway. Fire engulfed the entire barn. The yard was lit in bright orange light. A fierce roaring, punctuated by popping and snapping, spellbound me. I could feet the intense heat. Flames surrounded the barn, clinging to the structure as though it were not consuming it at all. A burning board near the peak pulled away and fell to the ground in flames. The rest of the barn stood like an animal in shock, waiting to be devoured by the raging fire.

Ma was in the pantry, frantically pumping water into a pail. She shouted, on her way by, telling me to put on my pants because people would soon be coming to put out the fire. Her words brought me out of my trance. Put out the fire? I wanted to tell her there would be no putting out this fire. I could see it was hopeless. Ma threw the pail of water on the wood shed attached to the house. The water turned to steam as soon as it hit the shed. I wondered how long before the house caught fire and began burning, too.

The town fire warden arrived with some copper fire extinguishers. Embers falling on the house roof were starting little fires. He put them out, one by one. Then he began shooting an extinguisher at the wooden saw rig platform that had caught fire. He hollered to ask if there was gasoline in the saw rig gas tank. Ma hollered back, "No." Somehow, the gas tank didn't blow up. Perhaps the gasoline had evaporated from the heat. Maybe we were just lucky. The exploding gas tank would have blown flaming gasoline onto the woodshed hooked to the house.

I ran upstairs to get dressed and to wake my brother and sisters to tell them to get out of the house. The image of people burning in the holy picture appeared in my mind. Would we be like the people in the fire? Was God punishing us, I wondered.

Firemen arrived from Turners Falls, five miles away. The firemen didn't lay a hose to the fire pond by the brook. "Too late," they said. My mother and Irene lugged a wash tub of water from the brook. The firemen threw a suction hose into the tub. Water shot onto the wood shed where it immediately turned to steam. In seconds the tub was empty. Ma and Irene gave up.

Cars kept coming. People parked along the road and in the fields. They helped Pa lug furniture out of the house. More people came to help. They put contents from the house out onto the front lawn by the road on the side away from the barn. I wanted to watch the fire because I knew it was a once in a lifetime experience. But my brother, Louis was crying hysterically. He didn't want to see the fire and didn't want me to leave him. I wrapped him in a featherbed quilt. He cried in terror whenever I tried moving away from him. So I stayed with him, watching people running, smelling the wood smoke, listening to the flames roar and crackle, seeing the yard illuminated, hearing the frantic shouts.

While I sat with Louis, two men began gathering chickens from the fenced range. They stuffed them into burlap bags. "Hey! What are you doing? I asked.

"We're saving 'em, kid," said one of the men. A cigarette sticking out of his mouth waggled up and down as he talked. His speech was slurred.

The other man laughed, "Yah, we're taking 'em to a safe place."

"No you're not; you're stealing them."

"Shut up, you little brat," the man with the waggling cigarette said. They jumped into their car and drove off.

Our dog Skippy ran up and down the road, dragging his chain and barking his head off. A second fire truck from Greenfield stopped a half mile away. Firemen sat on a distant neighbor's lawn and watched the barn burn to the ground. Someone took Louis to their car and comforted him. People ran in and out of the house, carrying out the contents. I realized, then, that the house would probably soon burn, just like the barn. I wondered if this was all a bad dream. How can you go to sleep in your bed and wake up to a nightmare like this?

The scene was one of increasing panic, confusion, and frantic shouts. People threw clothes and bedding on top of furniture scattered all over the front lawn. Someone took the girls clothes for safe keeping. We never saw the clothes or the chickens, again. Years later when a new family moved to town, the father talked with a cigarette waggling in the corner of his mouth.

Arnold Studer and his wife Mabel took us to their turkey farm, and put us to bed. Mabel put Louis and me in a bed together. It was about four o'clock in the morning by that time. After I used the bathroom, I tried to stay awake. It was almost dawn, and I was scared to death I'd wet the bed. I figured, to be safe, I'd stay awake. When it started to get light I closed my eyes for a second and dozed off. The next thing I knew, I felt wetness. I was wetting the bed! I jumped out of bed, got dressed and went downstairs, hoping they'd think Louis was the culprit. No one ever said anything. I don't know if they ever figured out who did it, but I always felt guilty about making it look like Louis had committed the dirty deed.

151

We went back home after Mrs. Studer fed us breakfast. Where the barn once stood, there was a big empty space with mounds of smoldering gray ashes surrounded by fine white ashes that lay like drifted snow. Some darker mounds were hens that had been in the barn. They stunk of burning feathers.

There wasn't a trace of the girls' despised high button shoes. Our home-made tractor, built from a Reo truck, had been parked in the barn. The tires were gone and the scorched metal sagged like chocolate in the summer sun. Aluminum parts had liquefied into strange shapes. I found one in the shape of a dinosaur.

A couple of my school mates came over to gawk at the ruins and what was left of the Reo. They made jokes about the smoldering hens being all cooked and ready to eat. I knew they were trying to cheer me up. I tried to laugh, but it didn't seem funny.

The cows gathered next to the fence, looking at their former home as though they were wondering what was going to happen next. I wondered, too.

Ma came out to tell us that Pa had had a bad heart attack and was in the hospital. Her eyes had dark circles. She seemed to be walking around in a daze, unable to accept that the barn was reduced to smoldering ashes, the house was in disarray, Pa was in the hospital, we had no money, and we were without a breadwinner. I knew that life would never be the same, again.

Ma told the boys that the cow had kicked over the lantern and set the barn on fire. That didn't sound right. I'd fooled around with lanterns and found that even if I held one upside down, they'd still stay lit and just smoke a little. Besides, no one could find the remains of the lantern in the ruins. I suspected they had carried a lamp into the barn and the heat from the lamp chimney ignited hay hanging down from cracks in the hay mow floor. Once ignited, there was no stopping the fire.

I felt like too much had happened all at once and I had to get away. When the boys asked me to come to their farm to visit, I asked Ma for permission to go. I thought going there would get my mind off of everything that had happened. But my brain seemed locked on the events of the fire. Ma offered to make me a lunch to take along, when I asked if I could go visit the boys. She began making chicken sandwiches, but had trouble cutting meat off from the bones. So she put a chunk of carcass, bones and all between two slices of bread.

"You can eat the meat off the bones," she said.

When we got to the boys' house, I stayed outside to eat my lunch. It didn't take a genius to figure out their father didn't like me, especially when other visiting kids were invited in to eat, and I got left outside.

"You make my father nervous, so you have to stay outside," one of them explained. "Crows, is what he calls you people. He says he doesn't like Polaks because you sound like crows when you talk. He says you people oughtn't talk Polish, you should oughta' talk American."

As I sat on the lawn ready to tackle my chicken sandwich, the younger boy came back out to call me into the house. At first, I thought his father wasn't at home. He usually just glowered at me. But, there at the kitchen table, he sat with a little smile on his face. This was the first time I'd ever seen him smile. I figured maybe he felt sorry for me because of the fire and Pa being so sick in the hospital with a heart attack. He had, after all, come to help fight the fire. It looked like he'd had a change of heart and we could be friends. They whole family sat smiling and watching. No one was eating, though their plates were full.

"Go ahead and eat your lunch.".

I took out the huge sandwich, not knowing what to do. I didn't want to open the sandwich and eat the chicken with my fingers as I had planned to do, knowing it was not polite to eat with your fingers. I opened my mouth wide. All eyes were on me. The chunk of chicken carcass between the two pieces of bread made it way too big to eat like a sandwich.

They burst out laughing. They laughed and laughed. I'd never seen their father laugh before. He was really enjoying himself.

"Take the sandwich apart and eat the chicken and bread separately," the mother said. She was no longer smiling.

I knew, then, they had lured me inside to have a good laugh at my expense. My mouth stayed dry while I tried to eat. The boys and their father kept looking at me and snickering. After the razzing about the chicken sandwich, I didn't feel like playing and went along home. They never invited me inside to eat, again, nor did I ever want them to. Though, it did make me bitter to see other playmates invited in for lunch, and not just to be made a laughing stock.

Playing with the brothers had always been fun. But the fire and the incident with the chicken sandwich changed all that. I realized I lived under different rules and more was expected of me, that I was part of a minority and subject to a degree of prejudice and ridicule.

Ma was gone when I got home from my chicken sandwich humiliation. The other kids said Mr. Lambert's nephew had driven Ma to the hospital in the Essex. One of the Greek grocery peddlers came by. He gaped at the mounds of white powdery ashes and bits of metal that stuck up like victims reaching for help.

"Where you poppa and mama?" he asked.

When we told him Ma was visiting Pa at the hospital, he asked if we had food to eat. We said we did, but he thrust a loaf of bread at us and insisted we take it. He took another long look at the ruins before getting into his produce truck and driving off.

I had enjoyed visiting the two boys, whenever I could get away, before being humiliated with the chicken sandwich debacle. The two boys never had to work the way we did—not even hoeing or weeding in the garden, much less a big corn field. They didn't have any chores to do, either. Their hired man did all that; they just played all summer.

On hot days when I visited, we'd cool off in the ice house by lying on the damp sawdust covering blocks of ice, or we went swimming, or fishing, in the brook. Sometimes we'd hike to the Fall River to swim in the icy water and bake on the hot girders of the iron bridge spanning it. A family lived by another iron bridge spanning that same river, several miles farther downstream.

The boys' mother invited me to go along with them for a ride to Greenfield in their nice new car. Her husband was at work. She would never have taken me along if he had been home. She handed me a shirt to wear, and said, "Come along." I guess she wanted me to look civilized, with a clean shirt, at least. On the way, the younger boy told me to watch carefully because we might see the poor kids living by the bridge.

"Look, look. There they are,"

I looked, but the kids didn't look all that different to me.

"Wow! Poor kids—you don't see that very often," their mother said with a little twinkle in her eye. I knew, right away, she meant me and I didn't feel very good about coming along.

Later, she bought ice cream cones for her boys and treated me to one, too. I could tell she realized that I knew she had made a cruel joke and she was trying to make up for it. When we got home, she cautioned her sons. "Don't tell Dad about going into town." But I knew that what she really meant was, "Don't tell Dad we took the dirty little Polish kid with us."

Usually, when I went to visit the boys, I returned home for lunch. The day before the chicken sandwich ordeal, the boy's mother called them in to eat, I told the boys I was heading home.

"Don't go home; go eat some apples in the orchard and cow grain in the barn,"

So, I went to the orchard, but the apples were green and gave me a belly ache. The cow grain from the bins in their barn wasn't that great, but checker-berry leaves and other plants growing wild weren't too bad, though I worried I would eat something poisonous. I liked to pretend I was an Indian foraging off the land, but excluding me from the house made me feel lonely. After they had tricked me into making a fool of myself, I seldom visited them. I stuck around home, hoping to get to go to the hospital to see Pa. I loved him and didn't want him to die. There wasn't much doctors did for heart attacks in those days, except offer bed rest and a little whiskey.

Chapter 52: The Hospital

On our first trip to visit Pa in the hospital, he was lying in bed in a ward with about 40 other patients. He took his illnesses very seriously, and this certainly was serious enough. He lay flat on his back with the sheet pulled up to his chin, looking grave. We surrounded the bed, overwhelmed by the hospital smell of ether and alcohol, and the whiteness of the place—white sheets, white beds, white walls, white ceilings, and rows of white beds. The nurses were all dressed in white with little white caps perched on their heads, padding about in their white shoes, carrying white bedpans and white towels. A janitor in dark street clothes shuffled in, pushing a dust mop that was three feet wide. He looked as foreign in his dark clothes as we did in this world of white.

When Ma leaned over to ask Pa how he was doing, anxiety showed in her voice. He replied between groans that he was grievously ill. He then rolled a bit to one side, raised his hip, groaned again and blew a big fart as if to show us just how bad things were. We tried to keep from laughing.

"Gas," he announced solemnly. Whereby we began to first snicker and then giggle uncontrollably.

"Not funny," he said, frowning.

Try as we might, we couldn't control ourselves. We periodically burst out in giggles and snickers, hoping he was too sick to climb out of bed and thrash us. He lay there, glowering between groans.

When we got ready to leave, Pa motioned for Ma to come closer. He whispered in her ear. I figured he wanted to utter his last words of will and testament.

"Bring me cigarettes and matches," he whispered. "They won't let me smoke—I got to have cigarettes."

The next time we came in, Ma passed him the cigarettes. He said he'd smoke them under the bed sheet after dark when everyone was asleep. I worried he would set his bed and the hospital on fire. Fortunately oxygen was not in use, then.

Stanley came to visit. He had once come to the farm on a rare visit when our parents were away. He smashed some aluminum parts on the old green Essex and taken then away in a burlap bag. We raised such a ruckus that he did not remove very much, and left. Now that he was here, again, we didn't trust him. But when he saw the tan Essex with paper thin tires, he took the car away. When he brought it back, the car had all good tires.

Since Pa couldn't go back to work, Ma applied for a job at the Keith Paper Mill where Pa worked before his heart attack. There weren't any job openings, they said. The Essex was nearly out of gas, and she was nearly out of money. The temporary WPA sewing project had long since closed down.

Ma went on foot to see the town officials to ask for money to tide us over until she could get a job. Going "on the town" was a disgrace, but she was desperate. They offered her six dollars a week, figuring a dollar per kid. That wasn't enough to feed the family. And the mortgage payment was past due. She came home, tired and discouraged. We had the chores done and potatoes on to boil for "brown soup." Ma made the "soup" by browning flour to make milk gravy. We'd been eating a lot of brown soup lately, but we didn't complain.

By now it was getting dark. She asked me to go with her to see Anne Franklin. That she would ask me to accompany her, made me feel grown up. I loved Ma and wanted so to have her love me. Maybe now that I was getting older, I hoped I wouldn't be getting into trouble, anymore, and would be good like Johnny.

Anne worked in the Keith Paper Mill office. She was a kind and gracious lady. She wore fashionable clothes, her lips and cheeks were always rouged, and her black hair was perfectly set.

Ma set out for her house at a pretty good clip. After about a mile, Ma stopped to rest.

"Tired, Ma?"

"Yes, I am, but I got to do something. We can't live on $6 a week. And I'm afraid the bank will take the house."

The thoughts of Pa not being able to work were bad enough—now, I had the added worry of the bank foreclosing. I wondered where we'd go or what we'd do, if that happened. I wondered what Anne could do for Ma. If the mill wasn't hiring what was the use of traipsing all over the countryside for nothing, I thought. Discouragement settled over me, worse than ever. We continued on to Anne's house. She invited us in and asked Ma to sit down.

"I'm sorry about the fire and your husband being in the hospital and all," she said. "Tell me; how I can help you?"

Ma told her about going to the mill to find there were no job openings and that they wouldn't even let her talk to anyone.

"Well, Mrs. Parzych," she said. "I can't promise you a job, but I can promise you an interview. Come to the office tomorrow morning and ask for me." She held Ma's hand in both of hers as she said goodbye.

157

Next morning, Ma was at the Keith Paper Mill office. I don't know what kind of influence Anne had, but she made good on her promise. Ma figured even if she didn't get a job, at least she would have a shot at one. But the super didn't have good news.

"There are no job openings; I've got men with families to feed, who are laid off."

"My family has to eat, too, and my husband is too sick to go back to work. Give me his job, or any job; I'm strong. Give me a job no one else wants. I'll even clean toilets".

The super gave her a job, sorting rags in the rag room—and cleaning toilets. She didn't like cleaning toilets—hated it, in fact—but it was only for a couple hours out of the day. And a deal was a deal.

My sister Mary's husband built a small shed out of slab wood to shelter the cows for the first winter. In a week or two, Pa came home from the hospital. He was weak, and seemed a changed man. He told us the doctor said about a third of his heart muscle was dead. He walked slowly and smiled a lot. The heart attack mellowed him, making him a different person—at least for a while. I showed him the cart I'd made to replace the one he'd made me—the one that had burned up in the fire. I was proud of the job I'd done. The cart was an almost identical to the original. I waited for him to praise me.

Pa looked at the cart and smiled as if to say it was a nice try but not anywhere near as good as the one he'd made. I should have known, by then, that he was not anyone who liked to hand out approval. I think he was afraid I would get a swelled head. I would have liked to have had him praise me, but at least he was calm and was not yelling or hitting me.

Pa bought some fallen pine trees blown over by the hurricane the previous year in the woods next to our farm. I spelled him on the crosscut saw opposite Ma as we sawed the fallen pines into logs that were two or three feet thick. We cut logs after Ma came home from work, and on weekends.

One day, after taking a turn at the saw, I sat resting in the huge hole where the stump had pulled out. I leaned back against the uprooted tree stump. It was cool and comfortable. Pa stopped sawing when there was just a little bit left to cut. He called out to me. I answered from my resting place, and he almost had another heart attack. It would have been my final resting place if he hadn't stopped to check on me.

When the tree trunk was cut through, the stump slammed back into the hole with a resounding "whump" that would have crushed me flat. There would have been no way to raise the stump. Though Pa scolded me for nearly giving him another heart attack, I was glad he cared enough to be concerned about me.

Pa bought an old Buick car and had it made into a homemade tractor in place of the Reo that burned in the fire. He was through with horses. With the Buick tractor and a trailer, he hauled one or two logs at a time to a saw mill about 5 or 6 miles away, where they sawed them into boards.

There was no fire insurance on the barn. Neither would the adjuster allow any money for a new roof on the house. He said the roof was old and needed replacing anyway. It leaked more than ever after the fire.

Mr. Lambert's daughter, May, had gone out to collect money to help us. She had collected $18 when she ran into a crabby old tightwad who ranted and raved at her. She began crying and quit collecting. She apologized, but we were grateful and thanked her for her efforts. This was not a gift to the poor, this was a customary collection taken up for people who had had a fire.

Pa bought some used timbers for the barn framework. During the day, Pa marked timbers and roof rafters for the barn. We kids sawed them, so they would be ready to put into place. When Ma got home from work, we all pitched in to raise the framework a bit at a time. We sheathed the roof with pine boards sawed from the logs we cut and hauled to the saw mill.

Though the neighbors marveled that Pa was able to put up a barn using kids to build it, not a single neighbor offered to help. One of them said, "I have to laugh; you folks must work during the night, because when I get up each morning I see more of the barn up."

Some distant cousins read about the fire in the newspaper, and drove up from Connecticut to help finish building the barn and two hen houses. One of the cousins was like Mr. Taradana. When Pa yelled at me, he would say, "Let him come work with me; I'll handle him."

By the second fall after the fire, the animals had a snug place to winter over, and we stored hay inside.

Chapter 53: A New Mowing Machine

We cut the hay with our one-horse mower towed behind our homemade tractor. With a short cutter bar, it took forever to mow a field and it was quick to clog with grass. The Miller family, about a half mile away, had given up farming, to move to the city. Pa attended the auction. He had his eye on a two-horse McCormick mowing machine which was in good condition. He tried his best to show disinterest.

Bidding started at one dollar and quickly went up by quarters and halves to $4.00. The auctioneer kept up his hypnotic sing-song, "Four-four-four-four-who'll give me five, four-four-four and a quarter, have I got a quarter here? Quarter, quarter, quarter," he chanted, pointing from bidder to bidder. His sing-song chanting got me excited. I wanted Pa to win.

Pa kept bidding. Someone bid a quarter more and someone else quickly edged up another quarter. Bit by bit, the price got up to $5.00. Pa had just $6.00 and the way the auctioneer was egging the bidders on, it didn't look like Pa would be taking the McCormick mower home.

When the auctioneer asked who would bid $5.25, Pa called out "$6.00." Bidding stopped. The auctioneer tried to get it going again, but the spell was broken.

"Sold!" the auctioneer cried out, "for $6.00."

Pa triumphantly towed the McCormick home behind the tan Essex. I'd ridden our one horse mower, but the McCormick was much bigger. Pa moved the iron seat down to the last adjustment hole but my feet still didn't reach the foot rest. Pa drilled another hole, lower still. I could just barely touch my toes to the axle housing. By sitting on one side of the bump in the middle of the seat, I could just reach the lever to raise the cutter bar.

That evening, I fashioned a seat out of a board and bolted it through the perforated seat. That brought me forward and lower yet, making it easier to stay seated and lift with the lever.

Neighbors called it a disgrace--- having a boy of 10 riding a mowing machine where he could get thrown onto the cutter bar. Hearing, their outrage, made me quite proud. I was doing a man's job; a dangerous job, at that.

The machine made a ferocious racket with a bone-rattling vibration to match. The treacherous knives flashed back and forth on the cutter bar at lightning speed. One day Pa decided to expand a hay field into an area where we'd cleared brush. I found out how fearsome the McCormick's knives could be.

The McCormick went over a hump and lurched down into a hole. The mower catapulted me forward. I hung onto the cutter bar lever. But that just swung me around to fall straight for the cutter bar with the razor sharp knives flashing back and forth.

I thought I was a goner, and thought about the man in town who'd come home from mowing a field to find blood on the cutter bar. He had gone back to the field to find his two little children lying dead with their feet cut off. I was sure that would be me, too—cut to ribbons. And I thought how the neighbors would be down on Pa for having a boy do a man's work. But Pa managed to stop the tractor in time and the nicks and scrapes I got were minor.

"Guess we better not to try mowing here any more," he said. "Not worth it. Better to make it a calf pasture."

It made me happy to know he thought it wasn't worth risking my life or limbs to make more hay field. As it turned out, we really didn't need the extra hay field, that year. The heavy clay soil produced a good crop of hay. We had enough to make a second haystack next to the roofed one. Pa showed us how to round the top of the exposed stack to shed the rain, the way they did in the old country in Poland.

First, he planted a tall pole in the ground to keep the stack from toppling over. We stacked hay around the pole, straight up. At the top, he rounded the hay like an umbrella. That winter, we cut the hay from under the roofed stack with a hay knife, cutting it into neat rectangles. As we removed hay, we lowered the roof. The cows fed at the smaller rounded stack in a fenced area, eating away the hay at the lower level until it looked like a giant mushroom before the top came sliding down.

The following year the barn was ready at haying time. Pa designed the barn with drive-through doors. He'd drive the home-made tractor and load of hay into the barn where we'd unload it into hay mows. The exhaust pipe on the tractor had been removed, letting sparks fly out onto the ground.

Out in the field, one day, the tractor stalled. As I restarted it, the engine backfired through the carburetor. Some gasoline puked out and sparks from the tractor exhaust ignited the gasoline and hay lying on the ground. The fact that sparks could also ignite a fire in the barn worried Pa. Backing the wagon in the barn didn't work out. The four wheeled wagon didn't cooperate at all. From then on, Pa stationed one of us with a pail of water to douse any fire that might erupt—but it never did—though a pail of water might not have been at all adequate.

Haying was an important annual event, but I never thought about it ending—never thinking about the day we'd all be gone from home and Ma and Pa would be alone to carry on. We were always be too busy worrying that there'd be too much rain, or not enough, as the grass grew to maturity. Then we'd worry about the weather holding until the hay was cut, turned, dried, raked, piled into haycocks, loaded on the wagon and trundled to the safety of the barn.

We had neither radio nor daily paper to warn of rain. Pa got pretty good at predicting weather. He looked for signs. Dew on the spider webs on the lawn meant fair weather. No dew meant rain. He told us to look to the northwestern sky to see what the future held. But sometimes a sunny summer day would suddenly cloud over and black clouds threatened. We'd all work furiously to get the hay loaded and into the barn before big drops of rain splattered and lightening split the sky with thunderbolts.

On such a day, Pa kept us hopping, racing to beat the storm. Wet hay was ruined hay. We'd have to turn it by hand, again, to try drying it before it mildewed. Even then, it often turned musty and made poor feed. The cows did not like it and sometimes it made them cough.

One fine summer day, I'd been riding the mower all day in our rush to take advantage of fair weather. Ma sent the girls out with water and a fresh dill pickle from time to time to slake our thirst. All day, I strained to pull the mower lever, standing on the attached J shaped bracket, designed to help lift the heavy cutter bar. Pa would holler "Up, up," and motioned with his hand if I didn't lift the cutter bar high enough to suit him.

Late in the afternoon, he finally parked the tractor and I climbed down off the mower, tired and stiff. My ears roared and my whole body tingled from the constant noise and vibration. My back felt as if it were permanently bent in the shape of a fish hook. My legs didn't seem to want to move.

"What's the matter," Pa said in Polish.

That he noticed how tired and stiff I was, told me how much he appreciated me doing a man's work. That made it all worth it.

"Are the stones you're walking on so hot that they are burning the soles of your feet?"

It took a minute for me to realize his words were dripping with sarcasm. I faced him squarely.

"Next time, you ride that beast of a mower and fight that worn out lever, and I'll ride on the tractor saying, 'Up, up,' all day and we'll see if the stones aren't on fire under your feet!"

I spoke in English—forbidden, by him at home. But, I was so enraged that I was beyond caring what he'd do. I stood with my chin out, waiting for him to hit me. He stood looking at me as though he'd never seen me before, then turned and walked out to the field where we piled raked windrows into haycocks. We worked silently side by side. I felt I'd shown him I was a man that day, though I was only eleven.

The next day when we were mowing, he began calling out 'Up, up,' again, motioning for me to raise the cutter bar higher. Something took hold of me, again; I jumped off and yelled out for him to stop.

"If you think it's so easy, come back here and you try lifting the cutter bar, just once."

He looked at me as if I'd taken leave of my senses, again, to speak that way to him. He did not hit me, but took hold of the lever. He had great difficulty even lifting it a little. Before we cut another blade of grass, he repaired the worn linkage that very day. The cutter bar lifted much more easily. But Pa seemed at a loss on how to deal with me, and I found him looking at me with a puzzled look.

Our hay rake had a dump lever to pick up the ten foot wide row of curved teeth. Pa added a pair of boards sandwiching the teeth to keep them from bouncing, making it seem to weigh a ton when it came time work the dump lever.

When a foot pedal on the rake was depressed, a dog caught in a gear on the wheel hub. As the wheel turned, it lifted the heavy apparatus effortlessly to dump the hay. Pa told me to never depress the pedal. He had once tried stepping on it, not realizing it needed only a quick jab. By holding the pedal down, the rake continued to dump up and down as it jumped from cog to cog.

One day when he was gone, I tied a rope to the foot pedal and ran it under the frame back to the tractor. By giving the rope a quick tug, the pedal engaged the dump mechanism. It worked magically. I raked the hay into windrows and then straddled the windrows and raked them into haycocks. When he got home he was clearly puzzled at how I'd single handedly done so much work.

The next time he put me on the rake, I kept my hand on the lever so he wouldn't catch me using the foot pedal, in case he looked back. When I used the foot lever I rested my hand lightly on the hand lever, letting it move my arm back and forth. But when he looked back, I panicked and made the mistake of moving the lever after I'd engaged the foot lever. The dump apparatus dumped and dumped again. He stopped the tractor.

"See? What did I tell you? The foot pedal is no good. Why can't you listen to me? Why do you always have to try to do everything the lazy way?"

The next day when I got home from school, I found the shaft that engaged the dogs---gone—hack sawed through and removed.

Chapter 54: Ruptured Appendix

Ordinarily Pa got us up at 4 A.M. to go up into the hills of Leyden to pick all blueberries. Fortunately, my sister Lora did not go with us, one day, because she wasn't feeling well. Someone had left a gallon jug of bleach on the porch next to a couch. As sunlight beat down on the glass jug, it served as a magnifying glass. Lora spotted the couch smoldering. By the time she got water to douse the couch, flames were leaping high, but she got the fire out. After that narrow escape, Pa always left someone home to watch the farm.

When it came my turn to be watchman, I wanted to surprise everyone by cleaning the house. I worked furiously, sweeping, dusting, mopping, straightening things up, washing dishes, polishing the stove with stove blacking and getting the house in spotless order. I couldn't wait to see their looks of surprise when they walked in. But when they got home, no one noticed.

Pa helped Irene out of the car. She had not been feeling well when they left and, now, she looked deathly ill. Her face was white and she hung onto her side with her eyes half closed. She was sick—very sick. I helped Pa get her upstairs to bed. She just lay flat on her back with her eyes closed, hanging on to her side and moaning.

She had asked Pa if she could stay home that morning because she was sick. But Pa told her she'd feel better when she got some fresh air up in the hills. "There's no sense to go, if you stay home," he said. "You're the best picker."

So she went.

Climbing the hills tired Irene. As the day wore on, she felt sicker and sicker. When she said she could go on no longer, Pa said, "You can go down to the car, but don't go empty handed." He gave her two water pails full of blueberries to carry.

Irene could only carry the pails a short distance before she had to stop to rest. The distance became shorter and the rests longer. She was beginning to faint. She'd run a little way and set the pails down as darkness closed in. When she came to, she'd pick up the pails and run again, over and over, each time going a shorter distance, until she got to the car. She said she thought Pa would never come back to the car, and on the way home, she felt every bump in the road. Now, she just lay in her bed, moaning and looking deathly ill.

When Pa went to pick Ma up at work, we were sure he'd come back with a doctor. But he didn't. When Ma saw how sick Irene was, her eyes got big. She held Irene's hand and felt of her forehead. Ma's lips began to move. I knew she was praying for Irene to get well and not die. I prayed Ma would tell Pa to take Irene to a doctor. I thought my prayers were answered when Ma looked Pa in the eye.

"We've got to get Irene to a doctor."

"What's a doctor going to do? She's just got a belly ache. She'll be better by morning."

They tried physics and other remedies but Irene just kept moaning. When they used an enema on her, Irene shrieked in pain and moaned worse than ever. I kept thinking about Julia dying and I guess Ma did, too. She finally convinced Pa to take Irene to find a doctor at this late hour. By luck, they found Dr Wolanski still holding evening hours at his office, though it was 10 o'clock at night.

It didn't take long for the doctor to diagnose appendicitis. Pa took her to Franklin County Hospital while Wolanski rounded up a surgeon. After a conference, the doctors concluded that she was really too undernourished for an operation, but without it, she would surely die.

Irene never ate very much because she was so fearful of Pa. He demanded we eat in silence and that made her too nervous to eat very much. Soured milk and potatoes, which we often had for supper, always gave her trouble. The yogurt-like soured milk would come right back up. Ma knew of her problem and would often sneak Irene a dollop of sour cream which Irene could tolerate. To avoid Pa spotting it, Irene would quickly mix the cream in with the mashed potatoes.

In any event, Irene's chances of survival were not great. The doctors told Ma and Pa an operation was her only chance, slim as it was, then, wheeled Irene off to the operating room. The surgeon found that her appendix had ruptured and stomach contents had spilled into her abdominal cavity. After sewing her up, the doctor went to tell Ma and Pa that Irene had survived the operation. But they were gone. I guess Pa figured that there wasn't much they could do at the hospital; it was in the doctor's and God's hands. Besides, it was past bedtime and Ma had to go to work in the morning.

Later, when Irene found out they'd left the hospital to go home while she was being operated on, she felt hurt and abandoned. She spent a long time recovering in the hospital. It took even longer to recover from the feeling of abandonment. We visited Irene after blueberry picking, and always brought her a basket of berries until she was discharged.

Irene had a drain in her side all summer to allow septic fluids to drain off. She spent a week or two recuperating with our sister, Elizabeth, in Great

Barrington and a couple of weeks with Johnny in upstate New York where he managed a big turkey farm.

The incision still had not healed over by the time school started, and Irene was too weak to attend. She missed the first month. It took a year, or more, for Irene to recover her strength.

Chapter 55: Chickens

Pa felt stronger after his heart attack, but the company doctor said Pa didn't pass his physical exam and couldn't go back to work at the paper mill just yet.

I don't know if the temporarily diminished blood supply affected Pa's judgment, but he got the great idea of raising chickens after looking through some brightly colored seed catalogues that also featured mail-order chicks. He immediately sent off for a thousand chicks.

A few weeks later, the mailman drove into the yard, causing quite a stir, because he usually left mail up at the mail box a quarter mile away and only delivered important mail like registered letters and packages to the door. His car was stuffed to the ceiling with cardboard cartons carrying baby chicks. Fluffy yellow heads stuck out of half-inch round portholes, peeping shrilly like excited tourists arriving on the Queen Mary. It was early spring and very cold, so we brought them into the house.

The brooder house wasn't quite ready, yet, so Pa built a big box on stilts, about six feet wide and eight feet long. It was about four feet high and just the right height for viewing the little golden chicks. Pa cut a hole in the middle of this contraption and fastened an inverted white enameled milk pail to the floor of it. A tall kerosene lamp place under the pail provided heat for our fluffy guests.

We were fascinated by the noisy chicks, peeping shrilly, and watched them for hours. My mother was less than enthusiastic about turning her living room into a chicken coop and their stay was short-lived. One more day of peeping, she said, and she'd take refuge in the brooder house, herself. To our dismay, the shrieklings were transferred to the brooder house in their ocean liner boxes.

The chicks grew fast—all except for the runts. Big chicks pecked the runts when they tried to feed and the runts did not grow. They came dashing out of hiding, screeching and flapping their wings as they ran the gauntlet of larger chicks pecking them. They would peck a few quick bites of feed while more chicks gathered to peck them unmercifully. They fell farther and farther behind, until they were dwarfed by the larger ones, growing thinner and weaker until we finally found them pecked to death, one by one. Pa began wringing the necks of the runts, even those just a little behind in growth. I begged him to stop.

"If the runts were kept apart from the others and could get enough to eat, I know they'd grow big and strong."

167

I didn't think ahead to the time they matured. I don't know what I thought would become of them if they had grown big and strong—I just wanted to save them.

"All right, I'll let you do that; it will teach you a good lesson," Pa said.

I segregated the runts in a big dog house, and made them a fenced area, but they never did catch up.

One evening I checked on my charges, huddled together for the night in their haven, where I'd fed, named, and kept my friends safe from all harm. There was Gimpy who had a bad leg, Whitey who had a few white wing feathers, but never matured fully out of the down stage, and the others, all named for their characteristics or imperfections.

Pa came to the enclosure. I didn't know what he was going to do, but I feared the worst.

"See? They're still runts, like I told you. They'll never amount to anything; just eat feed for nothing."

With that, he wrung their necks, every one. I was devastated.

The other pullets continued to grow. About half of them turned out to be roosters. We sold those as broilers, leaving the others for egg production. Production would have been great if we'd wanted to produce manure. By the middle of summer, the farm seemed in danger of being paved over with the stinking stuff. Ma urged Pa to fence the chickens as far away from the house as possible. He didn't need much urging and fenced them way out by the woods.

One night apparently rabid foxes got into the fenced area and went on a killing spree. They maimed more than they killed. Chickens lay scattered over the ground, dead or dying from bites to their body. Pa told us to gather up the dead chickens while he put water on to boil. Without refrigeration, the meat would soon be sure to spoil. We scalded the feathers and plucked the chickens clean, cut them up, cooked, and canned them. When the dead ones were all canned, Pa killed the wounded ones and we began canning those, also, never realizing the danger of salmonella, or rabies from the foxes.

Ma had been up since 4:30 that morning, when she'd brought Pa his breakfast in bed, walked more than a mile of her trip to the paper mill and worked until five in the afternoon. After a hurried supper, she began helping cut and can chickens. The hour grew late and the pile of chickens still loomed large. Everyone was tired from working all day and half the night. Pa grew irritable and began criticizing Ma. She remained silent, jaws clenched. He kept it up. At last, she turned to him, brandishing the knife she was using.

"One more word out of you," she said, pointing the knife at his chest for emphasis, "And you'll get it, with this knife."

He stepped back, astonished. She'd never stood up to him like that before. I stepped between them and calmed her down. I felt depressed that they were bickering, and at the same time felt admiration for the way she stood up to him.

We finished canning the last of the chickens in the early hours of the morning. Pa seemed to regard Ma with more respect after that, especially when she had a knife in her hand. We moved the surviving chickens to the safety of the hen house. That was not the end of controversy over chickens.

With World War II heating up, a labor shortage developed and Pa was able to pass the physical exam for work at the mill, the company doctor having apparently misplaced his stethoscope for the duration of the war. The coop-full of laying hens posed a problem. Who would take care of them? Pa asked Emmy to quit school to tend to them. She balked and Pa made her life miserable.

"What you want with school—if you can read, write and know numbers; what's the use of it, to go more? You probably going to get married pretty soon, anyway, and then it's all for nothing."

Pa held a dim view of education. He had quit school after just one day. The Russian teacher in his school in Poland caught him speaking Polish, which was forbidden. She made him spend the day kneeling on dried peas, leading him to decide he'd learned enough. His father let him stay home. "You can learn to be a carpenter, like me, and earn a good living."

After immigrating to America, Pa attended night school long enough to learn to sign his name, learn to read Polish and to do simple arithmetic. School beyond the basics was a waste of time, in his estimation—particularly for a girl.

But Emmy had her heart set on being the first in the family to graduate from high school. Soon, she left home to take a job as housekeeper and maid, continuing to attend high school, mornings. The lady of the house entertained often, with parties that sometimes lasted into the wee hours of the morning. By the time the party mess was cleaned up and the dishes done, it would often be nearly time to head off to school. With no time to study, Emmy fell behind in her studies, grew discouraged and quit school a few months short of graduation.

When Pa learned of her failure to graduate, he rebuked her. "See? You didn't finish high school, anyway. So why couldn't you quit when I asked you to?"

Meanwhile, Pa had proposed Irene a deal—if she would take a year off to tend the flock, she could resume school the following year. As an added incentive, he said he'd buy her May Lambert's Model A Ford as soon as Mae traded it in. Irene complied. The Model A Ford was a classy little coupe with tinted windows and a chrome grille.

With both Ma and Pa working, and money coming in from the sale of poultry and eggs, life improved. With meat rationing, we were able to sell any chickens that stopped laying eggs. No one asked the price; they just wanted the chicken. It wasn't unusual to have people come to the farm looking for chickens, or butter, and show gratitude for the privilege of paying exorbitant prices. Pa got out of debt, had a new roof put on the house and accumulated some savings.

One payday, Pa stopped for a little celebration of his new-found prosperity. He came home all smiles and breathing rather heavily through his nose. He stated that since things were going so well, he was going to start paying Irene for tending the chickens and grandly handed her a dollar—her first week's allowance. He turned to me.

"Since you only help her after school, you get 50 cents."

Later, Irene and I talked about the turn of fortunes.

"Life would be perfect if they'd quit drinking," I said.

"Joe, it's never going to happen. Don't rock the boat. Things are good now. We're getting an allowance; everyone's happy, keep quiet—don't rile him. He'll only get mad."

But I wouldn't listen and approached Pa about quitting drinking. Irene was right.

"Why you---I give you money, and you want to keep a working man from a glass of beer to relax after a hard days work. That's gratitude. You never get one penny more from me."

During the winter, our high school bus driver drove a bus-load of Gill kids to the Highland Park skating rink in Greenfield on Friday evenings. Irene loved to skate. She took her ice skates and boarded the bus. But when the bus got to the rink she'd shove them under the bus seat and run to the house where Emmy worked.

Irene would let herself in the back door and climb the steep stairs to the unheated attic which served as Emmy's "room." Rough rafters rose to the peak and nails white with frost stuck through the roof. A bare light bulb hung from a beam, illuminating the odds and ends of stored household goods. Irene usually found Emmy under the covers, keeping warm. Irene would join her in bed, and they'd talk and laugh. All too soon, it would be time for Irene to race back to catch the bus before it left for home.

Though Pa was still angry at Emmy for not dropping out to take care of the chickens, he wasn't so angry that he didn't come around each week, to collect her $3 in wages. The woman who employed Emmy saw what was happening and confronted Pa. "Those are her wages and I don't want you coming around to take them anymore."

Emmy began saving to buy Ma the gasoline washing machine. As soon as Emmy saved up a down payment, she hot-footed it down to Sears and Roebuck to arrange for delivery of the washer she'd promised to buy Ma. The payments were $5 a month.

The day the washer arrived, Ma's eyes glistened and she couldn't stop smiling. She put water on the stove to heat before the installer finished boring a hole in the floor for the exhaust. When Emmy got home, they sat in the kitchen, side by side, and listened to that mechanical marvel humming its "Chunka-chunk song.

Chapter 56: Burn Doctor & New Car

We got a new car a year or two after the barn burned. It all came about when Pa went out to drive the tan Essex to work. The engine ran but the wheels would not move. Pa went off to work on foot. A fellow worker picked him up and dropped him off for a few days.

Meanwhile I got badly burned when I was horsing around. Even though I was way too big to be acting like a little kid, I was under the kitchen stove with Louis. It was a fairly high legged stove and I was able to squeeze underneath it. I crawled out the front of the stove just as Gladys was getting a kettle of boiling water. She tended to react dramatically in situations like this, and dropped the kettle of boiling water on my back. I jumped up screaming, and reached around to put my hand on my back. My shirt stuck to my back imprinting the image of my hand. Some of the skin came off along with the shirt. When Pa came home, I begged him to take me to a doctor. He didn't reply.

The next say after he left for the mill, Ma said, "Pa will bring the doctor home with him when he comes home from work." In the meantime Ma slathered the burn with salted butter. The salt only made the blistered skin hurt worse. All day, I waited.

That night, when my father came in the house a man followed him.

"Here's Pa with the doctor," Ma said.

Both of the men smelled of beer. The "doctor" needed a shave and his clothes were soiled with grease. He held out a jar of Noxema.

"Here, kid, I brung you some medicine."

The man started smearing the cream on my back with his dirty hand, but Irene, who had not left home yet, took the jar from him and said she'd do it. The "doctor" left and Pa sat down to supper.

The next day, Pa went off on foot to Howe's garage in Riverside. He returned with Mr. Howe's son Kenny, who informed Pa that the Essex's cork-faced clutch had shredded into crumbs and now lay at the bottom of the clutch housing.

"The clutch could be replaced but would cost more than the car is worth," Kenny said.

"Better to junk it," Pa said, seeming to rejoice at the bad news. I hated to see our friend go to the scrap yard. But Pa apparently saw it as an opportunity to buy a new car with a clear conscience.

Pa got in Kenny's car, and off they went. A used car salesman gave Pa a ride home. In the days that followed, salesmen began arriving to show Pa cars.

Pa picked a sleek Ford V-8. He became very animated as he told of his shrewd dealings with car salesmen as he tried out different cars. He rejected them all, until he spotted the black beauty that now stood in the yard. It had plenty of power, speed, and style, he said. And now, having out-foxed the used car weasels, the car was his—his and the bank's, anyway. But he quickly went on to talk about the nice heater and defroster. No more freezing to death as we did in the Essex, he said. The one thing he neglected to consider was that it had mechanical brakes, notorious for their poor braking ability. I wondered how much Pa's friend Charlie's boasting about his powerful Ford V-8 truck had influenced Pa. I suspected it had more than a little to do with it.

I felt a pang of sadness to see our shabby but familiar tan Essex, still shedding wisps of red paint, being hauled away hanging from the tow truck's hook. I had hoped Pa would push the tan Essex behind the barn as he had done with the old green one. But Pa was not in the least distressed at its departure. Not only did the black beauty replacement Ford have a heater and defroster, but best of all it did not appear to have a skin condition like that of the shaggy beast Pa had created, now headed for the junk yard. Having paid out a fair amount for the fancy Ford, it was necessary to cut down on food expenditures to make the payments. We had soup of some kind, with potatoes, every night. Often it was brown soup, or kapusta--cabbage and sauerkraut soup, day in and day out. Once in a while Ma made a cream soup using juice from the sauerkraut barrel. One evening after another meal of kapusta, I didn't feel that I could stomach another mouthful. We sat crowded around the table, kids sitting on benches. Ma sat in a straight chair when she was not jumping up to serve food. Pa sat in his captain's chair eating sausage links and mashed potatoes. He needed more nourishing food to recuperate, and besides it was always important to have the breadwinner well-fed.

"Kapusta, again?" I asked

No response. I ladled cabbage and sauerkraut soup into a bowl, adding mashed potatoes. I chose a spoon from the coffee can filled with silverware that served as a center piece. The spoon had a large area of silver plating worn away. I put it back and selected another one. I hated the taste of the spoon's iron base metal.

"Don't be so fussy," Pa said.

I didn't reply, not wanting to start anything. Mealtime was a time of silence. Kids were supposed to silent. "Just shut up and eat," was the rule.

Pa liked mashed potatoes in the soup. Without teeth, it made the soup easier to gum. I finished the kapusta and mashed potatoes, then looked at Ma, and took a chance.

"Anything else? I'm still hungry."

Her eyes went to Pa and then at me, sending me a warning. Irene also gave me a quick glance, a sign to keep quiet. She quickly looked down. I knew she was terrified and couldn't eat, terrified he'd lose his temper and take it out on me. Irene was Pa's favorite. She didn't talk back to him, didn't argue, just listened and complied. He praised her as the obedient and dutiful daughter. He never knew how she really felt about him.

She stopped eating and coughed---another warning. I disregarded it and looked Pa in the eye.

"Hungry?" he said. "Have another bowl. There's more on the stove.

"I'm sick of kapusta; we had it all week."

"Maybe that's the trouble," he said, his face flushing with anger. "Maybe if you didn't have it for a week—had nothing to eat for a week—you wouldn't be complaining."

I thought he was going to go for the strap. But he didn't. He began to lecture.

"I was just about your age when the Cossacks came riding into the village and took my Tata right off the roof of the barn he was building. Took him away and threw him in a box car before he knew what was happening. And off to Siberia, he went. No letting him go home to tell us where he was going or to get warm clothing or anything. Didn't even let him tell anyone so they could go and tell your Babka so she could say goodbye. Dirty rotten Ruskies." His eyes blazed, and he sat silent, lost in thought. He began, again.

"Bieda. That's what it was—bieda! (misery). The Russian soldiers would stop at a house and say, "Feed us." And the people would give them what food they had in the house for fear they'd kill them.

"After the Cossacks left, people came out of hiding and came to tell my Matka. She cried, and put her hands together saying, 'Oh Jesus, have mercy on us'."

I tried not to let Pa see me sigh.

"We didn't keep many animals or raise crops--just a small garden. Tata made a good living. He was a good carpenter, and a good man. He came to Ameryka when he was young, learned to build, new style. Lumber is dear in Poland. Everybody wants him to build to save lumber and save money. Sometimes he takes vegetables, or meat, for pay. Always, they feed him, and give him some kind of food to take home—a shame on them if they don't. So we have plenty to eat without farming or having a big garden."

He smiled at the memory of affluence in his former life. I wished Pa had learned more carpentry so we could have something besides kapusta seven days a week.

"But then, it all stopped with Tata in Siberia—working like a slave, building jail houses for prisoners---people in prison for committing no crimes, like Tata. You think you got it bad? We had it really bad. Not so bad as he, though. He had no warm clothes, no decent food, working long hours, and he sees other prisoners die from cold and hunger, from sickness, and overwork."

Pa pushed back his chair; he was done eating. I eyed the sausage drippings on his plate. If we were good, we got to sop up the drippings with a crust of bread. "They died on the train going to Siberia, they died at the camps, and they died coming back. Tata didn't die, but his health was broken. "While he was away in Siberia, I was the oldest, maybe ten or twelve—and there was my younger sister and baby brother. We were ashamed to beg from neighbors. But soon, they came—a little something here and a little something there. We got enough to get by until he came back home—just barely. We went to bed hungry, more than once.

You learn not to worry what you eat---just so long as there's something to eat. Your grandfather came back, so skinny, dressed in rags like a scarecrow; his health broken."

I began to feel uncomfortable and went to the stove for another bowl of kapusta and mashed potatoes. I gave it a shot of ketchup to add a little zing. It didn't taste so bad, after all. At least we weren't starving. I sat down and Pa continued; his anger spent in the telling of the story.

Though Grandpa was glad to be home, he no longer was up to the strenuous work of carpentry. "Son, there is no future here," he says. "Better you should go to Ameryka. He gave me about 50 cents and a new pair of boots, telling me to go to Germany to earn ship passage."

Pa told how he cut off the tops of the boots to make them lighter. He gave the tops away to another boy, and set out on foot from his village of Zalesie which was near the Russian border. He traversed the width of Poland on foot, and on to Germany, sometimes getting a ride on a passing wagon.

I thought what it would be like leaving home as a boy to travel on foot across unfamiliar countryside to a foreign land where I didn't know the language and across the sea to another strange land where people spoke yet another language unknown to me. I realized my father must have been scared and discouraged at times during his lonely journey and I felt ashamed for complaining about eating kapusta day in and day out.

"When I come to Ameryka to live with Voey (Uncle), I work and save, and give him money to send home to my family. When they have enough money to send my sister—she is younger than me—she comes to this country. She tells me that Voey sends very little money, says I spend it on foolishness. I get mad that he lies to my family, so I move out. I send money for my younger brother to come to Ameryka but he stayed home to take care of our Tata and Matka in their old age. So I send him money when times were good and sometimes when times are not so good."

Chapter 57: Life Changes

One summer day Pa was trying to remove a cellar window to air out the basement. Much to Pa's irritation, the window, swollen with dampness, refused to budge. "Go outside and push on it," he ordered. When I got outside, there was nowhere to push, other than the window panes. I hesitated, not knowing what to do.

"Push the window!" my father yelled from the cellar. I wanted to tell him there was no window frame to push on—that it was all hidden. But I was afraid he'd get angrier. I put my hand flat on a window pane so that the pressure would be spread out, hoping it would not break. I pushed.

The glass broke with a crash. My hand went through the window. Pa turned around and headed up the cellar stairs. I figured that he was going to thrash me, but good. My hand felt numb. I looked down. My wrist was spurting blood. I clamped my left hand over the cut to try to stop the bleeding, and ran inside the house.

Pa came charging up out of the cellar. Afraid he could hit me, I let go of my wrist to show him what had happened. Blood spurted onto his shirt. He grabbed his chest and fell over onto the kitchen table, groaning. The blood on his shirt made me think of Julia dying and I figured I was going to die, too. Slashed wrists were among the options in the magazine showing suicide options.

Irene got a clean rag and tied it over the cut as tight as she could. Blood soaked through. She added another rag. Blood soaked through, again. She added more layers, tying them as tight as she could, until the blood stopped seeping through.

"My fingers won't move."

"Don't try to make them move. It'll only make matters worse."

"What's going to happen?" I asked Irene. I was scared.

"Pa, you've got to get Joe to the hospital, he can't move his fingers."

Moaning, Pa stood up and headed out the door to the car. Irene followed. She didn't say anything but I could tell from her face that things didn't look good. Pa took off down the road. He usually didn't drive very fast, but he didn't waste any time that day. He roared off down the road, but forgot to shift out of 2nd gear. We drove along for miles, engine roaring. I stood it as long as I could.

"Pa, you still got it in 2nd gear."

He looked down, shifted into high, and we began making better time with a lot less noise. There was no emergency room at the hospital. A nurse grabbed a doctor making morning rounds. The doctor took a look at Pa and then at me.

"Well, well, well. Can't be that bad. I don't see much blood on you. There's more on your dad than there is on you."

The doctor began unwrapping the rags. When he removed the last layer, blood spurted.

"I'm going to have to have some help on this one," he said to the nurse. He tied a rubber tube tightly around my forearm to stop the bleeding. The nurse hurried away, white uniform swishing.

"Who tied the rags on your arm?"

"My sister, Irene."

"Well, she did a good job," the doctor said. How old is she?"

"She's 13," I said, wondering why he didn't quit talking and get going on sewing me up. I tried to move my fingers again.

"Don't try moving your fingers. The tendons are cut. We've got to go up after them and pull them back down to hook them up again."

The nurse came back with another doctor. She held a sheet up so I couldn't see what they were doing. I could feel them cutting up inside my forearm and it hurt so I could hardly stand it. I let out a little moan.

"We've got to give him something to knock him out. This is going to take a while."

Someone put a mask over my face.

"Take a deep breath."

A strong hospital smell began to choke me half to death. My hearing became acute. The last thing I remembered was one of the doctors saying, "What've you got on the river raw." There was a popular nonsense song with reference to river raw. I drifted off trying to figure out what the doctor was talking about. I awoke with my wrist bandaged and my mouth dry. My parents came to see me that evening. I was afraid Pa would be awful mad at me for breaking the window and running up a big hospital bill, but he didn't seem mad at all. The arm got more swollen and sore by the day. The doctor squeezed pus out of the cut every morning. He'd start up by my elbow and work his way down to the cut on my wrist. Tears came to my eyes. I gritted my teeth to keep from making a sound.

"I know it hurts," he said, "but I have to get the pus out."

Nurses put hot water bottles wrapped in wet towels on my arm when the doctor wasn't squeezing pus. Pa and Ma didn't come every day, but my older sister Emmy did. No one could ask for a better sister. Emmy was married by then, and had begun working at the Greenfield Tap and Die inspecting machine gun ammunition boxes. World War II was on and the factory was turning out defense work. Emmy's husband had been drafted into the Army. He talked a lot about all the great things he'd done and even greater things he would do in the future. The Army stationed him in Colorado, much to my relief.

The GTD was not far from the hospital. Every noon, Emmy skipped lunch so she could run over to see me. One day, she brought me a fruit basket filled with all my favorite fruit. I got a lump in my throat. I couldn't talk and my eyes filled up. I loved Emmy, dearly. She was six years older and more of a mother than sister to me.

One day, Ma came in to see me. She was alone. Pa was out in the hall talking with the doctor.

"They going to cut off you hand," Ma whispered. "You got the blood poisoning."

At first, I was scared, especially by the whispering. But, then, I figured I'd be like Magrini, doing things like changing a tire all by myself with just one hand and having people say, "look at that guy, will you." And I would say, "I'm no cripple." Maybe the doctor would put a hook in place of the hand and I could be tough like "The Hook" in comic books. No one messed with The Hook.

The only part I didn't like was the blood poisoning. There wasn't much you could do about blood poisoning, back then, except die. A hook wasn't scary, but I wasn't ready to die just yet. I was getting sick of having my arm hurt when they squeezed the pus out every morning.

One day, as the doctor mashed on my arm, I asked him when I was going home.

"Pretty soon," he said.

"When's pretty soon?"

"Oh, a couple of days."

Later, I asked the nurse how many a couple was.

"A couple is usually two, like a couple is two people."

Two days later was Saturday. My regular nurse was off. I told the new nurse I was going home.

"Who said that?"

"The doctor."

"Oh really?"

"Sure thing. Saturday's the day. I can't wait to get out of here."

"Where are your clothes?"

"I don't know. Someone put them away when I came in."

Soon the nurse came back with my clothes—the old clothes I wore the day I came in. She held them out away from her white uniform.

"These clothes aren't very clean," she said, frowning. "And there's blood on them, too.   How come your folks didn't bring you clean clothes? And where's your underwear?"

"I don't have any".

"You don't wear underwear?" Her eyebrows went up.

"Just long-johns in the winter. But it's too hot for them in summer."

"Isn't it uncomfortable without underwear?"

"Nah, doesn't bother me a bit."

I was embarrassed enough about my dirty clothes without admitting it was uncomfortable without underwear. She just shook her head, helped me get dressed, and put a clean sling on my arm. I headed down the long dark corridor and out the door. I walked to Emmy's house, a couple miles away. Saturday was her day off. Her husband was still in Colorado, so she was glad to have company. Emmy took one look at me and said, "Let's go up street."

She bought me new pants and shirt. I put them on, right there in the store dressing room, and stuffed the dirty old clothes in a bag.

We went to a movie, and afterward had a sandwich and an ice cream soda at the Liggett's drug store soda fountain on Main Street. I was having the time of my life. This was the first time I had ever had an ice cream soda.

Emmy took me to Woolworth's 5 & 10, and bought me some kind of board game. It felt like Christmas morning. But I was happiest to just be with her.

When we got back to her house, a police cruiser pulled into the driveway. The cop said they had been looking all over for me. When Emmy drove me back to the hospital, the staff was all worked up—"blood poisoning... wasn't supposed to be out of the hospital... should have been having hot packs," and all that. They acted like it was all her fault. I was in trouble with everyone, including the doctor. The first thing he did was to give my arm a good squeezing. My hand had a "pins-and-needle" feeling and the squeezing hurt terrible. He did not spare me.

A few days later, the skin all peeled off my hand and stayed pale purple for a long time. Eventually doctors got the blood poisoning under control. I don't know what medicine they used, if any, besides the hot packs, but I was well enough to go home.

My hand still had the pins and needles feeling, and even though it was numb, it still hurt to touch it. The doctor gave me some iodized salve to apply each day. I don't know if I was supposed to see him for a checkup, and I don't know if he ever got paid.

One of the stitch holes opened up and juice started coming out. I didn't want to tell anyone for fear they'd start squeezing my arm again. So, I squeezed it myself. The hole didn't heal over for about a year. My fingers were numb and stiff for years after that, but I learned to write left handed, just as Magrini had done.

After a year or so, I got enough feeling in the injured hand to switch back to writing with my right hand. But the nerves didn't grow back correctly, so that when I cut myself in one place, it hurts somewhere else. The feeling never entirely returned in three fingers, and reflex action never returned in any of the hand. When I touched a hot stove, I would get some wicked burns before I took my hand away. The burns were slow to heal because of poor circulation. But I learned to be careful and the numbness never got in the way of anything I wanted to do. Like Magrini, I knew I could work around it.

I think one of the reasons I felt so close to Emmy was that when Ma and Pa went away for the afternoon or took off for days or even weeks at a time, it was Emmy who took care of us. She was only 12 when they began leaving her in charge, but because I was 6, she seemed all grown up to me.

I'll always remember her the day she was leaving to walk to grammar school. That was before I'd begun first grade. She wished me happy birthday and gave me the customary spanking. She just gave me a few love pats but she called it "spanking". I was already resentful of getting spanked at every turn and began throwing stones at her. She just dodged the stones and laughed good-naturedly.

Emmy looked after both us and the farm animals when our parents were gone. She was cheerful even when I knew she was scared to be alone with all that responsibility. She kept her sunny disposition and never complained.

Peddlers and strange characters would sometimes come to the farm. When they found out we'd been left alone and our parents weren't coming back for a good long time, they'd begin to look around with shifty eyes. It gave me shivers down my spine, and I was glad she was there to guard us.

One day, when we spotted a weird character walking down the road, Emmy told us to hide. She didn't answer the door when he knocked. We peeked out the window as the man prowled around the barn area.

"Keep quiet," she whispered. "Don't let him see us. He'll think no one's home and he'll go away." We scarcely dared to breathe. Soon he tired of rummaging and left without taking anything. Leaving us to fend for ourselves, made me feel that our parents had little regard for our safety. Having Emmy to guard us against all evil endeared her to me. I loved her with all my heart. When we got sick, it was Emmy who took care of us and comforted us. When I had a high fever, I had a tendency to hallucinate or sleep walk. One night I went to sleep feeling terribly sick and woke up feeling rested and refreshed next morning.

"How'd you sleep last night?" she asked.

"Oh, wonderful; I feel so much better."

Emmy smiled.

"What's so funny?" I asked, wondering why she had dark circles under her eyes.

"You hollered your head off and were going wild all night—even tried to jump out the window," she said with a laugh.

Though she was good natured with a ready smile, someone I could confide in. It was a sad day when she left home. I felt lonely and depressed after she left. Her rare visits home were a special treat.

Irene, who was two years older than me, took over Emmy's role as best she could after Emmy left home. She cooked meals, looked after us, and sometimes even baked a cake from scratch at age twelve. She had the job of filling the kerosene lamps, trimming the wicks and cleaning the soot from the glass lamp chimneys with crumpled newspaper.

Remembering Emmy's experience with the stove flaring up, Irene didn't dare build a fire in the stove or light the lamps, the first time our parents took off somewhere. We waited in the dark—cold and hungry until they came home.

Chapter 58: Good News

I was happy to have Irene living at home after her long convalescence. We got along very well and we also both got along well with Emmy, too. Irene and Emmy had an especially close relationship after the two of them had once nearly drowned one winter when they had fallen through the ice while skating. But I would soon lose Irene as she felt compelled to leave home as Emmy had. And it was all over chickens.

The September after Irene's year off to take care of the chickens ended, Irene got dressed for school. "Where do you think you're going?" Pa demanded.

Irene looked scared. "I'm going back to school like you promised."

He did his best to persuade Irene to drop out for good. He tried cajoling and bribing her, though he'd already reneged on his promise to buy her May Lambert's Model A Ford. Irene could not be swayed in her determination to finish high school. She went up to the corner and caught the bus.

Pa was hostile toward Irene after that and she soon left home. She got a part time job at Liggett's drugstore, and moved in with Mary, Ma's daughter by her first husband, our half sister, who was now married. At the same time I was happy to see Irene pursue her dream, I was sad to see her leave. One of the last moments we shared together at the farm was disheartening. Ma announced that she had some wonderful news. "This is for Irene, only," she said, unable to conceal her utter delight. "But you might as well hear it, too. The doctor says I have the change of life and I can't have any more children! Isn't that wonderful?"

"Yeah, I guess it is, Ma," Irene said.

Ma didn't seem to sense our feelings of guilt, dismay—and rejection. She'd always been so happy when Johnny came to visit that we thought her feelings of love enveloped us, too. Being so elated at not being able to have any more of us came as a jolt..

Whenever Ma got word that Johnny was coming to visit, she'd bustle about getting ready. She'd prepare sweet potatoes for him and him alone. She'd put on a clean dress and set the house in order for the big day. It was as if she were expecting the Dalai Lama. I thought some of that love was extended to us. I hadn't expected any of us to bring her that much joy, but it hit me like a punch in the stomach that we were so unwanted—that we had burdened her like a dozen kittens dragging at a mother cat, though I'm sure we had.

Though I knew that she'd been having babies for decades, ever since she was a teenager and had to work hard, I wanted to hear her say she loved us, just the same—that we brought her happiness like the family in <u>Cheaper by the Dozen.</u> I wanted to hear her say she was sad she couldn't have any more children to love and that she was sad to have that time end. Seeing her so happy at not being able to bear any more children made me want to run away, to hide somewhere. I envied Irene and wished I could leave home, too.

It was lonely at the farm with both Irene and Emmy gone. I missed the times Irene and I worked together doing farm chores or planned birthday parties when Pa and Ma would be away—the way she'd bake a cake, decorate it and invite kids for a quick birthday party, then clean up before our folks got home, the way Emmy had done before. It was nice to know that someone cared.

Late one winter night when I was on the way home from visiting friends, I decided to risk taking a shortcut across a flooded swamp. The ice held fine until I got to the brook. I could hear the rubbery ice cracking and knew it would never hold me where the ice would be thinner over the swift running brook.

I lay face down to distribute my weight and worked my way across in a swimming motion. When I stood up on the other side, my foot went through the ice and I felt water fill my shoe. I ran home, pants leg freezing. When I got home, I thought everyone would be asleep, but I found Emmy there. She had come to visit, and had waited for me, worried that I'd fallen through the ice. Ma told her where I'd gone, and Emmy figured I would probably try to take the shortcut.

She scolded me for crossing the brook alone, and reminded me about the time she and Irene nearly drowned falling through the ice on that very same brook. She didn't come right out and say she loved me, but she didn't have to—I knew by the way she scolded me and hugged me and told me she didn't want anything to happen to me.

Gladys had run away, by then—where, she'd gone, no one knew. Now, there were just two other kids, besides me at home—Lora, two years younger and Louis four years younger than me. Pa had long since given up his dreams of regaining prosperity. His heart disease, ulcers, hard times, poor decisions, and bad luck had all taken the fire out of his burning ambitions. I sometimes felt as depressed as he did.

Chapter 59: Turning Point

With criticism at home and continued harassment by the nasty new teacher at school, life looked pretty bleak. My marks nose dived. But, just when I thought school would be a nightmare forever, our red brick school house closed for good. Instead of having neighborhood schools with eight grades, the Gill schools were consolidated with the grades split up so that teachers taught two grades instead of eight. A Pontiac station wagon served as a bus to take me to Sunnyside School on the other side of Gill.

After studying my school record, my new teacher, Miss Quintillio, an enthusiastic red head, asked me why I did so poorly the previous year in fifth grade when I'd done so well before that. I didn't know what to say. She said she would help me get caught up. But she didn't need to. My marks went right back up.

Miss Quintillio lifted our spirits by banging out lively tunes on the school piano while we all sang. When she praised me, I felt as though I could accomplish anything. My only problem was being a newcomer, an outsider. The attention she gave me brewed resentment in the other boys.

One day, Miss Quintillio asked us to draw a picture of a panda bear. The crayon virtually swept around the paper by itself. When she praised me, the other kids asked me to help them draw theirs. I cranked out panda bears pictures, left and right. When the kids passed their pictures in, the teacher saw that they all looked pretty much alike and made the kids draw them over again with no help from me. Though she chided me for giving too much help, it felt good to be reprimanded for doing something well. I was the happiest kid in school—maybe in the world.

A photographer came to take school photos for twenty five cents each. Pa wouldn't buy any—saying it was a waste of money. But Miss Quintillio bought two---one for me and one for herself. She said I looked like a cute little bozo. I treasured that photo. Gladys took the photo to show friends and somehow lost it. I never saw the picture, again.

The other boys didn't like Miss Quintillio buying me my picture and, worse yet, announcing that she was buying one for herself, too. During recess, the other boys started mocking me, calling me "Cute little Bozo" and "Teacher's pet", and started pushing me around. I had started school at age five, so I was younger than the other sixth graders, but I was strong from working on the farm. I could handle them, one at a time—even the bigger ones. But, they ganged up, pinned me down and tickled me until I laughed, then spit in my mouth. They took off my pants and gave them to a girl. I was wearing long johns that were pretty gray looking. The girl brought my pants to me. I was mortified to have the kids see me in dirty long underwear, never mind that particular girl. I could scarcely face her after that. I wanted to die.

The ring leader wasn't done with me yet. When I began to play with a basketball, he demanded I give it to him. I had made the mistake of telling him earlier that the dentist Ma had taken me to had cautioned me about biting down on hard food and to be careful not to bump the tooth because it had an abscess.

The ringleader began punching me in the mouth. I didn't want to let go of the ball, and tried to defend myself with one hand. It didn't work. He pounded my mouth, unmercifully. Next day my face was so swollen I couldn't eat and my right eye closed completely.

The abscess made me so sick I stayed home in bed. After the other kids went off to school, the house was quiet. Soon, I heard Pa's footsteps on the stairs. He seldom came upstairs and I felt honored by this special occasion, figuring he was going to take me to the doctor.

He sat on the bed next to me. "I suppose you want to go to the doctor."

"Yes, I feel awful sick."

Just knowing he was concerned for me and was going to take me to the doctor, made me feel better.

"Sometimes, I feel sick, too," he said. "But I suffer it out, and after a while; it passes, and the money, that doctor charges, is saved. We don't have much money, right now. In fact, there isn't any money for food."

He looked at me and paused. "I know you have money hidden away. You'd be helping the family if you gave me that money to buy food."

Depression swept over me. I'd been saving the money for a long time. Suddenly I just wanted him out of there, to be left alone.

"The money's in the top drawer of the bureau, way in back."

Soon, I heard the car drive off. Later in the day, I was thirsty and made my way downstairs.

The day dragged on. At long last, the kids came home from school, saying my face had swollen more grotesquely than ever. Soon, Ma and Pa came home. Pa seemed surprised to see me downstairs, and transferred the sturdy brown paper bag he was carrying, to the side away from me. I heard bottles clink as he hurried into the pantry. I went back upstairs more depressed than ever.

The swelling eventually went down. In a few days I went back to school. But the tooth turned black and Ma took me back to the dentist, who pulled it. The ring leader still was not through with me. The seat of my pants was worn thin from bike riding and holes often appeared. With my mother working, I mended them myself as best I could. When the seat would break open, the ring leader would announce, "Joe, yer ass is out!."

Then a girl, who was in the inner circle, began saying, from time to time, "Hey, Joe, you've got a hole in your pants." My hand would dart behind me to feel for the tear. She would giggle for having fooled me, and the boys would jeer. One day, my mother came home with a new pair of dungarees. I couldn't wait to wear them to school. Next day, everyone admired my new denims until the ring leader spoke up.

"Those aren't store-bought dungarees; they got no rivets. They're from relief."

I could feel my face get red, and I wished we didn't have to wear relief dungarees with no rivets, and get surplus food, and haul wood from the dump in our car.

The next year I transferred to a bigger school where the seventh grade was now taught. My old classmates—including my tormentors—went along, too. But there were kids from other schools there, too. One of them, Hugo, joined in the abuse. Worst of all, the teacher who nearly flunked me was there to torment me all over again. The bed wetting didn't start again, but I gnawed my nails to the quick, and my grades took a nosedive. When the Christmas play began, I asked for a part.

"Are you sure you can learn it?"

"I always did before."

"I'll give you a part, but you better get busy and start memorizing it better than you've been doing on your other work."

I really worked at memorizing the part, practicing it, over and over. There was one part that I sometimes got confused with a similar line. But I thought I had it down. The night of the play, Pa decided to attend. With him in the audience watching and the teacher following every word I said, I got nervous and stopped reciting my lines about three quarters of the way through. I stopped dead. My mind went blank. There was utter silence in the room. I was paralyzed, not sure of the next line. No words would come out of my mouth. After an eternity, the teacher prompted me with a word. After that, even though I knew the rest of the lines, I repeated her prompts, word by painful word, to the bitter end. My father sat in embarrassment. I wanted to die. No one said much on the way home. I rode with my head down.

The next Monday, the boys at school teased me about it. The gang from the previous school got together with the guys at the new school and started holding me down; spitting in my mouth. Hugo, who weighed about twice what

I did, stood a foot taller. He helped hold me down. I began hiding in the school building at recess and noon hour.

The teacher kept an eye on the playground from the window and noticed me missing. She found me hiding in the basement and ordered me out to the playground. "Don't be such a sissy. You've got to learn to fight your own battles."

The school and yard were on a small plateau with a farmer's field below. I strode out of the school and felt a rage building up inside. A feeling of calm came over me. I was no longer in fear of the bullies. I felt a surge of power and strength filled my mind and body. My muscles seemed to swell. I was determined to end their bulling by any means possible, once and for all. Hugo stood at the top of the embankment at the edge of the school yard. Sharp stubble covered the slope where the farmer had recently cut off the brush. Hugo spotted me. "There he is; guys. Let's get 'em!"

When Hugo approached to throw me to the ground, I stood my ground. As soon as he reached to grab me, I punched him as hard as I could. He lost his balance, toppled over and rolled down the bank like a barrel. When he reached the bottom of the stubbled slope, he looked like a tiger had attacked him. Seeing Hugo out of the brawl gave me a tremendous shot of adrenalin. Two more of my tormentors came at me. The bigger of the two was the one who liked to spit in my mouth. He was eager to teach me another lesson, and came at me with arms reaching for me. I kicked him in the crotch---hard. He fell to the ground clutching his groin, groaning in agony. The ring leader was next. I lusted for revenge over his punching me in the mouth when I had the abscessed tooth. I grabbed him around the neck in a head lock, and began strangling him. The rest of the gang ran away. Other kids stood watching at a safe distance. He began turning blue. I didn't care. He gasped that he would never touch me again. I made him say it again, choking him harder. The other cowards, who liked to join in when I was safely on the ground, had run away and were watching from afar.

The teacher came running out. She ordered me to release my hold. I let him go. My tormentor slunk away, disgraced. Hugo had climbed back up the bank, bloodied and torn. The teacher ordered me inside and began tending to his wounds. She cleaned Hugo up the best she could and sent a note home to his mother. The teacher kept me after school. The bus left without me, meaning that I would have to walk home the four miles, or more.

"Hugo's mother is coming to deal with you," The teacher warned.

Hugo's mother arrived dressed in hat, gloves and pocket book. The teacher apologized, repeatedly. Hugo's mother mostly listened. She took me into the coat room, sat me down, and took a seat opposite me. She reached into her pocket book. I wasn't sure what she was reaching for. The pocket book wasn't big enough to hold a strap. Still it made me nervous.

She brought out a donut wrapped in a napkin. She smiled and held it out to me as if she were trying to tame a savage beast. I thanked her and ate the donut as slowly as I could. As starved as I was I didn't want to gobble it down like the wild animal she probably assumed I was. While I was eating the donut, I could see she was looking at my clothes. They were shabby and nowhere near as nice as what her son wore. At least, before he rolled through the stubble.

"So you're the one who beat up my Hugo," she said, trying not to smile.

"Yes ma'am."

"Can you tell me why?"

I told her the whole story. How I finally did what the teacher told me to do—fight my own battles. She did not like the part about the boys spitting in my mouth, but she smiled when I told her how her son had rolled down the hill.

"Perhaps he won't be so ready to bully others, now."

She didn't seem at all angry. Then she quietly asked me where I lived. I hoped she wasn't going to go tell Pa, or I'd wind up in worse shape than Hugo. On my way home, I left the road and cut across through the woods where I had to cross a swamp I didn't know existed. It didn't save me any time but I didn't want anyone to see me walking home and know that I had been kept after school.

When I got home, I wasn't very popular with Pa for being kept after school. I didn't tell him why and he didn't question me. I didn't mind Pa complaining about me coming home late. It felt good to get back at the cowards who were making my life miserable. On my long walk home, I had made up my mind that I wasn't going to let them get away with ganging up on me, again—ever. And I decided I wasn't going to let Pa hit me any more, either. But that decision nearly got me into reform school.

Chapter 60: Reform School

Not long after settling scores with my tormenters at school, Pa cornered me. He took a swing at me and I blocked it. The same calm determination I had felt on the playground came over me, but without the wild aggression. I was going to put it end to it right now, but not by striking back. I still respected him as my father and would not hit him. I just blocked the blows. He tried a few more times but each time I'd raise my arm to block the punch.

"Raise your hand to your father, will you? Get your things and get out."

When I didn't move, he went upstairs and threw my clothes out the window. I picked them up and brought them back inside.

"Get in the car. We're going to the Police Station; you're going to reform school."

Our town didn't have a police station. We didn't even have a policeman. All we had was a constable and he never arrested anyone. Pa knew he wouldn't be any help. Besides, the constable didn't even have a uniform, nor did he have a gun. He was apt to just smile and get people to work things out.

The adjoining town of Turners Falls had a police station, complete with a police chief. He had a uniform, a gun and substantial girth. Pa marched in ahead of me, jaw set and scowl on his face. The veins on his neck were bulging and his eyes were bugging out a bit.

"I want you to put him in the reform school,"

At this point, I'd resigned myself to going and even began to look forward to it. Chief Walter Casey leaned back in his office chair. The chair creaked as he rocked back and forth with his hands folded over his ample stomach. He listened to Pa rant on about me raising my hand to him.

Casey knew Pa, but he never brought up the fact that we were in the wrong town, and that as Police Chief, he had no jurisdiction over Gill.

"Can't do it," Casey lied. "They don't do that no more."

Pa threw up his hands, and walked out. I followed him to the car. We drove home in silence. He more or less gave up on me after that, and never tried hitting me, again. And we actually got along better, to my surprise.

I got along better at school, too. I enjoyed a feeling of power after the playground battle. When I came out onto the playground, I got respect. The cowards slunk away. There was no more ganging up on me. I even picked on Hugo, once in a while, just to let him know what it was like to be on the receiving end.

My marks were still a problem. At the end of the year my grades were so low the teacher passed me "on trial", again. I felt a failure. When she found out I wanted to go to Mount Hermon, she said with scorn, "Mount Hermon will never take you."

I hated to think she was right and felt depressed, especially knowing Hugo had a much better chance of being admitted because his marks were better and his father was on the Mount Hermon School faculty.

After our school let out for the summer, Hugo's mother came to our farm. I thought she was coming to tell Pa how I beat up her son, and what a rotten kid I was. Instead, she gave me a nice plaid wool jacket and other clothes that Mount Hermon students had left behind in their dorm rooms when they left for home at the end of the school year. She told me that a group of campus women sorted, cleaned and mended clothes to give to needy kids. I appreciated her giving me the nice clothes, but I did not like being labeled a needy kid.

Chapter 61: Panther on the Loose

The summer after the playground battle, some of boys who had once ganged up on me, invited me to go with them on a bike ride to see a movie in Greenfield. We set out from D.O. Paul's store in a body, like the Five Musketeers, one of them said, for an adventurous trip to the city. I had mixed feelings about having the group accept me, when I remembered how mean they had treated me in the past.

We arrived in Greenfield long before the second show began. Someone suggested we had time to visit "Bud", who had previously lived in Gill. He was glad to see us and came along to see the double feature. The first movie was an action thriller featuring a keg of dynamite with a fuse that sizzled forever, as we sat on the edge of our seats, chewing our nails, waiting for the explosion.

The second movie involved a black panther that'd escaped from the circus. We never did set eyes on the sinister beast as he stalked people in the dark. First, a young woman walked into the darkness of a railroad underpass—a scream, a gurgle, and then blood came running out of the shadows. Next, a mother sent her daughter to the store for cold meat and a jar of mustard. The little girl heard rustling in the brush along the way and ran back home. Each time she stopped to listen, the beast made a faint rustle. She ran in spurts until she got home and beat on the door, begging her mother to let her in. The scene shifted inside the house.

"Go back to the store," said her mother, shouting though the closed door. "I won't let you in until you bring back the meat and mustard."

The camera angle shifted to the bottom of the locked door—a scream, a gurgle, and blood flowed from under the door. At the movie's conclusion, there may have been traces of mustard on the Five Musketeer's seats.

When we got out of the theatre, night had fallen. Sinister shadows hid lurking danger in every alleyway and behind every bush. Bud asked us to escort him home.

On the way, stories of panthers and tigers that had escaped circuses became the subject of discussion. Gradually the conversation crossed over to local beasts of prey—mad dogs, bobcats, mountain lions, cougars, and lynx—that freely roamed our area in droves. Members of the brave Musketeers began looking over their shoulders

At Bud's house, first one, and then another of my faithful friends asked to use the phone to get permission to spend the night at Bud's house. Because my family had no telephone and I'd not dare ask permission, anyway; I headed for home—alone.

Where the street lights illuminated the road, I rode feeling comparatively safe. But the street lights ended at Factory Hollow, and inky blackness engulfed the road. My pulse beat faster. I and my pedal rate increased.

A faint breeze stirred, making the leaves rustle in the underbrush beside the road. The rustling seemed to increase from time to time. When I stopped, the rustling stopped, like that of an animal keeping pace—a curious squirrel or a restless rabbit, perhaps---certainly not a lynx or mountain lion. That would be silly.

I rode on up a hill where the woods thickened. My eyes grew acclimated to the dark and I could make out limbs of branches overhanging the road where a creature could easily lie in wait. My heart beat faster and my breathing grew louder, making it difficult to distinguish it from an animal panting.

The hill grew steeper and my breath became ever more labored as I made more and more effort to keep going. The bicycle went slower and slower. Sweat began to run down my armpits and I began to breathe harder and harder.

I was past the place where I usually got off to push my bike and walk, but the night air had given me additional energy. I pushed harder and harder on the pedals. The bike chain stretched and didn't mesh quite right with the sprocket. It went cronk, cronk—every time I pushed down on the pedals. I looked up at the tree limbs as I slowed, knowing that soon I had to get off the bike and walk.

Then I saw it. Concealed in the overhanging trees, a dark shape loomed ahead on a tree limb. I could barely make it out, but it looked exactly like the panther in the movie, tensing his body, ready to spring. A burst of adrenalin surged though my body. Cronk, cronk, cronk, cronk—faster and faster, up over the crest and onto a relatively flat section where I sped away leaving the panther far behind, probably gnashing his fangs in frustration. When I got home, still damp with sweat, I felt a certain confidence in myself for having braved the night, alone. I had a snack of the cereal and milk I'd stashed in the barn, and went to sleep in the hay mow.

When I next saw the rest of the group, they asked if I'd been scared to ride home that night, alone.

"Scared? What of? I'm no sissy—like you guys."

I knew then that I would never be "one of the gang" but would be a self-reliant individual like Magrini. I began spending more time with my friend Ray, who lived in the adjoining town. And I decided to apply at Mount Hermon. At times, I also spent time with another friend who had an interest in cars and the here-and-now. He thought me a little strange for wanting to attend Mount Hermon. My talk of college left all my classmates cold, and they mocked me by calling me "Professor" for having such ambitions. They looked forward to quitting school and getting a job to earn money to buy a fine car.

Raymond and I had loftier aspirations, though I often felt we were daydreaming and wondered if our dreams would ever materialize. With my marks down, the chances of being accepted at Mount Hermon, or college, seemed slim.

Chapter 62: Elusive Mount Hermon

Fortunately, the old mean teacher didn't teach eighth grade. Miss Rule, who taught at Riverside School, was tough but fair. My grades went back up and Mount Hermon accepted me. My father's words that I wasn't smart enough or rich enough came back to me that fall when I didn't have enough money for books, fees, and clothes, too. To ask him for money was out of the question. Mount Hermon had eluded me, after all, and I enrolled in Turners Falls High School, instead.

One of the reasons I hadn't earned enough money was that I made the mistake of accepting a summer job at Mount Hermon, working on the farm, without first asking what the pay scale was. When I received my first month's pay, the check was made out for $16.

"There must be some mistake; I worked a whole month."

The payroll clerk looked up the time sheets.

"No, it's correct-- $16."

"Correct? How the heck much are you paying me an hour, anyway?

"Your pay is ten cents an hour."

"Ten cents? How much do the men get?"

She hesitated a moment. "The men got 35 cents."

"I've been doing a man's work. The farm manager had me working as a teamster and shoveling coal like a man, how come I don't get a man's pay?"

"Because you're a boy and you don't have a family to support—you get ten cents an hour."

"Not anymore, I don't. I quit!"

Depressed at having wasted a whole month working for a lousy 10 cents an hour, I went home.

Tony Kendrow, a farmer in Gill, heard I'd quit and came to the farm to ask me to work for him. He said he knew I was a good worker and would pay me 45 cents an hour; I was thrilled.

Before the end of the week, he raised me to 50 cents per hour. Kendrow later told me Hugo had applied for the job, but he'd turned him down. How sweet that was. Kendrow also held the job of town road boss. When haying was over, he put me to work for the town grading gravel on town roads even though I was only 13. The pay scale was 50 cents an hour.

"If the State man shows up and asks how old you are, tell him you're 18."

The town had only one small dump truck delivering gravel. Spreading gravel beat haying. In fact, the hardest part of the job was looking busy. When any of my friends drove by with their parents, I swelled with pride to be seen working with men, earning a man's pay. I swaggered a bit, feeling like a big shot.

Still, the month I'd wasted working for 10 cents an hour left me short of the money I needed to attend Mt Hermon. Discouraged, I abandoned the idea of ever going there—they were a bunch of cheap skates, anyway, paying me 10 cents an hour, I said to myself, though I'd really had my heart set on it.

That fall, I began Turner Falls High School as a freshman. By now, I'd become fast friends with Raymond, now a student at Mount Hermon. He told me not to get discouraged and urged me to reapply.

The following school year, I had earned enough money working for Mr. Lambert to enroll at Mount Hermon—the only student attending from our town. Lambert's factory job paid on a piece-work basis. He had the opportunity to make considerable money working overtime. He farmed part-time and had a dozen cows that needed milking when he worked overtime. He paid me a dollar to do the afternoon milking and barn chores. It took less than two hours. The barn was equipped with a Surge milking machine, automatic drinking cups for the cows, and a radio to keep us company. I loved it. He employed me at other times to work around the farm. Once, I helped a plumber install automatic drinking bowels. The plumber put me to work cutting and threading pipe, and fitting the pipe to the bowels. It all added up and I soon had money enough to start Mount Hermon School.

I went shopping for school clothes, knowing they had to be better than what I wore while attending Turners High. I bought a suit at Carson's store in Greenfield. The salesman said tweed was what I needed if I wanted to fit in at a prep school.

"Tweed is warm and durable, too," he said, "and very classy."

I also bought a brown plaid sport coat, yellow lamb's wool sweater, brown wing tipped shoes, socks, tie, and a tan reversible all-weather coat to go with the tweed suit. I proudly showed Mary and Johnny the clothes, I'd bought with my own earnings for going to Mount Hermon. They joked about my suit, calling it "Seedy-tweedy". Johnny tried on the reversible coat. The sleeves were too short for him. They laughed, and I left, disappointed that they did not congratulate me on being accepted to Mount Hermon.

The first day of school, I wore the suit to meet the headmaster. My parents didn't go with me. Pa wasn't at all happy that I was enrolled. Bible study was required at Mount Hermon, and "Bible" was a dirty word at home. Just Jehovah Witnesses read the Bible; Catholics weren't allowed. Only a priest was smart enough to read a bible and understand all that holy stuff. Besides, Pa considered it folly wasting my time studying heathen Bibles when I could be earning good money in the paper mill getting 62 cents an hour. "Just think, sixty two cents an hour. That's more than a penny coming in every minute of the day. Times are good. Once you get in the mill, you'll have a job for life." But the thoughts of enduring a lifetime of the racket and stink of the mill didn't appeal to me.

High school students had bus service. Since I had enrolled in a private school, it was up to me to get there as best I could. I got all dressed up in my nice new tweed suit and tie, put on my new wing tipped shoes, carefully combed my hair, and took off on my bike. This was a big step in my life— *First Day at a Prep School, Meeting the Headmaster.* My stomach jumped around just thinking about going up to him and shaking his hand. I tried to think of something impressive to say to such an important guy.

A few miles from home the sky opened up and I got caught in a downpour. The tweed suit turned into a soggy mess. I looked like I was wearing wet burlap. The handlebar grips were made of some kind of synthetic rubber that stained my hands black. I arrived at Holbrook Administration Hall looking like a half- drowned rat flushed out of a sewer.

As I was leaning my bike against a big elm tree in the parking area, a stately black Cadillac pulled up. The driver, decked out in a black uniform and chauffeur's cap, got out to hold the rear door open. A man and woman got out, dressed like the Duke and Duchess of Windsor, followed by their Little Lord Fauntleroy. I went on ahead of them to the receiving line, shoes squishing, water dripping off my baggy suit, hair plastered to my head from the downpour.

When I moved up to the headmaster, he grabbed my hand still stained black from the handlebar grips and started pumping it. He looked past me to the royal couple. "You must be this fine young man's parents."

"Good heavens, no!" her royal highness replied, stepping back to disassociate herself from this ragamuffin standing in front of her. She brushed imaginary dust from her finery, as though fearing she might have contaminated herself by getting too close to this homeless creature who had obviously mistaken the admissions office for a soup kitchen.

I never saw the royal heir, again. His parents may have had second thoughts about having their delicate darling attend Mt Hermon after seeing the white trash the school was accepting, and gone in search of a more appropriate school for their precious darling.

I arranged to have all my classes in the morning so I could work afternoons. After lunch, I'd go down to Jackson's potato farm and change into work clothes to help harvest potatoes in fields adjacent to Mount Hermon's lower athletic fields. While my preppy classmates chased soccer balls, I heaved bags of potatoes onto a truck. Jackson paid me 35 cents an hour. I was doing the same work as men he hired for 45 cents per hour, but I was a kid, needed the money, and Jackson knew it. The men also had families to support, he could have argued.

After getting home, tired and dirty, I'd wash up at the pump in the pantry, eat supper, and fall asleep studying. Pa would get out of bed and blast me for sleeping at the table. Next morning I'd get up at 4:30 to milk the cow and walk a quarter mile up to the corner to catch a ride part way with Mr. Lambert, wait a half hour at a gas station and catch another ride to Mount Hermon. I was tired all the time. I struggle to keep my grades up. It was discouraging and I knew I could do better. I was glad to have potato harvest over. We began sorting the potatoes in Jackson's basement storage but the work was not as hard. By December, potato work was all over until spring when seed potatoes were cut up for planting.

Many of the Mount Hermon boarding students came from affluent families. The dress code called for suit jackets and neckties in the dining hall. One classmate was forever "forgetting" his sport coats in classrooms, the library, or the dining hall. He had coats scattered all over campus, when I'd thought I was doing pretty good to own one. The school required students to work for ten hours a week. He once showed up at the school farm in a suit, tie, and dress shoes, apparently figuring the farm manager would recognize his higher station in life and give him a cushy job. The farm manager put him to work in the manure pit. "That'll educate him," he said. At the student's store, the wealthy student spent money freely and talked of his travels abroad, while we still did not have electricity or running water at our farm. I envied him until he went home for Christmas vacation and blew his brains out.

Chapter 63: WWII Creates a Great Job Market

Mr. Lambert dropped Ma off to walk about a mile to the Keith Paper Mill. Part of her hike was across the Turners Falls-Gill Bridge spanning the Connecticut River. Strong winds coming off the river swept the bridge with icy blasts, carrying spray from the falls. She'd often be shivering so much by the time she got to the mill that the foreman wouldn't let her begin her job of slicing cloth on the big upright razor sharp knives until her hands stopped shaking. Later, when Pa passed a physical exam and resumed working at the mill, they rode to work in Pa's car. There were no openings for his old job in the beater room. The mill super assigned Pa to the rag room where women worked, apparently, figuring it would be easy work in light of his heart condition. But the foreman gave Pa the job of wheeling heavy bales of rags to the cutting tables on a two wheel hand truck. The bales often weighed a half ton or more. It took a considerable effort to tip the bale onto the truck. Once balanced, wheeling the bale wasn't too bad, except when a wheel dropped into a hole in the floor, pulling him to the floor or pitching the heavy load forward---and him with it.

The exertion caused angina. When Pa stopped to catch his breath and wait for the pains to subside, he'd get dark looks from the foreman. Another heart attack ended Pa's working days for an extended period.

During the war years there was a severe labor shortage. To prevent job hopping, an employee couldn't quit and take a job elsewhere unless the present place of employment granted a written release. Students working seasonally were an exception. I got a job at the Keith Paper Mill while Pa was working there. Though I was 15, the personnel manager didn't ask my age. With the shortage of labor, he wasn't fussy. I went to work in the finishing department, wrapping rolls of paper. It was the most boring job I have ever had in my entire life. To ward off boredom and to earn extra money, I began using the mill suggestion box. Payment for ideas accepted was a percentage of money saved. But few employees seemed to be interested or imaginative. I saw plenty of places where the mill could do things more efficiently, and stuffed the box with suggestions. Many times, my suggestions resulted in more money for me than my paycheck. Unfortunately, most of my suggestions were for the manufacturing department. The finishing department super said he did not like me dreaming up suggestions while working for him when it only helped manufacturing be more efficient.

He sometimes put me to work hauling paper on a wagon from one machine at one end of the factory down one or two floors to a machine and then back again for some other operation, before going back down to the shipping room at the opposite end of the mill. I suggested that they line the machines up next to each other so that work flowed from one machine to the other, ending next to the shipping room. It greatly benefited the finishing department, but the super was embarrassed that a high school kid had come up with an idea that should have been plain for him to see. Rearranging the machines was a major project involving upper management, further bringing attention to his ineptitude. He was not pleased. On the last day of my summer job, an hour before the quitting time, he saw me getting a drink from the water fountain. He asked me what I was doing.

"As little as possible," I said with a grin, "I'm going back to school; this is my last day."

He turned white with fury, "This is your last hour," he roared. "You're fired!"

That was the only time in my life that I ever got fired. But I was a good worker and during a two week semester break in college, I was hired in the same mill to work in the millwright department. When the finishing department superintendent saw me back at work, the color drained from his face. I gave him a cheery "hello," but he stalked past me without replying.

Chapter 64: Working on the Railroad

During winter break at Mount Hermon, I was 16 and it was wartime. Someone told me that if I wanted a good-paying job, I just needed to walk into the B&M Railroad Division Engineer's office and ask for one. In I went, without knocking. Mr.Wilkens, sat behind a big desk with stacks of papers strewn about. He was barking orders into a telephone. My heart began pounding a hole in my chest. I wondered if I should turn around and leave before he hung up and threw me out.

"What do you want?" he growled. I wanted to tell him I could do the work of a man, but his demeanor scared me.

"I'm looking for a job," I blurted out.

He seemed to soften. "We can sure use some help," Wilkens said. "Go down to the section shanty and tell Casey, the foreman, that I hired you. If anyone asks, tell 'em you're 18."

He didn't say where the shanty was, but a railroad worker standing on the station platform pointed it out to me. He wore a striped railroad cap. I was all excited. I couldn't wait to begin wearing a railroad cap. The section gang foreman wrote my name and social security number in the time book. I didn't know what the pay scale was, but I think I'd have worked for nothing just to be part of the prestige and excitement of working on the railroad. The workmen showed me how to swing the special hammers when driving spikes, how to space the rails to an exact width and the essential details of the job that insured the safety of workmen and passengers, alike. The section gang was a rough hard-drinking bunch. They mostly maintained tracks around the railroad station. When a steam train pulled in at the station, a great hubbub arose. Crowds of people milled about, some getting off the train and others getting on. Steam hissed out of various places of the locomotive as it sat in the station panting like a big black beast. The enormous steam cylinders and connecting rods that drove the massive iron wheels were all out in the open. Soon, the conductor called out "Allaboardt," and the train chugged out of the station, whistle tooting. With the train gone, calm and quiet descended on the station. The lunch room lost all its urgency and the counter help relaxed after the big rush.

We took a coffee break as we worked late, one night, keeping rail switches clear of snow. The station was quiet during a lull. The buxom blonde waitress bantered with the section gang. They egged her on to show me her butterfly. She raised her skirt, but I looked away. I didn't realize she wanted me to see the butterfly tattoo on her inner thigh. I hadn't been exactly sure what she wanted to show me and I didn't dare look. The men howled when my face turned red. Later, I wished I'd taken a peek.

Working on the tracks was a dangerous job. Dropping a rail could smash toes or break a leg. Sometimes a train bore down on a different track than expected, catching trackmen unaware, especially when fatigued while working around the clock. Mr. Calaboosa, a track inspector riding on a little put-put car, was run over by an unscheduled train when he failed to check with the office. Whenever the foreman wanted to take a chance on not calling the office to see if the track would be clear, a cry went up, sounding like a slogan, "Remember Calaboosa!"

Not only was railroad pay higher than what other occupations paid, but after eight hours we got paid time and a half, and after sixteen hours we got paid double time. Then it went back to straight time and started all over again. When it snowed, the section gang's job was to keep the rail switches clear of snow and ice. If a switch didn't close all the way, a train could derail. We lit kerosene smudge pots to keep the rail switches from freezing. If it snowed all night, we worked all night. The railroad lunch counter closed about ten o'clock, but Smitty's Diner never closed. Smitty sold a delicious bowl of beef stew and a big chunk of crusty bread for 40 cents. It felt good to have a pocket full of folding money, eating out instead of carrying a lunch bucket, working all night with the section gang doing a man's job even though I was only sixteen. My classmates looked up to me. Working on the railroad was heady stuff.

When it looked like a snow storm was letting up and we might not work all night and lose out on the time and a half and double time, the gang would take up a collection to take Casey out for a few drinks. While they were getting him mellow, my job was to fire up the coal stove in the railroad shanty. With the shanty was warm and cozy, Casey would soon doze off and snore through the night.

The men took turns checking the smudge pots and switches while the others curled up on benches to catch a snooze—on double overtime. I stoked the pot bellied stove though the night between snatches of sleep. At about two o'clock in the morning, a train came thundering by, making a horrendous noise. It shook the shanty, threatening to take the shanty with it. Someone stirred, "There goes the bootlegger." The Montreal train got named "the bootlegger" during prohibition when people took the Montrealer to Canada to bring back whiskey. The train roared off into the night and quiet descended on the shanty. The foreman's snoring continued unabated.

The next morning, Casey was grouchy, until the crew took him out for breakfast and a cup of Irish coffee. My first week's paycheck equaled more than what my sister Irene earned in a month as a store clerk. I never did buy a striped railroad cap, but whenever I saw a train rumbling by, or heard a whistle blow, that old railroad feeling stirred in me.

Chapter 65: The Farm Gets Electricity

With our family on solid financial footing, Pa contacted the power company to extend power lines to the farm, right after WWII in 1945. They charged him for the poles but spread the charges out in monthly installments. The pole charge equaled or exceeded the charge for electricity.

Pa bought a Frigidaire refrigerator and a radio. Later, he bought a chest freezer. But it didn't occur to him to install an electric water pump or telephone. Ma and Pa saw the need for a telephone when they were overcome by coal gas one night and couldn't get out of bed until the end of the next day. Toward evening, Pa was able to get to a neighbor's telephone to summon Louis. That's when Louis moved back home to keep an eye on things. He had a phone installed and later hired a man to install plumbing while Ma was in the hospital. Soon after that, Pa had an oil furnace installed. He'd lost all confidence in the safety of burning coal after the narrow escape.

Mail service to Poland was interrupted during World War II. When Pa next heard from his family, his brother wrote that the old folks had died and he was so impoverished he hardly had clothes enough to cover himself to go to the post office to pick up his mail. Pa sent his brother his only suit and his good overcoat in the first of a series of many packages. Shortly afterward, I saw Pa walking down the street in an old threadbare overcoat looking like a seedy bum. I avoided him, ashamed to be seen with him. He later got another overcoat and when I got a little older and a little smarter, I bought him a new suit.

"Now I have a suit to be buried in," he said, fingering the material.

In the end, the parcels Pa sent didn't bring his brother much luck. The Germans who had occupied Poland during the war confiscated his tools and all the horses in the land. Pa sent all manner of carpenter tools, enabling his brother to begin earning money again. Pa sewed tightly folded money into the seams of the clothing sent in the parcels, which Ma later mentioned in a letter.

The family began tearing the clothes into a million pieces, looking for hidden money. Pa then instructed Ma to give more specific locations of the hiding places when she wrote. Pa even sent a mare through the relief organization, CARE. A horse was a symbol of prosperity in Poland. After WWII, the Germans were required to return confiscated horses, but many had died or were slaughtered for meat during the war. My uncle had been sorely in need of a horse. The mare that Pa sent gave birth on the way. Now, our uncle had two horses. The communist authorities suspected him of criminal activity to be prosperous enough to own two horses. He sold one to distant relatives. The horse fell ill soon after and died, causing hard feelings with his relatives.

Pa's brother wrote to tell us to stop sending packages. His son had reported his father to the authorities saying his father was a U.S. spy. The son ran away to join the Russian Army and was accidentally shot during training. He came home a cripple. Fate was not on their side. Not long after that, Pa's brother and his wife were struck by lightning. They never fully recovered and died shortly after. We never heard from the son. Pa felt especially sad for his brother, a good man, who had stayed in Poland to give care and comfort to their parents in their declining years as best he could during those trying times. I think Pa felt sad, as well as guilty that his brother had been repaid for his sacrifice with hardship, pain, suffering and death.

Though we didn't have it as difficult as our uncle and his family, the tough times motivated me, and I could see more and more that Magrini was right. Education was the only way to get ahead. Magrini further reinforced that idea when he established a monument business in addition to the insurance agency that he and Helen ran.

Just before Memorial Day, Pa drove us to the cemetery to tend Julia's grave. Much to our surprise, there, on Julia's grave, sat a pink marble gravestone with her name engraved, appearing as though by magic. Mama's prayers had been answered. She smiled through the tears, relieved that Julia's grave would not be lost in the brush. Later, we learned that Helen and Magrini had set the stone, as a surprise. I looked up to them all the more after they set the gravestone.

Chapter 66: Car Dealer

Now that Pa was not asking me to turn my money over to him, my pockets were jingling. I found that I could pick up extra money buying and selling used cars with my newly acquired riches.

I was 15 when I bought my first car. It was a 1936 Studebaker. "Mac" McDonald, who sold the car to me, said he'd driven it behind the barn where it was parked. His wife, Elsie, said she'd pushed it there, herself, and his father-in-law said his faithful horse had towed it there.

I dragged the car home with our tractor and tried to get it running. When all attempts to start it failed, I took off the cylinder head. The valves and seats were burned beyond repair. I figured the entire family had been telling the truth, and that it had taken the three of them, along with the horse, working in concert, to get the car moved to the spot behind the barn. I sold the car to a junk dealer for about what I had paid.

The next car I bought was a 1931 Chevrolet Cabriolet, a convertible club coupe with leather upholstery and a top that only leaked when it rained. The connecting rod bearings sounded like a flock of woodpeckers on steroids and the car wouldn't go over 50 miles per hour downhill with a tailwind, but I loved that car.

With WW II on, gas was rationed. It was summer, I was still 15, had no license, and the car wasn't registered. Without registration I couldn't get gas ration stamps. The ration board gave Pa plenty of stamps for his car, the farm tractor, and the saw rig.

"Louis," I'd say, "Siphon a couple of gallons of gas from the saw rig and drain a gallon of kerosene from the 55 gallon kerosene drum, and dump it in the Chevy. After supper we'll go for a ride."

Louis followed my instructions. The Chevy ran a bit sluggish on the mixture, but it ran. We draped the top down over the empty number plate bracket, but the canvas top billowed out behind us, probably attracting more attention to the lack of plates then if we'd stowed the top properly. Driving that car, hanging onto the steering wheel and pressing on the gas pedal filled me with excitement—my very own car, carrying me wherever I wanted to go. It seemed like a dream.

After a number of evening joy rides, Louis informed me the saw rig gas tank was running low. I instructed him to alter the ratio—one gallon gas to one gallon kerosene. Next, it was one gallon of gas to two gallons kerosene. The Chevy didn't have much in the way of top speed or pickup with the increasingly poorer mixture. The car acted as if it had a governor and would not go very fast, but we didn't care; we just wanted to ride around. With no police in town but the constable, who had a zero arrest record, we roamed farther and farther from home—even risking an occasional trip to the adjoining town.

Soon, the saw rig gas tank had little more than a film of gasoline lying on the bottom and we dared drain no more. We began running the Chevy on virtually pure kerosene. I dumped moth balls in the tank hoping the naphtha would give the kerosene a little boost. We could hear them rolling from one side of the gas tank to the other when we went around corners. Sometimes, the engine was hard to start and I'd have to prime it with a little gasoline to get it going. Pa must have marveled at a car that ran on little more than air and got such good mileage. I waited for Pa to put a stop to my joy rides without a license, but he had long since given up on me after failing to send me to reform school. The day finally came when Louis brought me the bad news; the kerosene drum was empty.

"How you're going to explain that one to Pa when he finds out?" Louis asked.

The dreaded day arrived. I came home to find the kerosene drum, standing upright with the end chopped out. The axe leaned against it. I knew I was in deep trouble when I saw the grim look on Pa's face.

"Look at that! Kerosene's all gone."

I didn't know what to say, knowing he must have been in a blind rage to go at the drum with an ax.

"That drum's no good—it's got a hole in it. All the kerosene leaked out," he said. "I'll use it for a rain barrel."

I don't know what he thought the Chevy had been running on, but I figured it was time to register the car and apply for a ration book. Registering the car, at 15, was easy. The insurance agency asked no questions about age. Since they got the plates from the registry for me, I didn't have to answer any questions there, either. The Gill ration board issued me an A book. I got a friend with a license to drive to D.O. Paul's general store to fill up the tank.

Learners could drive at age 16 when accompanied by a licensed driver. My friend knew the test route. We drove the route, over and over, until I had all the required maneuvers down pat. On my 16th birthday, I drove to the Registry of Motor Vehicles to take the test during the noon hour.

"Age 16, today; are you?" the Registry official asked, reading my application. "How'd you learn to drive? You didn't learn just this morning."

"Oh, I learned on the farm, driving tractors and stuff."

He may have been tipped off that I was familiar with the test routine when I went on to the next part of the test before he instructed me. He cut the road test short. I figured he'd flunked me and have me arrested for driving around the test circuit before I was 16. But, apparently, he could see I could drive with a fair amount of skill, and he issued me the license.

Louis and I had a grand time driving around in the Chevy. We'd go down to D.O. Paul's general store for a quart of ice cream and a quart of soda and polish them off before going swimming in the Connecticut River. Mrs. Paul warned us not to go swimming for an hour after eating or we would sink. I drove the car to classes at Mount Hermon, ending my round-about ride to school and the long walk home.

Pa didn't like the idea of me having so much freedom and persuaded me to return the Chevy. He was especially nice to me and offered me his 1937 Ford V-8 for the $150 I'd paid for the Chevy. He had contacted a lawyer who had informed him that minors could not enter into a binding contract. Pa informed me that I had to return the car. I wasn't so sure about making a deal with Pa. Still, it wasn't a bad deal; his Ford V-8 was newer and much nicer, and had a lot of pickup. I'd heard that Ford V-8's would go 75 miles an hour in second gear whereas the Chevy wouldn't go much over 50 miles per hour down hill in high gear, even on pure gasoline. I returned the Chevy. The dealer wanted $25 for his troubles. I figured it was worth it, for all the fun I'd had over the past month.

It soon became apparent that the Ford wasn't entirely mine. Pa retained the right to use it whenever he liked, which often was just when I wanted to go somewhere. I decided the deal wasn't working and asked for the money back. But not before I ascertained the truth that a Ford V-8 would go 75 miles per hour in second gear. It did.

Riding my bike beat arguing with Pa about who was going to use the car. Soon, I found a nice 1934 Ford for $50. I didn't tell him where I'd bought it and he didn't ask. Apparently he wasn't about to spend any more money on a lawyer to rescind another deal.

Soon, I found another bargain—a 1931 Buick for $50. I sold that for $75. Then I sold the 1934 Ford for $150-- three times what I'd paid—and bought a 1928 Buick in pristine condition for $20. Soon, I was buying and selling enough vehicles to keep me in spending money. Pa called me a junk dealer. I didn't care; it was an exciting way to make a little money and made me feel grown up. Cars were scarce and I could have charged more, but I was happy with a modest profit. Between buying cars and working afternoons and weekends, I didn't study as much as I should have and usually didn't get to bed until late. My marks suffered, and my counselor pointed out that I was performing way below my potential, ranking 75th out of 150 students. To top it all off, I fell asleep in Louis Smith's deadly dull Advanced Grammar class as he droned on about the principle parts of a past participle, or something equally stupefying. My eyes closed in a state of utter exhaustion, as he lectured me for falling asleep.

The lack of sleep wasn't the only difficulty. I had an undiagnosed low blood-sugar condition. I ate breakfast at 4:30 AM before doing the milking at home and setting out for school. By the time I got to my 10 o'clock Advanced Grammar class, I was ready to pass out from either lack of sleep, hunger, or boredom---or all of the above.

The students called Mr. Smith, "Laughing Louie." He had a perpetual smile on his face, even when he was livid---which he was that morning—grimacing more than grinning. He sent me to see the assistant headmaster for a talk. The assistant headmaster wanted to know why I was falling asleep. It did not appear that I was a serious student, he said. I explained the circumstances, but he did not comment and gave no hint of what lay ahead.

Chapter 67: Childhood's End

I was savoring the liberty of being on vacation for the summer, out in the fresh air raking hay with our home made tractor and a one-horse dump rake. It was a rake Pa bought at auction, after having sawed the trip rod off the old rake to keep me from using it, saying I was too lazy. He saw the error of his ways and bought a replacement rake when Mr. Lambert hired me to rake hay with his tractor. Pa saw me using a rope hooked up to the trip lever on Lambert's rake and decided using a rope to trip the rake was not such a bad idea.

I loved driving and raking the hay into piles. The warm sun and gentle breeze felt good. First I raked the hay into windrows, letting up on the gas as I yanked on the trip rope. Then I straddled the windrows to gather them into piles. I aligned the haycocks in rows, leaving room for the hay wagon to pass. Seeing the haycocks in neat alignment filled me with pride. I loved the aroma of new mown hay and the feeling of freedom, away from stuffy classrooms, out in the open air under sunny skies doing something useful.

Life couldn't get any better than this, I thought, humming a little tune. The noise of the engine seemed to harmonize with my happy melody. I thought about times past when the whole family took part in the haying ritual. It usually began the first part of June, and I always looked forward to the hustle and bustle that went with it. I loved the excitement and noise—the clatter of the mowing machine, its pitman arm and cutter bar knives flying to and fro in a blur of moving parts. There was always a sense of urgency. Pa would scan the sky for signs of rain as the family hurried to get the hay raked, piled into haycocks, loaded on the wagon and hauled into the barn before a sudden summer rain storm could spoil it.

But now the kids were gone. They'd all left home except for Louis and me. But I didn't dwell on it. I knew we could still get the hay in, even if it took a bit more time, as long as the weather held. And nothing could ruin this perfect day.

Pa came trudging out to the field, and I wondered why. There was no need for him to be out here. His last heart attack had slowed him, and he really looked his years. He held out a letter and I shut off the engine so we could talk.

"This came in the mail for you," he said, and watched as I opened it. The letter was from Mount Hermon informing me that they felt I'd be happier going to school elsewhere.

"What's it say?" my father asked.

It's from Mount Hermon School. They don't want me to come back."

"What you gonna' do?" he asked

"I don't know, Pa," I said, starting up the engine to resume raking hay. The truth was, I didn't know what I was going to do. I'd felt good about being the only boy in town accepted to the school. Now they were telling me they didn't want me. I knew I could have done better. Getting the letter made me feel like a total failure. Why hadn't I studied harder? The humiliation of going back to Turners Falls High School and facing my former classmates was not something I wanted to do. Still, I wanted to finish high school and go on to college. I tried to concentrate on pulling the trip rope so the piles would be evenly spaced. But my timing was off. All sorts of thoughts ran through my mind. Feelings of frustration, shame and anger came over me. The sun felt hot and hay chaff now clung to my sweaty skin in an annoying way. This is a stupid way to try to farm with a tractor made out of an old car dragging an old horse rake when neighbors drove Farmals and Ford-Fergusons pulling hay balers making neat bales, I thought.

When the hay was gathered into piles, I went back to the barn to get the wagon. Depression weighed me down. Louis, Ma, and Pa came out to help get the hay in. Pa drove the tractor towing the wagon through the field. I pitched hay onto the load while Louis and Ma built the load and tramped down the hay. Usually we dressed the load. But I really didn't care what the load looked like; I just wanted to get the hay into the barn and be done with it.

A few days later I drove my Model A Ford pickup truck to a gas station to have an inner tube vulcanized. It was less than a year since the end of World War II, and the only tire tubes available were made of synthetic rubber. A regular patch wouldn't hold; it had to be vulcanized.

A friendly Army recruiter struck up a conversation. "You look a little down in the dumps," he said.

When I confessed I'd been kicked out of Mount Hermon, he assured me that I could complete my education in the Army, get free room and board, medical and dental care, shoes, clothes and $75 dollars a month, besides.

"That's the perfect solution," he said. "And we got a special deal. If you sign up right now, we are offering an eighteen month enlistment. But, because you're only 17 you'll have to get your folks to sign for you." I hadn't counted on needing my parent's signature and I was afraid they wouldn't sign.

The next night after supper, I got up enough nerve to show them the enlistment papers and told them I wanted to join the Army. I thought I'd have a tough time convincing them it was a good idea, but they agreed without any coaxing. I'd have felt a lot better if they'd shown at least a slight hesitation.

The day I was to leave, soon came. Pa offered me a ride to Greenfield where the recruiters had an office above the Post Office. Ma came with us. That surprised and pleased me. It dawned on me that they both loved me and that this was a momentous day for them as well as for me. I wanted to tell them I loved them, but I didn't know how and sensed they felt the same. We rode along without conversation. To break the silence, I said, "This would be a good day to make hay." Then I remembered that they were getting on in years and had depended on me to help get work done. How would they get the hay in with Pa's heart condition and Louis only 13? Who would pitch the hay onto the wagon and then up into the hay mow? Guilt came over me for deserting them and for thinking only of myself.

At the Post Office, a big olive drab bus sat waiting. We got out of the car and stood not knowing what to say or do. I shook Pa's hand. Ma hugged me and tried to smile, biting her lip to try to keep from crying. Her eyes filled with tears. My eyes got a little watery, too, and I hoped the others on the bus wouldn't notice. I climbed aboard, went to a window seat and looked out to wave goodbye. But they were gone.

Epilogue

After Army basic training in Ft Belvoir, VA, my records were lost and I did not go to heavy equipment school as the Army Engineers had planned. Instead, since I did not know anything, they sent me to Washington, D.C. There, I drove a staff car at the Army War College. After a couple of months, they sent me to California by train, giving me a great opportunity to see the country. In California, I received a high school diploma from Pittsburg Evening High School. I sailed under the San Francisco's Golden Gate Bridge to Japan. There in the U.S Army of Occupation, I took parachute and glider training to become a paratrooper. I was stationed on Hokkaido, the northern island. An officer learned of my enrollment in a course at Hokkaido University and my ability to organize my fellow soldiers in all sorts of endeavors. He sent me to Troop Leadership School. My job consisted of public relations writing and public information talks to fellow paratroops on Saturday morning. If my advanced grammar teacher had ever learned the Army had me working as a public relations writer, he would have had a stroke.

In November, 1947, I was honorably discharged from the army at Fort Lawton, Washington, after 16 months of service. I was 18. I re-applied at Mount Hermon for the second semester but they turned me down. I enrolled in Turners Falls High School in the senior class two weeks before mid-year exams. I had left Mount Hermon as a sophomore, but since I had earned a diploma from Pittsburg Evening High School, the Turners Falls High School principal said that if I could pass the senior mid-year exams, he would give me credit for the first half of the school year. I studied hard, and barely squeaked by. I soon got on the honor roll and began working in a garage. Soon, I became a partner in a used car business with the owner. I went back to Mount Hermon to tell them I now had two high school diplomas, graduated with honors, was involved in a successful business, was ready to apply myself, and promised to stay awake. I graduated from Mount Hermon in 1949 I took an accelerated program at Bryant College--now Bryant University--where I crammed four years into two grueling years to earn a Bachelor of Science degree in Business Administration. I married Edna Carleton, and we moved 10 times in the first five years of marriage–twice to California--seeking our fortune. After a succession of jobs, I established a business as an excavating contractor in Gill. My fortune turned out to be the treasure of our four children; Deborah, Joann, Joseph, and Christine who was multiply handicapped. I continued taking courses at various colleges and universities, and became a National Honor Society member. I began pursuing photography and writing. A variety of newspapers, journals and magazines publish my work. Yankee magazine and Reader's Digest published excerpts of my memoir in another format. Marianne Phinney, director of languages and linguistics at the University of Texas at El Paso, selected one of my Yankee articles for her textbook on writing, along with work by Isaac Asimov, Russell Baker, Martyn J. Fogg, Edie Clark, and others.

Of the fifteen children, only Elisabeth, Louis, Lora and I are still alive. Emaline was murdered. The others, like my parents, died of natural causes. My daughter Deborah and her husband Mike took me on a trip to Poland where we found my mother's ancestral log home in the mountains. We did not find my father's village. Deborah died of complications of breast cancer treatment on June 13, 2005, to my everlasting sorrow.

Author's Note

This memoir is primarily episodes of my childhood to age 17. Some names have been changed out of concerns for privacy of others. I have tried to present this book in a chronological manner, but with so many family members and events, times overlapping and memory lapses, sometimes events are not in exact order. Since I could not possibly remember dialogue verbatim, I have tried to reconstruct it to the best of my recollection. I want to thank my wife, Edna, who listened to me read and offered feedback. I want to thank my daughters Joann and Deborah who read and critiqued the manuscript, and I thank my son Joseph for encouragement and other family members, dead and alive, who helped me to recall and to ascertain events of childhood. Special thanks to Clara Clairborne Park who edited and critiqued the manuscript. I loved my parents and realize, now, that I was a willful child, and they brought us up as best they could under trying circumstances. With our four children, we had a great time raising them. I ruled out corporeal punishment, long before they were born, and they turned into happy, loving kids who made us proud of them-- every one.

215

Printed in the United States
200430BV00005B/1-129/A

9 781591 139379